MW01233735

Finding Home in Redemption

Whitney Morgan

Merry Christmas
Morgan ♡

Copyright © 2017 Whitney Morgan

Edited by Red-Headed-Liners

All rights reserved.

ISBN: 1974679772
ISBN-13: 978-1974679775

Mandy, what your friendship means to me could never be put into words. I would have never finished a book if it weren't for you. I would have never published a book if it weren't for you. I would have never found the faith in myself as an author if it weren't for you.

You are incredible, and I'm so beyond thankful for that day at work when we bonded over vampires and our love of reading.

I hope you never doubt that when I remember Bentley's story and every story after, I will remember the amazing friend that was with me every single step of the way.

This book is for you.

To every girl and boy who had the misfortune of growing up without your father, Pop is for you.
I hope he's everything you dreamed a father could be.

CHAPTER ONE

January, seventeen years ago

"Sylvia, crank up that television!" Hank yelled to his wife from the kitchen. Sylvia, dressed in her diner apron, rushed to the old box TV they had sitting in the corner and turned the volume up. Standing in front of the courthouse in the next city over, James Harris, the news anchor, was finishing up his six o'clock segment. They were only able to catch the end.

"-we covered the tragic scene where a young girl, who we now know as Erica Duncan, was killed early last week. Duncan, sixteen, was heading home from a friend's house when she was struck head-on by another vehicle. William Short was driving well over the speed limit when he missed his stop sign and collided with Duncan. Short, eighteen, is being charged with aggravated vehicular homicide. Authorities have informed us that Brennan Sanders, Short's passenger, is being held at the Juvenile Delinquent Center and is facing charges of possession of drugs with intent to distribute. No other details are being made public at this time, and we will continue to follow the story as new information is released."

Sylvia looked at the booth where her three young sons sat doing homework. She couldn't imagine or comprehend what the mother of the young girl must be facing. The thought alone sent a dart of pain through her heart.

After saying a prayer for the girl's family and the boys involved in the accident, she resumed her duties.

"It's a horrible situation," her husband said walking into the dining area. He closed the short distance between them and pulled her into a hug. Looking at his children, he worried about the problems they might face in the town where they lived. Hoping from the bottom of his heart his children would never struggle with addiction; he whispered into his wife's hair, "someone needs to get this drug problem under control."

CHAPTER TWO

March, seventeen years later

When I woke up that morning, I knew he was going to murder me, my boss, that is. Although I worked for my father, being tardy didn't show good form considering I'd received a promotion the day before. Isaac Douglas Cooper II, founder, and owner of Cooper's Cars & Stuff ran a tight ship. Pop typically let me get away with a lot, but I couldn't imagine him being okay with his Assistant Manager running so late on her first day. I reassured myself that it wasn't my fault.

After setting my alarm, I laid awake in bed. I'd worked at Cooper's since I was sixteen years old and this move up was a huge step for me, especially since I'd one day own the business.

Excitement prohibited me from being able to close my eyes but eventually, after at least two hours, I was able to pull back my thoughts and retreat into a deep sleep. Little did I know, the universe had plans to ruin my day and around two o'clock in the morning, those plans became evident.

It all started when the couple that lived above me began fighting. In my two years living below them, I'd never heard them fight, so being caught off guard by their behavior; I tried and failed to ignore it. An hour later they were still going strong. Irritated and confused, I walked to my kitchen and grabbed the strainer I'd used for dinner the night before. Climbing onto my counter, I started banging on the ceiling.

I knocked a few times, ignoring the few wet noodles that fell onto my shirt before they got the hint and took mercy on me by shutting up. I wish I could say that was where my misfortune ended, but sadly, that's not the case.

My brand new alarm clock failed me on this of all days. I woke up thirty minutes later than I should have and rushed to get my shower started. To make it, I'd have to skip washing my hair, but as I waited for the water to heat up, minutes continued to disappear.

Eight minutes was how long it took me to realize my water heater wasn't working again, and thanks to the useless piece of junk my landlord had yet to fix, I took the coldest shower of my life.

Finally dressed and in my kitchen, I planned to defrost myself with a hot cup of coffee, but when I opened my pantry, all there was, was an empty canister.

"Did I wake up in a parallel universe?" I asked my empty apartment. I didn't get an answer.

Even though I was the one who put the empty coffee canister back into the pantry, I scoffed at the idiot who did it. Only idiots did that, right?

With no time to grab a coffee from The Market across the street from where I worked, I did what I had to do. After two years of turning left out of the apartment building, that day, for the first time, I turned right.

My building happened to sit on a line dividing two tiny towns in the middle of Nowhere, Ohio. While I technically lived in Taylorsville, if I moved three feet to the right, I was in Hillview. The differences were astonishing. Taylorsville was light, homey and welcoming, whereas Hillview was the opposite.

Other than the diner that was diagonal from my building, the homes and businesses within sight were boarded up and abandoned. There weren't many people wandering around Hillview, outside of the people who worked in the diner and the homeless man that called their parking lot his home.

There was a policy that the residents of Taylorsville seemed to follow. Residents didn't cross the line into Hillview, and I had never witnessed anyone break that unspoken rule.

Since I was already running late, I made the executive decision to go where I'd never gone before. Bucking Bandits, the diner that doubled as a gas station, had a certain charm to it. If the name didn't give you pause, then the dirty windows would certainly do it.

As far as I could tell, they hadn't sold gas since the beginning of time since the pumps were older than dirt. I was sure I was their first customer in no less than ten years.

Bucking Bandits may have looked rundown, but I put my chances of walking back out alive at about sixty-percent, and that was enough for me. It was all for the love of caffeine.

The homeless man, whose long hair shielded all of his features, was present, as usual. Although I had yet to see him awake, I thought he brought the whole image together. I'd be lying if I said I wasn't cautious when I walked by, and I felt bad for judging him before I knew him.

When I walked up to the diner, the dog acknowledged my existence before lying back down by his owner. Two signs sat beside them. One that read, "will work for food" and the other, that was nearest to the dog, said, "I'm friendly."

Complete silence met me when I opened the door and walked in the diner. I was very pleased to see the inside looked far cleaner than the outside. Old, but clean.

The only others who were present were the people who owned and worked there, and those three pairs of curious eyes stared at me.

I'm sure I looked lost, but I smiled and walked up to the man at the counter anyway.

"Hello, can I just get a cup of coffee to go?" I asked. He nodded and grunted something to the waitress beside him, who then turned and shrugged at the cook. I turned around and spotted the man and dog through the window. Feeling nothing toward him proved to be impossible, and before I could stop myself, I said, "excuse me, I need to add a few things to my order."

Ten minutes later I was walking out with two coffees, two cups of water, and two orders of their biggest breakfast. I went over to where the man was sleeping on the ground and, as politely as I could, nudged his leg with my foot.

"Good morning! Hello?" When there wasn't any movement, I adjusted the containers as much as possible and sat it all on the ground. I squatted down beside him to make sure he was alive by feeling his neck for a heartbeat. After confirming he was breathing, I lightly shook his shoulder and looked at the dog, as if he could help in some way. He didn't seem to notice anything other than the boxes of food sitting a foot away from him.

"Sir?" I asked, shaking him a little harder. He rudely reached his hand out and swatted at me as if I were a pesky fly of which he was ridding himself.

"Hey, that wasn't very nice! I have some food for you." It was not lost on me how ridiculous I must have looked. Me, in my pencil skirt, suit top and bright blue tennis shoes, shaking and yelling at a man sleeping in the parking lot by a dog. I could feel the eyes in the diner watching the spectacle.

After resigning myself to the fact that he wasn't going to wake up, I opened the to-go boxes and started preparing the food for them both. Biscuits and gravy, toast, eggs, sausage, and bacon for two. I placed a plate in front of the dog and nudged the man one last time.

"Breakfast is ready, sleepyhead," I said. He started to stretch, so I grabbed my coffee and walked away.

My trek to Cooper's, which was made up of a body shop, a used car lot, and my dad's house, which is the house I grew up in, was about a twenty-minute walk for me from my apartment.

Main Street, the only street to run through town, housed every business, house, and apartment in Taylorsville. The only exception was Greater Road, which took you about twenty miles into the country and dead-ended. My hometown was incredibly small.

Miles and miles of cornfields surrounded us, and, even though we were in our little world, it didn't feel suffocating. I'd grown up in this very town, and although I knew just about everybody in it, no one bothered to intrude in anyone else's business. Peacemakers and secret keepers were what the population was made up of, and I came to realize it was a blessing. I liked that I didn't have nosey neighbors. I didn't have to deal with running into the old woman at The Market who would pretend to care about your problems until she could run and gossip to the first person who would listen.

By the time I arrived at work, I was well over an hour late, and Pop was furious.

"Bentley," he huffed. The vein in his head was so much more visible since he'd shaved off his hair.

"I'm sorry, Pop. You don't understand the kind of morning I've had."

"If you would just-." I cut him off with my hand before he could finish his sentence.

"You promised me you wouldn't bring it up again," I said, referencing a conversation we'd had weeks prior, where he tried to convince me to get a car. At twenty-two years old, I felt like I was using that day from my childhood as a crutch, but no matter what, I felt terror grip my chest with the mere thought of getting behind a steering wheel. I may have forced myself to get my driver's license for emergencies, but that didn't mean I was over my fear of driving. Maybe one day I'd feel different, but I knew it would probably take a miracle.

"You can tell me about your morning after you've vacuumed out the cars," he said, bringing me back to the present.

"What?" I asked, incredulously. "I just vacuumed them all out yesterday. You know, when that was my job?"

His chuckle met my ears, and I knew it was a lost cause. "This'll teach you not to be late again, Squirt."

"Oh, whatever, Old Man," I grumbled before opening the closet door. I silently wondered how much I would need to pay one of the mechanics to destroy the vacuum, but figured Pop would just send me to his house to get his vacuum, so, breaking it would be pointless.

CHAPTER THREE

I hadn't planned on returning to the diner across the street, but every morning when I tried to head straight to work, I felt like he was tugging on my heart, pulling me in the opposite direction. I couldn't start my day without making sure the man in the parking lot had a warm meal, and eventually I became friends with Sylvia, the diner waitress.

That day, back in March, started a whole new routine for me. I'd wake up and head to Bucking Bandits for coffee and to pick up breakfast for Man and Dog; the unfortunate names I came up with for them.

After Man had swatted at me that first morning, I chose not to try waking him up again. I'd cut up Dog's food and pour the gravy over the biscuits for Man; then I'd leave.

Pete, Bucking's owner, said Man would wait until I was out

of sight to sit up and eat then he'd lay right back down and stay there until evening. Sylvia, who happened to be Pete's wife, said they let him use their restroom anytime they were open, but we had no idea what happened to him after seven at night when he would vanish.

Other than what Pete and Sylvia could tell me, I didn't know much about the guy. If it hadn't been for the note, I would've never known he did anything other than sleep.

One evening, after having gone to the diner a few times for dinner, Sylvia walked up to the counter where I was seated wearing the world's most infectious grin.

"What's got you so happy tonight?" I asked.

"You won't believe who came in today and you definitely won't be able to guess what he wanted!" She reached into her apron pocket and pulled out a folded piece of paper.

The weight gave away the fact that something was inside, so I opened it to reveal a small but beautiful turquoise stone. The note read,

"I wanted to say thank you. I saw this rock a few days ago and thought you should have it. It isn't much, but thank you."

I felt my eyes water before I could stop them and looked out of the front window to watch him for a moment. Turning back to Sylvia she smiled and shook her head.

"Go on and sit out there with him. Just bring me my dishes
back when you're finished." She'd read my mind.

"Will you add a grilled chicken and fries to my bill and
bring it out when it's finished?" I asked. "I want to make sure
he has something tonight."

When she nodded, I picked up my plate and walked outside.
Taking a seat beside Dog, I told them about my day while I ate
dinner. All the mundane things I didn't realize I wanted to talk
to someone about tumbled out of my mouth.

I started eating dinner beside them at least once a week,
leaving a bag of food for him to eat when I left. Man never
moved a muscle and Dog loved the attention.

Me? I was content.

On the days I didn't have dinner outside, I'd realize how
lonely I truly was. This friendship, no matter how one-sided it
was, meant a lot to me.

Throughout April, I always worried about Man's health. He
fashioned some boxes and trash bags in an attempt to keep
himself and Dog dry, but it didn't seem like it would be enough.
I asked Sylvia to let me know if he ever appeared to be ill and
one night I got a call from her, telling me he'd been sneezing.
The next day, I went to The Market to buy some generic cold
medicine, and I put the pill on his breakfast plate every

morning for a week.

The next couple months seemed to fly by and when Independence Day rolled around it was scorching hot. If caring about this man had taught me anything about myself, it was that I'd be a worry wart when I became a mother. I was constantly looking at him through my window when I was home. I was always checking to see if he was shaded from the sun or protected from the rain, and I had no idea what I would do when it was below freezing. I was going to have to move and forget about this place if I ever wanted to be productive again. I knew that was a ridiculous solution, so continuing what I'd been doing; I worried, fed, and checked on him every day.

One Saturday in mid-August, Pop and I spent the day together. It was his forty-ninth birthday, so the plan was to eat some dinner and watch whatever was on television. After walking to his house and seeing how empty his cabinets were, I demanded we go grocery shopping instead, so we made our way across the street to The Market.

"I am perfectly capable of doing this stuff on my own, Bentley. I'm forty-nine, not ninety!" he hissed when I put three containers of Metamucil in his cart.

"It's on sale, and I know you use it! Stop your grumbling and just say thank you, Old Man." I rolled my eyes at him and headed to the toothpaste aisle.

I had started a collection of things I planned to get for Man in the front of the shopping cart by my purse. A toothbrush, toothpaste, and deodorant hadn't raised any questions, but it started to draw attention when I added body spray.

"Are you planning on smelling like a man for a while?" I looked at my father and decided it was past time I tell him what I'd been doing.

"There's this homeless man that lives by Bucking Bandits. I've been feeding him for a while now, and I guess I just worry about him a lot. I don't know why I never thought to get this stuff before today. I kind of feel like a jerk now."

"How long have you been feeding him?" he asked while stopping in the middle of the tampon aisle. If that wasn't awkward enough, we were talking about something I had been keeping pretty close to my heart for the better part of five months.

"Since March," I answered.

"First of all, it's foolish for you to think you're a bad person for not providing anything outside of food. I'm sure he appreciates everything you've given him. Secondly, I'd like to get out of this aisle. Let's continue this conversation around something I'm more comfortable looking at."

"Pizza," we both said at the same time. As we walked to the
frozen pizza aisle, Pop started questioning me about Man.

"Alright, so what do you know about this guy?"

"Well," I said in a voice I hadn't used since the eighth
grade, when he'd caught me kissing Dave Hilton behind the shop,
"I'm not sure about much of anything, to be honest. I know he's
homeless and he has a dog. He's never once been awake when I'm
out there, so we've never had any interaction with each other.
Now, Sylvia, that's the waitress I told you about, she said he
comes in from time to time to use the restroom. He gave me a
thank you note once with a beautiful stone in it, and that's the
extent of his acknowledgment of my existence."

"Are you attracted to him? Is that what this is?" he asked.

"Honestly Pop, I've never even gotten a look at his face. I
know he's scruffy, but that's because Sylvia said so. All I'm
certain of is no one takes care of him. I mean, he barely does
that himself. Financially, it isn't a burden for me to feed him
so I feel like I should."

"Kid, I'm not stoked about you doing so much for someone
you don't know. I think you should think things through before
you do them. Unfortunately, even if you have a good heart,
people will try to take advantage of you." I could tell he was
debating what else to say so I gave him the time he needed to

sort out his thoughts. "You see yourself as helping someone in
need, but I see it more as enabling him. Right now he probably
doesn't worry about eating because he knows you'll be there to
provide his food. What would happen if you didn't feed him one
day? What if you completely stopped? Would he get angry? Come
looking for you? I'm sure he's watched you walking in and out of
your apartment building. It wouldn't be that hard for him to
find out which one was yours. I'm proud of you because you have
a good heart, but you are also the gatekeeper to your heart.
Your voice alone has given away your emotional connection to
him. Don't let just anyone in, make them earn that access."

"That was kind of poetic," I smiled.

"I know, I surprised myself there for a minute," he tugged
my ponytail and took over pushing the cart for a while. We
talked more about being careful with my heart, and he scoffed
when I told him what I'd been calling them.

"It worries me that you couldn't come up with anything
better than that. Man and Dog. How insulting," he said.

All in all, he was right about me needing to be more
careful. I didn't notice how much I had begun emotionally
relying on my moments with Man. I didn't put anything back, and
I continued to pick up a few items here and there for him and
Dog, including real dog food.

I decided I would give myself a deadline. I would stop feeding Man after winter. I couldn't enable laziness, and if that's what this was, I couldn't support it. I may not have known what his story was, but I had made up my mind.

When Pop dropped me off at home, Man was long gone. After saying goodbye and telling him "Happy Birthday" for the hundredth time, I went upstairs, blasted music and put all of Man's new things in an old backpack I had. Crackers and apples made it into the bag along with the personal hygiene items. I hoped that maybe a few of the items would help job prospects if he'd been having trouble in that area.

A few days later something came over me. I don't know what I was thinking or why I decided to do something so crazy, but when I got home and thought about my actions, mortification settled over me.

I was washing my dishes when all of a sudden I thought about the possibility that Man had a wallet. If he had an ID, I could figure out a little bit about him, so I made my way over to his sleeping body and sat down.

"Alright, Man. I'm going to look through your stuff. If you want to stop me, you're going to have to do so now." I waited for a beat and then added, "My dad said some things the other day when I told him about you. It was just a bunch of girly

/ FINDING HOME IN REDEMPTION / 22

stuff about my heart, so I won't bore you, but I need to figure
a few things out."

Again, I waited a moment longer before I reached my hand
over and felt up my homeless friend's butt. I started patting
him down, looking for that familiar shape of a wallet and I came
up empty. Next, I grabbed his bag that was halfway tucked under
his belly and pulled. His weight was hard to fight, but I won in
the end.

"You sure are heavy," I huffed. I unzipped the bag and
began searching.

Nothing. There was not one thing I could take away from my
crazy moment. Finding only items I'd bought for Man, and random
things that he'd probably picked up along the way, there wasn't
anything informative about his belongings.

"Well, aren't you a mystery," I said before sudden
embarrassment flooded my cheeks. I stood up and walked back to
my apartment, promising myself I'd never look through a sleeping
man's things again because, well, who does that?

By Halloween, I had well gotten over the incident, and
things were back to normal. I spent the morning helping Sylvia
put goodie bags together for their neighborhood trick-or-
treaters, and then I headed home after giving Man his very own
bag of candy.

I was almost certain there weren't any children in my building or, for that matter, on my block. Instead of handing out candy as I did with Pop when I was growing up, I did adult things. Meaning I paid my bills online, prepared a couple of simple meals for the next few days, and did my laundry. One of the perks of the building was that each apartment had a personal laundry room. After adulting, I decided to revert to my teenage years, and I picked up my favorite novel to read.

It was nearing midnight when my cell phone started ringing. Since my father was the only one who would call me, I was surprised to see a blocked number on the caller ID. I didn't answer, and they didn't leave a message, so I forgot about it and went to sleep.

CHAPTER FOUR

Work, for me, typically started at eight in the morning. I'd respond to all the missed calls and emails, and schedule appointments for people needing repairs or maintenance. I'd take coffee and donuts to the shop out back and let the boys fight over who got what while I cleaned up the office and did their stock inventory. It never failed that when I finished, there was always one donut left; a plain glazed, which happened to be my favorite.

Our lot specialized in selling used cars, but they were new enough to generate plenty of profit while remaining affordable to our customers. I don't think I had ever witnessed a car come through with more than 20,000 miles on it and it was rare for us to have a client who was upset. With three sales associates who were always busy I'd say there was a need for a place like

Cooper's.

The shop was at the back of the property and was mostly run by our mechanics. Pop and I didn't have the talent or knowledge it took to work on a vehicle, so we left it to the boys.

When Pop first opened the shop, he decided retired military and reformed convicts would make up his employee base. He believed in second chances.

It made him angry to see the men and women that spent their lives protecting us go through unemployment. Having served time himself in the Marines, he hated watching his brothers struggle to find jobs and provide for themselves and their families. If there was one group of people that deserved immediate employment, it was the men and women that served our country. Another thing that frustrated him was that the people that earned second chances, once out of prison, hardly ever received one. After extensive research on an individual and a reference letter from their parole officer, he hired Simon, Drake, and Raj. Pop's heart gravitated toward helping the underdog, so naturally, I was the apple and he was the tree.

I had never seen him waver in his obsession with cars, hence my name, Bentley. The woman who gave birth to me let Pop give me my name and thank God for that. I would have been a Violet Clementine otherwise, so crisis averted in my opinion.

Named and raised by a car fanatic, you'd think I would be obsessed with them too, but I wasn't. I loved the business and interacting with people, but it wasn't about what we sold. Those customers gave my life purpose every single day, and that is what I cherished.

I would usually clock out at 5:00 P.M., but six days into November that wasn't the case. From start to finish I was always running. We had shipments of parts coming in, customers that weren't scheduled showing up and Pop sold more cars that day than he had in the last two weeks put together.

I didn't get to leave until well past 9:00 P.M., which meant it was freezing and dark. I argued with myself the whole walk home about not having a car. If I could have swallowed my fear, I would have used one from the lot, but the fact was, I couldn't deal with getting behind the wheel.

To keep my mind from racing on the walk home, I wondered what Sylvia had made for dinner. Every now and then I would eat with them, but that was out of the question tonight. Since I had my Crockpot full of food I was planning to pack for lunches all week, I'd be settling for a lunch meat sandwich and a can of soda.

As soon as I saw the figure on the steps of my apartment building, I knew something was about to change. The dog bounding up to me gave the identity of my visitor away.

He was altering the dynamic of our relationship forever.

"Hi there, Dog!" I said, laughing as he searched through my bags, almost knocking me down in the process. "I don't have any food right now, I'm sorry buddy." I didn't notice Man had stood and started making his way toward us. It was late, and even though I'd been feeding him for months, I couldn't stop the immediate reaction of fear I felt. What if he was on something and that's why he was waiting for me? I hated the thought as soon as it popped into my head.

When we were a few feet away from each other, we both stopped and waited. My heart was beating so hard I could feel the pounding in my head.

I won't lie, I had romanticized him a bit. It wasn't anything serious since I had never seen his face but standing so close to a streetlight meant I could see him. I stood there and stared up at him. His beard was touching his chest, and I couldn't imagine how long it had taken to grow out. The skin that was visible was dirty, and his brown eyes looked tired. He looked tired.

"I didn't mean to scare you. I just," he paused and reached his hand up to rub the back of his neck. His voice was deep, raspy even, like he hadn't talked much lately. I was having a hard time focusing on anything because this was the man that had been in so many of my thoughts for months, and here he was in front of me. "You dropped this, this morning." He stretched his other hand out toward me, and I pulled my debit card from his fingers. It didn't go without notice that he was returning something he could have used to steal from me.

"Oh, wow, thank you! It must have fallen out of my purse earlier. I appreciate that, Man."

"Man," he said, his voice laced with humor.

"I don't know your name, so I had to call you something," I replied.

I'd read books where people spoke before thinking and did ridiculous things without contemplating the consequences. Even with the fear of him being somewhat unknown to me, it wasn't enough to stop what was about to tumble out of my mouth.

"Would you like to come inside? I have a pot roast in the Crockpot that I was going to use for my lunches this week, but we can eat it tonight if you're hungry." His eyes widened a bit, and I feared he would say no, but he surprised me with a nod.

I walked ahead of him and Dog, and we made our way up the steps to my apartment. I immediately put my things in my bedroom and went back to the kitchen to get plates for each of us. Turning to walk into the archway that connected my kitchen to my dining room, I was startled when I ran into his chest. I let out a scream.

"I'm sorry," I said. I felt like my heart was going to jump out of my chest, so I placed a hand over it and laughed. Man didn't reply, so I took a deep breath and stepped out of the grasp I didn't notice he had on my arms. I looked up to see him looking at my arm, and when I looked down, I saw there were smudge marks from his dirty hands. Dirt was nothing to me, but I could tell for whatever reason, he didn't like that he'd gotten something on me.

"It's not a big deal. You can wash up in the bathroom; it's right down that hall," I pointed toward the restroom, and he walked in and shut the door.

I sat Dog's bowl on the floor and filled it with the dog food I had for him. He devoured every last bite in a few short minutes, so I quickly got more. After I had set the bowl down, Man came out and stood awkwardly watching me.

"We can sit at the table," I suggested. He sat at the head of the table, and I brought out two plates piled high with roast, veggies and buttered bread, along with a glass of milk for each of us. He started eating immediately, and I couldn't help it; I didn't know what to do or say, so I just watched him like the freak I am. After a bit, he finished his food and

looked at me again. I slid my plate toward him, and he finished
my food as well.

"So, I have questions," I said. He sat up straight like he
knew what was coming. "What's your name?"

"Aaron Fitzpatrick," he replied.

"How old are you?"

"Thirty-two."

"What about the dog?" I asked.

He glanced over at him. "He's probably three."

I hid my smile behind my hand and said, "No, I mean what's
his real name?"

"Oh, it's Charles."

"What? Charles is not a name for a dog."

"Neither is Dog," he replied, and I laughed.

"What was I supposed to call him? You were never awake to
tell me differently. Well, I guess we've established you've been
awake more than once since you knew where I lived. You just
ignored me." I didn't mean for it to sound like it hurt my
feelings because, after a few weeks, it hadn't. What bothered me
most was I sat and told him so much about myself, and he'd been
listening. He picked up on it and shook his head.

"I came here to give your card back, but also to thank you
for feeding us every day. I want to pay you back somehow. I

don't have any money, but if you ever need something fixed
around here, I can do just about anything."

"I didn't give you food looking to get paid back," I
paused, barely catching myself before calling him Man, "Aaron.
In all honesty, you should be thanking the people at Bucking
Bandits. They've been giving me discounts on your meals.
Sometimes it was even free."

"I've already thanked them," he replied with a nod.

"Okay, well," I tried to think of something else to say but
fell short. It felt so awkward and weird. I'd waited this long
to have a two-way conversation with this man, and now I couldn't
think of anything to talk about. "If you want, you can take a
shower."

That was my speaking and not thinking again. He looked
surprised, and I didn't blame him seeing as I had just offered
him the use of my shower.

"Is it that bad?" he asked.

"Oh my gosh! No! I wasn't even thinking about that. I was
just offering you what I would want, I guess. Sorry, I didn't
mean to offend you." He nodded like he understood what I was
saying. "I have some clothes that used to be my dad's. I sleep
in a lot of his old sweats, but you're welcome to them. I'll
even wash what you have on and anything else you need."

"Why?" he asked. "Why are you acting this sweet? You know I could be a psycho or something, right?"

"Well, I thought about that, and I figured you wouldn't kill me since I just fed you. You returned my debit card when you could have used it, which tells me you're a decent human being. Plus, Dog likes me so he might try to bite you," I laughed when Dog barked at his name. "For as long as I can remember my dad has tried to give more than he could ever receive. The saying people use, 'he'd give the shirt off his own back?' I've witnessed him do it on more than one occasion. He is just pure goodness, and that's what I want to be. I've heard people say that giving is selfish because it makes you feel good and yes, it makes me happy, it also breaks my heart to see people hurting. If I could bring happiness why wouldn't I try?"

Aaron sat and looked at me for a few minutes. I guess he was trying to figure out if I was telling the truth, but I'd never actually said those words aloud until then. I would have to let Pop know that I could wax poetic from time to time, too.

"Okay," he eventually replied. He stood, walked to the restroom and shut the door. Apparently, he was taking me up on my offer. I ran to my room and grabbed the biggest sweatpants, sweatshirt, and t-shirt I could find. I thought of socks halfway down the hall.

Sliding to a stop, I turned and ran back to my room to find a pair of thick socks before grabbing towels out of the hallway. I rushed to the laundry room and started the washer before I knocked on the restroom door.

"Come in," he called out. I let myself in and found he was already in the shower.

"I brought you some clothes and towels. Here's a wash rag, too," I said throwing it over the shower rod.

I heard a deep laugh and smiled in response. "This whole situation is so odd compared to what I imagined would happen," he said. I nodded my agreement because he was right; it was weird.

"What did you think would happen? I asked.

"I thought I'd hand you your card and we'd go about our business."

"I'm sorry, I guess that's my fault. I feel like I know you. I've spent the last eight months thinking about you at some point during the day; deciding what to get you for breakfast or even dinner sometimes. I've sat and talked to you over meals you didn't emotionally attend. I forget that you don't even know me. I'm Bentley by the way," I waved even though he couldn't see me. "I'm going to take your clothes now. Do I need to check the pockets?"

"I got everything out and put it in my bag."

"Okay, well, I'll be out here with Dog then," I said, starting to pull the door closed.

"Bentley?" Aaron's use of my name stopped me in my tracks. I looked back into the room and saw his head peeking out of the curtain.

"Yes?" I asked.

"Thank you." With that, he shut the curtain, and I took his clothes to the laundry room losing my fight against a smile the entire way.

While Aaron was in the restroom, I had cleaned up the dinner dishes, thrown his clothes in the washer, and sat down to twiddle my thumbs. I was excited and nervous having this interaction with him. I was truly butchering it with my awkwardness, but I think he was handling that nicely.

When he came out, I had to do a double-take. His damp, brown hair was slightly wavy and hung past his broad shoulders, allowing the water to fall onto his shirt. His beard, although still very long and caveman-like in my opinion, looked a bit neater. His face was clear of dirt, as were his muscular arms that were holding his wet towels. In all of my romanticizing of him, I'd never imagined him as handsome as the man standing in front of me.

CHAPTER FIVE

After I got rid of the towels, I invited Aaron to have a seat on the sofa while I brought in a kitchen chair. Minutes full of awkward silence went by before I couldn't take it anymore and started a conversation.

"Is it okay if I ask you more questions?"

"Of course. I think it's only fair that you get to ask some questions."

I started with the question that was bothering the most. "What are you going to do when it starts snowing?"

"I guess I'll do what I did last year and the year before that. I've lived through winters before; I can do it again," he gave me a reassuring smile that didn't make me feel better at all.

"I remember you being out there last winter but I didn't

think twice about it. I'm sorry for that."

"There's no need to be sorry. You're not the one that put me out there."

"Why are you out there?" I whispered.

"That's a long story, and it's not something I'm proud of." I wondered if he was talking about something other than being homeless. You didn't end up on the streets without some form of harsh reality.

"How old are you?" he asked.

"Twenty-two. I'll be twenty-three on Christmas Day," I said, smiling.

"A Christmas baby, huh? Your parents must have been excited."

"Pop said I was the biggest surprise ever. My mom didn't even know she was pregnant until she was almost seven months along. So," I said, changing the subject. "Do you work anywhere? I notice you're gone every night."

"I do different things from time to time. It doesn't make much money, but I get by," he replied stiffly.

"Oh, okay," I could tell he didn't want to talk about that either, so I turned the television on for him while I went to switch his laundry over. I stayed in the laundry room a little longer than I should have. I couldn't help but wonder about the things he was hiding. It wasn't my business, I knew that, but it was hard to remember that we didn't know each other. And that's what I wanted; I wanted to know him.

"Are you okay?" I started, having not heard Aaron come up behind me. I had been resting my elbows on the washer and my head in my hands, so when I jumped up, I hit my head on the shelf directly above me.

"Oh my gosh, that hurt, ow, ow, ow!" I grabbed my head and started jumping around the small area.

"Crap, are you okay? I didn't mean to scare you! Come on, let's go get some ice." I felt his hand gently grab onto one of my elbows, and he led me to the living room.

"Wow, I didn't think the shelf was that sturdy. I'll have to tell my landlord it's a fundamental part of the structure of the building," I tried to joke, but before I could stop myself, I started crying because of the pain.

He dropped me off at the sofa before walking into the kitchen. He must have found the sandwich baggies I kept on the counter because I heard him rummaging around in the freezer. I laid down and closed my eyes, wiping away a few more tears. Of course, I would cry on the night I finally got to have a two-way conversation with this man.

"You need to stay awake. If you have a concussion, it's not

a good idea to go to sleep. Here, let me see if you're bleeding." He reached over to help me sit up and brushed his fingers through my hair. Looking for the bump, he accidentally grazed over it, and I flinched.

"That's a pretty nice goose egg, Bentley. I think you need to go to the hospital," he sounded worried.

"I'll be okay. Let me put some ice on it for a while and take some medicine. I've suffered worse before."

"Tell me where your medicine cabinet is, and I'll get some for you. I feel so terrible about this, I'm sorry," I smiled and patted him on the arm.

"Don't worry about it. Seriously, I was just in my head and didn't hear you come up behind me. The medicine is in the cabinet above the microwave." He left the room while I held ice on my head.

"Here you go," he said when he came back to the living room. He handed me the pill bottle and a glass of water.

"Thank you," I said after I took a couple of painkillers. "My head is already feeling better thanks to the ice."

I looked over to where Dog was sleeping, and I laughed. "He is definitely not a service dog."

"Why do you say that?" Aaron asked, eyes wide.

"He slept through the whole thing. He didn't help me at

all."

"Yeah, I guess he probably shouldn't. Hey, I hate to do this, but I have to leave soon." He looked at the clock I had hanging on the wall and let out a frustrated sigh. "I would feel better if you went to the hospital. What if you have a concussion? Maybe we should call your dad."

"My dad?" I asked, a little surprised. Aaron stopped pacing and looked at me like he was embarrassed.

"You, uh," he paused. "You talk about your dad a lot when you eat. I can tell you love him."

"Well, of course I love him. He's my dad," I laughed. "I'll call him okay?"

"Please don't get offended but I'd rather you call him before I leave. I don't want you to fall asleep."

"Okay, well can you hand me my phone? It's behind you on the table." He placed the phone in my hand, and I dialed Pop's number.

"Hello?" he answered, his voice gruff from sleep.

"Hey, Pop, sorry to bother you this late. I was just calling to let you know that I hit my head pretty hard. I didn't want to go to sleep without telling you."

"Dang it, Bentley! How'd you hit your head?" he sounded aggravated, but I knew it was because he hated to worry.

"It's okay, I promise. I was in the laundry room, and I hit my head on the shelf above the washer. It's okay, I just wanted to call and let you know so you can call and check on me in the morning."

"Alright, well do you want me to come stay with you tonight?"

"No, that's-," I paused when Aaron squatted down in front of me and nodded his head yes. I shook my head at him and smiled. "No thanks, Pop. Just call me in the morning. Okay?"

Aaron rolled his eyes and stood up. I watched as he sat on the chair by the door to put his shoes on.

"Okay, kid. I'll call you super early, too. I love you. See ya tomorrow."

"Love you, too," I said before hanging up.

"I wish you would have let your dad come and stay with you," Aaron said.

"I wish you wouldn't have been listening to my conversation," I shot back.

We stared into each other's eyes and he started to smile. "I wish you wouldn't have gone through my belongings."

My face instantly heated up and I averted my gaze. "Touché."

"I really do think you should call him back and ask him to

come stay the night, just in case."

"I know, but he's already in bed, and it's cold outside. I don't want him out in this weather." I didn't realize what I said until after I said it. Aaron was going out in it. "I'm sorry, Aaron."

"What? Why are you sorry?" he asked. "You don't owe me any apologies."

"I know, I just hate that you have to be outside when it's this cold. Would you like to take some food with you?"

"No, that's okay. Thank you." He walked over to the sofa and sat down beside me. "I do have to go now, but please promise me you will call your dad if you start to get dizzy or your vision gets blurry, okay?"

"Okay, I promise," I laughed. "You sound like a doctor."

"I've had my fair share of concussions," he admitted. I don't think he could have said anything else that would have stopped my laughing as fast as it did. I had no idea how long he'd been living on the streets and the thought of, 'his fair share of concussions,' didn't leave me with a warm, fuzzy feeling.

"Will I see you in the morning?" he asked, standing again. I looked up at his bright face and wondered if I could spend a morning doing anything other than going to see him and Dog.

"Definitely."

"Okay. See you tomorrow, Bentley." He grabbed his things, locked the door from the inside before turning to give me a small smile, then he left and shut the door behind him. When I turned around to get comfortable, I saw two huge brown eyes looking at me like I was his world.

Aaron had left Dog, who seconds ago had been asleep, with me. While I thought it was incredibly sweet, I had no idea how he knew to stay, and I worried about Aaron being alone. At least Dog was always there to protect him, Then again, he was a decent size, and one would have been an idiot to mess with him.

I had just gotten up to head to my bedroom when my cell phone rang. I looked down to see my father's phone number, and I laughed. I hadn't thought about this outcome.

"You're going to call me all night long, aren't you?" I asked.

"How are ya feeling, pipsqueak?"

"Oh, you know, just adjusting to blurry vision and all," I joked.

"That isn't funny, Bentley. How's your vision?"

"It's good, Pop. Thanks for checking on me."

"I'll call you again in an hour. Keep your phone turned up," he said before hanging up.

"Good grief," I said to my empty apartment. Well, empty

other than Dog and myself.

I had only been in bed for forty-five minutes when Dog ran

into my room and jumped on the bed with me.

"Oh no! No, no, no. No dogs on the bed," I said to him. He

stood still and started to whimper. When he looked toward the

window and whined louder, I understood. "You have to go to the

bathroom, don't you? Where am I going to take you?"

I got up and put my long coat on, shoved my feet into my

rubber rain boots, and ran for the door. When I pulled the door

open, I paused. A man was sitting on the floor in my hall. To be

more specific, Aaron was sitting on the floor across from where

I was standing.

"What the heck are you doing-," I was cut-off by someone

walking up the stairs.

"Bentley? Are you okay?" Pop's voice boomed loudly in the

small hallway. He sounded panicked.

"Oh, for the love of Pete! What are you doing here, both of

you?"

"Who's he?"

They both asked the question at the same time, which made

me laugh in spite of them being there.

"Pop, this is Aaron and Dog," I said, pointing, as he stood

and held his hand out to shake.

"My name is Aaron, sir. It's a pleasure to meet you finally," he said, grabbing Pop's hand.

"Didn't I just say that?" I quietly asked Dog. Dog, who was sitting there like he didn't have a care in the world. Dog, who not five minutes ago needed to use the facilities. "Oh, no."

"What's wrong? Is it your head?" Aaron asked.

"Why don't you go lie down?" Pop asked, guiding me into the apartment. That's when it happened. I found out why Dog didn't need to use the bathroom anymore. There was a puddle in my foyer, directly under my feet.

"Well, that's lovely," I said, giving Dog a disapproving look.

"Charles!" Aaron exclaimed.

"Who is Charles?" Pop asked.

"The dog," Aaron and I answered at the same time.

"I thought the dog's name was Dog," Pop looked confused.

"His real name is Charles," I explained. He looked skeptical, but I continued, "Aaron, I thought you had to be somewhere tonight? And Dog, I'm telling you what, you are getting only dog food from now on. No more yummy treats for you." Dog had the audacity to act like I'd wounded him and he walked back into the living room, head hanging in shame.

"I'll go grab some paper towels," Aaron said, passing Pop and me as if he lived here. It made me smile, but my father did not look amused.

"Leave it alone," I said, elbowing him in the stomach.

"I'll leave it alone until morning. Go to bed," he answered. It didn't matter if I was in my twenties, when Pop told me to do something, that's what I did.

Aaron quickly cleaned up the mess and took Dog with him when he left. Apparently, he was going to be late to wherever he had to go. Pop stayed in my spare bedroom so he could keep an eye on me and after a few minutes, I fell asleep.

CHAPTER SIX

Pop woke me up earlier than I'd planned, explaining that he needed to have a talk with me. I wasn't looking forward to being reprimanded, but I sat and listened anyway.

After an hour of arguing over my stupidity, I agreed to be more careful, and he promised he'd not look at Aaron like a villain unless he did something that deserved it. I wouldn't entirely call it a win since he still thought I'd made a mistake by being so vulnerable with a stranger in my home, but I took it anyway.

When Pop left, I got ready and headed to the diner. No matter what my father said, I was excited about having a real conversation with Aaron again. When I walked in, he was already sitting at a table, and the crew was wide-eyed and confused.

"Hey, guys!" I said, giving them all a little wave. "I'm

going to be having breakfast with Aaron in here today." I didn't know how it was possible, but Sylvia's eyes got a little wider.

"Aaron?" she mouthed the question. I smiled and nodded to her.

"Good morning," he said when I got to the table. "I'm not sure why but no one's come over yet. I've only been here a few minutes though."

I handed him his bag of clothes he'd forgotten the night before and turned to get Sylvia's attention. I waved her over, but they were all still staring. Shaking my head, I laughed and said, "I think you broke them."

She finally arrived at the table to take our order and hurried away. If it hadn't been strange, I probably would have been bouncing in my seat a bit. Breakfast inside was Aaron's idea, but I'd been secretly nervous that he would have gone back to sleeping all day; forgetting I existed.

"Thanks for bringing me my things, I completely forgot about them last night after you hit your head," he gave me an apologetic smile. "So, how do you feel?"

"I feel great," I replied. "My bump went away for the most part."

"That's good! I'm glad." We sat in silence until Sylvia brought our food and we dug in.

"So, there's something I wanted to talk to you about," he said, pushing his plate aside when he finished.

"Okay, shoot," I stated before taking another bite of my pancake.

"I want you to stop buying me things. Food, deodorant, all of it." I choked on the bite I had just swallowed. I was not expecting that.

"Um," I paused for what felt like forever. "Why? Did I do something?"

"No, you didn't do anything. I just can't let you do this anymore. I've let it go on for too long."

"How will you eat?" I asked, feeling like my heart was breaking.

"The same way I did before you; when I can. You can't worry about that. I can take care of myself, I promise. I just can't have you buying things for me all the time."

"Do I annoy you or something?"

"Sure, if that's what's going to make you stop then, yes."

That hurt.

"Did you even have somewhere to be last night, or am I that unbearable that you made something up?" I asked. I was still curious about his whereabouts, but I was also wounded and wanted to understand what was happening.

"I did have somewhere to be. This isn't about you being unbearable; I shouldn't have said that. Last night I was willing to miss something I needed to do so I could make sure you were okay. I only left because your father arrived. I just can't let you spend any more money on me. I owe you too much as it is."

"Is that what this is about?" I asked, getting angry. "You think I want you to pay me back? I already told you I don't expect you to so why is this a problem? I'm just helping someone that needs it!"

"I'm not a charity case, Bentley. I'm a person. There is more to me than being homeless!" he stood and started putting his coat on. "Don't worry about the bill; it's taken care of."

He whistled for Dog to follow and walked out of the diner. I'm not sure how long I sat there before I finally got up. Sylvia hugged me, and I thanked them for breakfast before I left. I wasn't expecting Aaron to be sleeping out front. I figured he would have gone somewhere else, at least for that morning, but he wasn't going anywhere.

I immediately noticed something different. Aaron had made an addition to the sign so the word, 'work,' was underlined by angry looking lines. He was emphasizing that he would only work to eat.

I wanted to appreciate the fact that he didn't want to take

advantage of me. If I didn't feel like I was losing my only
friend, that's the only thing I would have thought. I had waited
so long to share something with him, and I felt like we'd had a
great night. We may not have figured each other out completely,
but it felt like friendship to me. At that moment, it felt like
it had all been for nothing.

I walked past him and decided to head to work early. I
couldn't sit there and beg him to let me feed him every day.

I was irrationally irritated, and I knew that. I planned to
tell Aaron how ridiculous I thought his pride was when I got
home, too. I was sitting in my office, spinning in my desk chair
when Pop walked in.

"How's that noggin?" he asked.

"I'm all right," I sighed. "Just a bit dizzy."

"Well, I'm no doctor, but I'd recommend you stop spinning
around in your chair," he said, grabbing the backrest, so I had
to stop.

"Agh!" I held my head still while I felt the room spinning
faster than I had been. "You can't just stop a spinning person!
It's rude."

"I don't understand how I had such a weird kid," he said
under his breath. He walked to one of the chairs in front of my
desk and sat down.

"What can I do for you, sir?" I asked.

"What's wrong? You stomped straight in and slammed the door when you got here. All before noon, too. So what's the problem?"

"I'm just in a bad mood today. First, you tell me I'm stupid, and then I go and have Aaron telling me to basically leave him alone," I complained.

"I never said you were stupid; I said you were making stupid decisions," he corrected.

"Same thing," I grumbled.

"Why did he tell you to leave him alone?" Pop asked after a minute.

"Aaron said he couldn't pay me back for everything I've done for him, so he wanted me to stop doing things. He told me to stop bringing him food." I felt tears fill my eyes and I angrily blinked them away.

"What if I told you there was a way you could help him without making him feel like he was receiving handouts?"

I sat up straighter in my chair and asked, "How?"

"Simon and Drake came up with an idea for the place. They think we need a couple more employees, and, if you can find it in the budget, you can offer Aaron one of the positions. If he can do basic things like changing tires and oil, then I think it would work out."

"I agree we need more people to help with the workload. They've even had the guys from sales helping them at night."

"That's what Drake was telling me this morning. Do me this favor and try to figure out how many more employees we could hire. Preferably a full time, seasonal employee, if there is such a thing."

"I can do that, but what made you change your mind about Aaron?"

"If he's here, I can get to know the guy that's taking up so much of my daughter's thoughts and time. I love you, Bentley, and if you want to be his friend, I have to find a way to be okay with it. Having him work here is just the only way I know how at the moment."

"Thank you," I said. "I think I'll be able to get this done in the next couple of hours."

"Well, I'd sure hope so. You're the one with the business degree."

"Pop, you have a business degree, too," I said. "Plus, you do realize what a huge difference there is between your master's and my associate's degree, right?"

"Yeah, but here's the thing; if I wanted to worry about all this crap, I wouldn't have had a kid."

"So, you only had me so I could share the workload?" I

asked, laughing now.

"Basically, I had you so you could do all the work while I got rich. Get it done, dork." Pop stood and shot me the peace sign before leaving my office.

It was hard to believe he thought I was the weird one.

As soon as I finished the budget, I grabbed my papers off the printer and ran to the back of our lot, into the shop. Things were happening everywhere. The garage was full, and we had five cars parked in the waiting area. Lucky for the customers, Cooper's was across the street from the grocery and a few stores so they wouldn't be too bored. I found Pop and Drake in the office in the back and barged in.

"Sorry to interrupt, boys but I have some great news. According to my calculations, we can hire two full-time employees for the winter months. I figure we can post two positions from today until the first day of March, then, maybe we'll reevaluate where the shop is and consider a permanent position."

"That's excellent news! I was just telling Isaac that we needed more hands around here," Drake said, nodding in excitement. "I promise I wasn't planning this, but I have a daughter that's into cars. She's honestly as good as I am at fixing them. She just decided to take some time off from school so she can figure out what she wants to do as a career. I could see if she wants to take one of the positions, if that's okay, Boss."

"That works out perfectly because I have someone I want to offer the other position to."

"As long as he's qualified," Pop added.

"Right," I agreed. "I'll call you tonight after I talk to Aaron and let you know."

I turned to run out of the shop office and heard Pop yell my name, so I popped my head back in the doorway.

"Yeah?" I asked.

"I need you to finish the jobs I put on your desk, so I need you to talk to him after you get off tonight," he said.

"You got it, old man," I smiled and was relieved when I got one in return.

I was jittery all day. Yeah, I was still upset about what happened at breakfast, but this was a great solution. He would be able to work for the things he needed or wanted, if he accepted the job.

When five o'clock finally came around, I was ready to go. I looked a little weird with my dress pants and tennis shoes, but I was in a hurry. I bolted out with nothing more than a frenzied wave to everyone, and I ran home. Let's make something clear; I am not nor have I ever been a runner. I was dying by the time I got home and didn't know if I'd ever get enough oxygen into my lungs.

"Oh God," I huffed, the breaths almost painful. "Why do people enjoy this?" I placed my hands on my knees and listened to what sounded like a wind tunnel in my ears. When the dots started dancing in front of my eyes, everything went dark.

I didn't hear Dog's barking until he was above my face looking down at me.

"What?" I looked from side to side and realized I was laying on the ground. "When did this happen?"

"Bentley?" Aaron shouted from across the street. I heard his feet pounding the pavement to get to me. "Why are you on the ground, is it your head?"

"No," I sighed, embarrassed that I was still wheezing. "I just ran the mile home. My head is perfectly fine, thanks. I'll just chill here for a minute or ten."

He laughed and grabbed my hands, pulling me into a standing position. I gave myself another few minutes to catch my breath while he sat on the steps with Dog. I looked at the stairs that led up to the third floor, where my apartment was.

"This building needs an elevator," I said to no one in particular.

"You should probably stretch so that you won't be stiff tomorrow." Aaron was smiling at me, and I thought for a minute that this morning couldn't have happened. Then I remembered why I had run home and got excited again.

"Okay, Aaron-,"

"Wait," he said cutting me off. "I needed to say something. I've been thinking about things all day, and I feel horrible about how I walked out of the diner on you this morning. I shouldn't have been a jerk but I want you to understand, I want to be friends with you, but I do not want you buying me anything else. Can you work with that?"

"Absolutely," I responded immediately.

"Really?" he seemed shocked. "No argument, just a simple agreement?"

"Oh no, I have a better idea. Let's go upstairs, and I'll tell you about it."

He walked behind me as I hobbled up to my apartment, and I vowed to myself that I'd never run again. Once we got inside and got settled, I looked him straight in the eye and turned on my employer switch.

"Aaron, I'd like to offer you a job. You said you were good at fixing things so first thing's first, do you know how to change a car's oil?"

"What? Yeah, I know how to change the oil on a vehicle. I don't understand-,"

"Do you know how to rotate tires?" I asked, cutting him off like he'd done to me downstairs.

"I've taken tires off and put them back on if that counts."

"Great. How are your people skills? Do you do better working on your own or can you work well in a group setting?"

"Either works well for me. Bentley, what are you-,"

"Fabulous! Okay, you need to be ready to go to work at six tomorrow morning. I know that's insanely early, but I have a lot I need to show you and, possibly Drake's daughter, if she takes the job. Hopefully, everything goes smoothly." I was standing and heading to shake his hand when I thought of something else. "You don't have a problem working with reformed convicts, do you?"

His eyes widened. Shaking his head no, he took my hand in his.

"Pleasure doing business with you. Please be here at six. We have to walk to work so make sure you wear your tennis shoes."

"Yeah," he said. He looked like he was in shock, so I just let it slide. He'd warm up to the idea through the night, I was sure.

"So, are you hungry?" I asked, heading to the kitchen.

"We need to talk about this a little bit, Bentley. You can't just give me a job because you feel sorry for me, that's worse than before. I couldn't repay you for that."

He was right about that. I decided it was best to be completely honest with him. After a sigh, I began my explanation.

"Right now, the shop at Cooper's is struggling. We're struggling positively, but it still looks bad for business when we can't get to all of our customers in one day. We've been so busy, and our guys aren't able to leave when their shift is over. Pop asked me to do some research today and here's the deal, we need seasonal workers. We don't know how long this busy period is going to last, so, in about four months we'll see where we are. If we're still busy, we might make the positions permanent. If not, then you'll have 30-day notice to look for some other work. This isn't strictly a charity offer, but I won't lie to you and say you aren't the first person that came to mind. You told me you were handy, so I want you to take the position."

We didn't talk through our dinner of turkey sandwiches and potato chips. He ate and watched me while I ate and watched the television. I felt his eyes throughout the entire time and every minute that he refused to speak was more stressful than the last. Finally, after rinsing the dishes and allowing them to soak in the sink, he took a deep breath.

"Okay, I'll take the job. I have a condition though," he said.

"You can't manipulate your boss, Aaron," I grinned.

"If I'm going to work for you and your father, you cannot buy anything for me. You have to promise me you won't spend a penny of your own money."

I had won! "Of course. I promise that after your first paycheck, you'll never see me pay for your things again."

"Right," he said. He tried to hide it, but I could see his smile. "I'll be here in the morning."

He and Dog left to do whatever it was Aaron did at night, and I got ready for bed after I called Pop to let him know the good news. Running had worn me out, and I was confident the devil himself invented it.

CHAPTER SEVEN

I was sitting in the foyer putting my shoes on when there was a knock on the door. I opened it to Aaron and Dog, both of whom looked like they were ready for our day.

"Wow, you look beautiful today," Aaron said before his eyes widened in shock. "I'm sorry. That was inappropriate. You just caught me off guard," he ran his hands over his hair that was pulled up into a bun.

I looked down at my outfit. Other than my tennis shoes, everything looked normal. I was wearing my favorite burgundy sweater dress and black leggings. My boots were in my bag, but those wouldn't go on until I got to work. I'd curled my hair and put a little blush and eye shadow on that morning. I told myself it was so I looked professional for my new employees, but really, deep inside, I knew it was for Aaron.

"Thank you." There was a moment of awkwardness, not knowing where to take the conversation after that and I laughed. His smile reassured me, and I motioned them inside.

"So, what are we going to do about Dog?" I asked, looking at the giant German Shepherd laying on my floor. "We could either take him with us, or we could leave him here. I already know how good he is at holding his bladder so he'd need to stay in the bathroom and I'd feel guilty. Okay, so we'll take him with us."

Aaron laughed, and I looked up at him in confusion. "I'm glad we could talk that out," he said.

"Oh, sorry, I tend to have conversations all by myself sometimes. You already know that though." I grabbed my bag and headed for the door. "Let's go."

"It's getting chilly out so you might want to get your coat," he said. I looked at him in his jacket and frowned.

"Where's your coat?" I asked. I could hear the sadness in my voice, and he started shaking his head.

"It's in the hallway, Bentley. All my things are in the hall." I peeked my head out of the doorway, and sure enough, his belongings were sitting against the wall, coat included. I walked out and grabbed the two backpacks and his coat and brought them inside.

"You can leave them in here anytime you need to. Now, grab your coat and let's roll." We walked out onto the sidewalk and started our trek to work.

"So, you walk this every day?" Aaron asked after a few minutes.

"Yeah. It's not that bad, to be honest. The walk home gets a little creepy sometimes when it's dark."

"You really should get a car. Doesn't your dad sell cars?" When he noticed the look on my face, he explained. "You told me about the place a few months ago."

"Were you ever sleeping when I was talking to you?" I asked, avoiding the car conversation and covering it up with honest embarrassment.

"Sometimes, yes. After a few times, I would lay there and listen. To be frank, I thought you were a little off in the head at first. You would just talk and talk. I got used to it, eventually."

"Why didn't you ever talk to me? I mean, why wait so long?"

"I expected you to go away," he said, and Dog chose that moment to start barking at a squirrel, saving me from responding.

We walked the rest of the way in silence. I didn't think what he said was rude or malicious in any way, but it had hurt my feelings nonetheless. When we reached Cooper's, I looked at Aaron to gauge his reaction.

"This is where you work?" he asked, shocked.

I looked out over the place and smiled. The car lot sat at the very front. The morning frost covered all the cars, and Jerry, the guy that ran the lot and my father's best friend, was already inside turning the lights on. Behind that was my childhood home. A simple three bedroom, one level house that was in dire need of fresh paint and a few decorations. Plain is how Pop liked his house, and since it was his, I couldn't argue. Last was the shop on the far left corner of the property. The garage had six bays, and two were already open with a car waiting in each.

I wanted to arrive before business hours to ensure that I'd have time to show Aaron around and let him get comfortable, but now that was out of the question.

"Aaron, Welcome to Cooper's Cars & Stuff," I said, holding my arms out like I was presenting to him a crown jewel. In my mind, I was.

"You would fit in perfectly if this were a cheesy movie," I laughed at his joke and walked toward the shop.

When we made it to the bays that were open, I saw Drake talking to a girl around my age.

"Good morning!" I greeted.

"Hey, kid!" Drake said enthusiastically. "This is my daughter! Sam, this is Bentley Cooper. My future boss and your current boss," he laughed and nudged Sam's shoulder.

"Hi, I'm Sam. It's nice to meet you," Sam was about an inch taller than my 5'5, and she had the world's coolest pink hair pulled up into a ponytail with a green bandana holding it all back. She had a simple silver hoop through her septum, and when I shook her hand, I noticed the sleeve of tattoos that didn't stop until it reached her fingers. If I had a spirit animal, it would have been her.

"What's a spirit animal?" Sam asked.

"Uh, say what now?" I replied after a moment.

"You said I was your spirit animal?" she laughed. "What does that mean?"

"Oh my goodness, that was supposed to be an inner thought. Well, meet me in my office when you finish up here." I turned, grabbing Aaron's hand and began dragging him away, toward the sales building.

When we reached my office, I turned and shut the door behind me. With my embarrassment evident on my face, I looked at Aaron and noticed he was smiling.

"What are you smiling about?" I asked.

"You can let go of my hand now. I won't run away, I promise." He squeezed my hand, bringing my attention to the grip I had on him. I let his hand go and took the few steps to my desk.

"Sorry about that. I didn't mean to uh," I paused. "You know. Okay, so we need to do a few things before you start work. Just some liability and paycheck stuff."

I pulled the few papers out of Aaron's folder I had already started on yesterday, in hopes he would take the job, while he sat on a seat in front of me. Dog walked over to sit beside me, placing his head on my leg. I had a feeling he knew there was a honey bun in my desk somewhere. I searched a few drawers and pulled it out for him. It took only seconds for him to eat the sugary treat, which convinced me that he didn't chew at all. I smiled when he placed his head back on my leg.

"So, this is just stating that we aren't responsible for injuries you sustain off our property. You're covered, even without insurance, while you're working." He read carefully over the page before signing his name on the bottom.

"Since you don't have an ID I can get the information off of, I'll need to ask you some questions," I said.

"I think we should talk about the fact that you know I don't have an ID." I could see the laughter in his eyes, and I decided to ignore further embarrassment for the day.

"It happened, and it's in the past. I'd rather not discuss
me patting you down like some freak. If you've forgiven me then
let's not talk about it." I could feel heat crawling up my chest
and neck. I still couldn't believe I had searched him and to
know he was awake was an awful feeling. Did I regret it?
Honestly, yes, but only because I couldn't gather information
from the incident. Did I think I would ever do it again? No.
Well, probably not.

"I need an address for you, Aaron," I said. His eyes
snapped to mine, and I didn't know what to do.

"That's going to be a problem, Bentley."

"I know. Let me think about this." I tried figuring out the
best course of action. I needed an address.

"What if I used yours?" he asked, cutting off my thoughts.
"If it's okay with you, can I use your address for the time
being?"

"Smart! You're only a few yards away from me so that would
work." I inwardly rolled my eyes at my choice of wording and
hoped Aaron missed it.

"Great," he replied.

I was just finishing the paperwork when there were three
taps on the door and Drake, and Sam walked in.

"Hey Bentley, I told Sam you might want her to do something about the piercing since all the guys take theirs out," Drake said.

"Oh, well, honestly the only the only reason we ask that they are taken out is that we don't want anyone getting hurt. When you're in the garage working on the vehicles, I think it's safer not to have anything on that can get caught in something," I explained.

"That's not a problem at all, boss," she replied.

"Awesome. So, I didn't get to introduce him, but this is the other new hire, Aaron. Aaron this is Drake and his daughter Sam. And this is Dog," I said, patting Dog on the head.

"His real name is Charles, but Bentley likes to rename other people's animals," Aaron added.

"Charles is a terrible name," I said, looking at Aaron. I waited for him to say that I was wrong but he only smiled. "Well, Drake, I need Sam to fill out some paperwork, so if you finished showing her around outside, we could trade off. I figure you can show Aaron around, too."

"Sounds good, kid. We'll be in the shop when you girls are finished."

"Okay, thanks."

"Nice beard man, how long have you been working on that

thing?" I heard Drake ask Aaron as they were walking down the hall. I didn't hear Aaron's response because Sam and I started laughing.

"My dad is a little goofy," Sam said, breaking the ice.

"He is, but I love him for it. He's made me and Pop laugh quite a bit," I said. "So, there are a few papers I need you to fill out, and if you have your ID, I can complete the stuff I need on the computer."

"Yes ma'am, here you go," she said handing me her driver's license. I gave her the papers and I started putting in the information I needed for payroll. Her birthdate made her a year younger than me.

"So, your dad told me you're taking a break from school?" I asked.

"Yeah, I am. I was going for nursing, and even with good grades and all that, I decided I didn't want to be a nurse. I think I was living up to my mom's dreams. I like, no, I love cars. Dad came home a few days later telling me he got me a job at the shop and I was so excited for the opportunity. I think that's when I knew for sure I wanted to be a mechanic."

"That's great, Sam! I love this place. I think more women need to get into fields like this, you know? Start teaching this kind of stuff in school and then more people will know how to do simple things in emergencies."

"I've always said schools need to teach oil changes, at least," she said. "I think we might be mind twins."

"Mind twins?" I asked.

"Yeah, we think alike."

"Hey, mind twins sound way better than spirit animal," I joked, and we both started laughing. We talked all the way back to the shop, and when I had to leave Sam, Aaron, and Dog to do my work, I was shocked at how sad I was. I had a moment where I thought about going to school to be a mechanic, so I could hang out with the cool kids instead of having the cool kids working for me.

CHAPTER EIGHT

From that day on, Aaron met me at the door of my apartment.
We would have breakfast, he would shower before getting ready,
and then he would leave his things in the foyer before we headed
to work. He fit in well with all the guys, and according to
Drake, he was excellent with cars.

When he received his first paycheck, we walked to the bank
on our lunch, and I cashed it for him. He couldn't cash it with
the lack of identification, and since I knew the check was good,
seeing as I wrote it, the teller didn't have any problems
cashing it. He spent part of his first check on breakfast from
Bucking Bandits for the both of us, and I made sure Dog had
actual dog food. Aaron agreed it was time for him to start
eating food that was good for him more often. A bonus was he
started calling him Dog.

The days turned into weeks, and before I knew it, it was just a few days before Thanksgiving. Every year Pop and I had a real Thanksgiving dinner. Turkey, mashed potatoes, stuffing, deviled eggs, the works. He was my only family, so he wanted to make sure I had a memorable dinner every year, and it was always awesome.

The Tuesday before the big holiday, Pop was sitting in his office across the hall when I walked in and sat down.

"Hey, squirt," he greeted.

"I was wondering how you would feel about me inviting Aaron over for dinner this year," I replied.

He sat back in his chair and rested his hands behind his head. "I don't mind. I figured you'd want to do that anyway. I'm shocked you haven't invited him already."

"I just wanted to make sure you were okay with it before I did. Have you set the turkey out yet?" I asked, getting excited.

"It's in the fridge until tomorrow morning. You coming over tomorrow night?"

Since moving out, the tradition was, I would spend the night with him, and we would start cooking early in the morning. I wasn't sure what I should do since I was inviting Aaron and Pop solved my dilemma.

"Bentley, ask Aaron to spend the night. He can sleep in the

other bedroom or on the couch if he wants."

"What? Really?" I asked, already excited and hoping Aaron would agree.

"Well, yeah you nut. I'm not going to make the guy sleep on the porch." Pop got up and walked over to hug me when I stood to leave. "I know you care about him and he's your friend. I wouldn't let him sleep outside on your favorite holiday. Plus, he's a darn good employee. Jerry said he caught him vacuuming out the cars the other day."

I laughed because I walked in on him picking up trash on the lot the day before. "He's a good man, Pop. That's why I don't understand what went wrong in his life."

"Sometimes things just happen to people. It's out of their control, but it's also up to them how they handle it. Just because life throws something horrible at you doesn't mean you have to use it as a crutch, but sometimes people can't see past their pain to realize that. Maybe you're helping him understand what he can be."

"Maybe you're right, Old Man. Thanks for letting me invite him this year." I squeezed him and left to finish my paperwork for the day. I was walking through the door when my cell phone started ringing. I rushed to it and saw it was an unknown number. I sent the call to voicemail and a few minutes later noticed they didn't leave one.

I called the few customers that had called in that day and scheduled appointments for all of them. Even a few weeks after hiring Sam and Aaron, we were still busy. They took a lot of the load off the other guys, and it seemed things were running smoothly. I was hanging up the phone when Sam walked into my office.

"Hey, Bee," she said sitting in one of the chairs. Sam had become an instant friend, and we got along perfectly. Her hair was in a high ponytail, putting the ends at her mid-back. The silver hoop was in place, and her smile was so big that her eyes crinkled in the corners.

"Hello, Samantha," I said, laughing when she made a face at the use of her full name. "What's up?"

"So, I think we should go into the city this weekend. Maybe go Black Friday shopping? I've never had enough money to go, but now that I have a steady job I can get some sweet gifts this year for my parents. Maybe even my little sister. She's a brat, but I think she'd cry if I didn't buy something for her."

"Yes, let's do that! Oh my gosh, Sam, I haven't been to the city in probably two years," I said, and it dawned on me how true that statement was. Living in a small town in the country was all right with me, but going shopping at real stores with more than two employees sounded exactly like the fun I needed.

"Awesome! Alright, I'm heading home. Mom's going to the grocery tonight and needs my help. I'll come pick you up Friday morning."

"Okay, see you then!" I waved goodbye and changed my shoes from one-inch high heels to my tennis shoes. When I stood to leave, Aaron was waiting in the doorway watching me. His dark blue coveralls were slightly unzipped, showing his grease stained white shirt underneath. His beard, trimmed down to a few weeks worth of length, was spotted with oil and something else that was blue. His hair was pulled up into a bun on the back of his head, and he was smiling at me.

"Hi," he said when I made eye contact.

"Hi," I replied. I put my coat on and grabbed my bag. We started our journey home, and when we were a block away from Cooper's, I started talking.

"I have a proposition for you."

"Don't tell me you're offering me another job," he joked.

"Ha. Ha. Very funny," I said, elbowing him in the ribs. He faked being hurt and reached over to tug on a piece of my hair. "I wanted to invite you to Pop's house for Thanksgiving dinner Thursday." I continued. "Not only that, though. Wednesday night I spend the night with him so I can start cooking early, and he

wants you to come too. He said you could use the spare room or
the sofa, whichever you prefer."

"That's a nice offer, but I don't want to ruin something
you do with your dad," he said.

"You wouldn't be ruining anything. I want you there, and
Pop likes you a lot. He said he was surprised I hadn't invited
you already."

"If you both are okay with it, I'd love to spend the
holiday with you and your dad." I felt my face stretch into the
biggest smile I could offer. I wrapped my arms around Aaron's
stomach and squeezed as hard as I could. I felt his arms wrap
around me and return my hug.

"I'm so excited for you to be there! Thanksgiving is my
favorite holiday, and I'm glad I get to spend it with you too
this year." I released my hold and looked up at him with a grin.
"You're going to love my mashed potatoes."

"I've loved everything you've made me so far, so I'm sure
you're right," he replied.

When we got to my apartment, Aaron said he had something he
needed to take care of, and he and Dog left. I tried not to
think about it and wonder what he was doing, but it bothered me
anyway.

When Wednesday night finally arrived, Aaron met me in front

of my building, and we walked to Pop's house. We each carried one backpack with our overnight and Thanksgiving Day clothes; Aaron had been buying items here and there to add to his wardrobe. I warned him that Pop was very into taking pictures all day long, so he found a beautiful red and cream flannel and paired it with dark jeans and boots from the local thrift store.

"Tonight, we're probably going to watch some movies and eat burgers. Nothing fancy since we're having a big feast tomorrow," I said when we were almost there.

"I'm not complaining. I'd be okay with a ham sandwich," he replied. He was honest, too. Most nights, when Aaron stuck around for dinner, if I asked what sounded good to him he'd always answer, "anything." He thanked me every single time, even the time I forgot the biscuits in the oven, making them much too hard to eat.

When we arrived at Pop's, I opened the door to let us in. I could hear Pop in the kitchen listening to one of his harder rock playlists.

"He must have just worked out," I said to Aaron, and sure enough, when I rounded the corner to the kitchen, Pop was there in his basketball shorts throwing burgers on the griddle.

"Hey, Pop!" I yelled over the blaring music. He looked up from what he was doing and smiled.

"Hey, squirt," he yelled back to me. "Give me a minute," he finished piling the burgers on, turned to the sink to wash his hands, and then proceeded to shut off the music. He walked around the island and grabbed me up in a hug.

"Oh, I'm going to kill you Pop!" I screamed. He sat me back on my feet, and I looked down at myself. I could see his sweat on my arms. "I think I might puke. Go shower you freak." Pop laughed all the way down the hallway to his bedroom and shut the door behind him. I didn't even get a chance to turn around when he opened the door again and came back out.

"Hey Aaron, I didn't mean to be rude," he shook his hand and pointed to the food. "You wanna keep an eye on that meat for me?" Aaron must have answered, although I didn't hear him because my dad chuckled and walked back into his room. Aaron's eyes were huge, and he looked completely freaked out.

"What's wrong?" I asked after I washed off my arms.

"Bentley, your dad's muscles have muscles," he turned to look at me then back down the hallway.

"Um, yeah, he works out." I was confused by his behavior. "You know you've seen him before, right?"

"I've never seen him without his shirt on and right after a workout though. How old is he?"

"Like a hundred or something," I said when he walked to the

griddle to stare at the food.

"He had an eight pack." I heard him whisper to himself.
"He's almost one hundred-years-old with an eight pack."

"He's not technically that old. He's only forty-nine. He
spent a while in the Marines, and he is hardcore about working
out," I laughed, remembering the awful time I tried to work out
with him. "He made me lift weights with him once when I was,
like, fifteen. He pushed me so hard I literally cried. It was
the worst experience ever, and he swore he'd never make me work
out again, if stopped eating potato chips at three in the
morning."

"Well, who eats junk food at three in the morning?" he
asked. "Especially with that monster as a father?"

"I get hungry sometimes," I replied, walking to the pantry
to look for a bag of chips. "Can we stop talking about how
stacked my dad is? It's freaking me out."

"Sorry, hey, where did Dog go?"

"Uh," I looked around the wall separating the kitchen and
living room and spotted Dog sleeping in front of the fireplace.
"He's sleeping. Must have had a big night."

"Yeah, we were up for most of it."

"Doing what?" I asked, trying to be casual about it so he'd
answer.

"A few errands. I won't have to do them every night for the next six weeks though. Probably just once a week."

"What do you do at night?"

"Errands, Bentley," he replied, his tone cutting off any further questions. I looked down at the floor and tried to convince myself his secrecy didn't hurt my feelings.

Pop walked back in wearing a dark gray wife beater and a different pair of basketball shorts. I looked closely at the man that raised me and noticed, for the first time, that his arms were probably about the size of my head. The muscles on his shoulders bulged when he reached up to grab the plates out of the cabinet, and I felt a little sorry for Aaron. He was muscular, but I realized Pop would have been intimidating to anyone.

When the food was ready, we all sat at the table and ate. We talked about work, and Aaron smoothly avoided any questions about his family. Every time he avoided a question, Pop would make eye contact with me and raise an eyebrow.

After dinner, we watched Pop's two favorite movies, and then he headed to bed. I started flipping through the channels and found another one of my favorite movies playing.

"You guys have a weird obsession with him," Aaron said after a few minutes, referencing the actor that had been in all three films.

"Well, he's our favorite actor. Plus, he's insanely hot, so that's a huge plus for me." When Aaron didn't respond, I looked over to see the horror written across his face.

"He's old enough to be your grandfather. That's the most disturbing thing I've ever heard." I started laughing at the face he was making, and he shook his head and turned back to the television.

I don't remember what part of the movie I fell asleep, but I remember the part of my dream that woke me up. I sat up as fast as I could and urged my eyes to stay closed. The car wasn't real; the semi didn't hit me, I'm here on the sofa with Aaron. Pop is in the other room. I am okay. I repeated in my mind. The car wasn't real. It wasn't real.

I didn't notice Aaron was speaking until I opened my eyes and looked at him. He seemed scared to touch me, but when he saw the look in my eyes, it must have broken his resolve. He slowly wrapped an arm around my shoulders and pulled me so that I was leaning against his chest.

"Bad dream?" he whispered.

"It was a nightmare," I replied, my voice wavering.

"You don't have to talk about it if you don't want to, but are you okay?"

"I'm okay, now." Every breath he took was deep and controlled, moving my head and making me smile.

"I can feel you smiling. What's funny?" he asked.

"You're moving my entire body with your breathing," I said, giving a small laugh.

"Sorry," his arms tightened around me and I heard a throat clear behind us. I jumped up like I'd been caught doing something wrong. Pop laughed, and I felt my cheeks redden.

"I hope you always react like that when it comes to your old man," he said, turning around and going back to bed.

"Love you, too, Pop," I said, rolling my eyes and sitting back down beside Aaron.

"Why do you call your dad Pop?" he asked.

"I've had so many people ask me that question, but the answer isn't as cool as you'd think. He called his dad Pop, and it stuck for me, too. I called him Dad once, and he acted as if I'd slapped him. He said it wouldn't bother him if I called him Dad but I think he secretly loves being called Pop. I don't know; he just looks more like a Pop to me."

"You're right."

"About what?"

"That was a lame reason." I rolled my eyes and hit Aaron with the throw pillow I had been holding, and he pulled it out of my hands with little effort, tossing it back at my head.

"I think I'm going to go to bed now. I'm pretty tired, and I have a lot to do tomorrow."

"I can help you tomorrow with the cooking if you want," he offered.

"That would be great." I turned to walk toward my room and stopped. Looking back at Aaron making his bed my heart kind of did this weird spasm thing. I was so happy he was here, and I decided to tell him that. "Hey, Aaron?"

"Yes, Bentley?" he asked smiling in my direction.

"I'm happy you're here with me. I just want you to know that. Thank you for coming."

"Thank you for inviting me." Was his soft reply and even softer he whispered, "Goodnight Sweetheart."

CHAPTER NINE

I woke up and immediately got to work. 6:00 A.M. came early, and I had much to do before lunch. Turkey? Check. Potatoes? Check. Boxed stuffing? Check. The list went on and on. The front door opened and I heard Aaron and Dog come back inside. I was staring at the largest turkey I'd ever seen when he walked into the kitchen.

"Good morning!" I said. He seemed so rested and happy. His long hair was messy and free of a hair tie, and his clothes were wrinkled. He looked adorable. "You want coffee?"

"Morning, coffee sounds great," he replied.

"I want one too, cupcake," Pop yelled from down the hall, making his voice sound sweet and girly. I rolled my eyes, got two more cups down, and poured their coffee for them.

"Happy Thanksgiving kids," Pop said when he walked in. He

walked over to pat me on the head and take his cup out of my
hand.

"You're not all that much older than Aaron you know?" Pop
cocked an eyebrow in question.

"How old are you, Aaron?" he asked.

"Thirty-two."

"Thirty-two? That's a relief. It's hard to tell under all
that hair."

"Pop!" I was so embarrassed.

"What? I didn't mean to sound rude, Bentley. I don't care
what his hair looks like."

"Well, it sounded mean to me!" I said, my voice going an
octave higher. I looked over to see Aaron's amused expression.

"What's so funny?" I asked him.

"I'm just enjoying the show." Aaron and Pop laughed and
drank coffee as if nothing had happened, and I decided men were
stupid. I got back to work and started pulling the innards out
of the turkey.

"Well, I hate to be the bearer of bad news, but Jerry
called and said he needs me to come in and approve a few things
this morning." Pop said walking out of the kitchen.

"What? It's only 6:30 A.M., why on earth is he at work on
Thanksgiving, especially this early?" I asked, confused.

"Oh yeah, I forgot what time it was," he said to himself. "Uh, he called last night. I'll be back in about an hour."

I followed him to his room, carrying the innards with me, and pushed the door open when he tried to shut it.

"Why are you leaving?" I asked. I couldn't believe he was about to blow me off on my favorite holiday.

"Why do you look like you're about to cry?" he asked when he turned to look at me. "I was just trying to give you some alone time with your friend. That's all."

"But I don't want you to leave. I mean, I appreciate the offer, but Aaron and I get plenty of alone time."

"That's disturbing. I'd like to pretend you didn't say that."

"Well, Pop, we have the walk to and from work together, and every day we eat breakfast, sometimes even dinner, together."

"I have heartburn," he said, grabbing his chest like he was in pain.

"You," I said, pointing my finger at him, "were about to leave us alone!"

"Yeah, but I wasn't going anywhere! I was going to be spying through the window!"

"Oh, come on, Pop!" I started laughing so hard my stomach started to hurt. By the time I calmed down enough to look at my father, tears were running down my cheeks. "That is the stupidest thing I've ever heard."

"It's not stupid. It's tactful," he replied with a smile. "I guess we better get back in there. He's probably wondering what's happening."

"No, I would say he probably heard every word, and he's decided to run away." To my surprise, Aaron was still in the kitchen, and an even bigger surprise was, all the peeled potatoes he had stacked beside him.

"I see you didn't make a run for it," Pop said.

""Well," Aaron replied, smiling in my direction, "I would have, but it started snowing."

I began to smile in return but looked outside to see the early morning light and hundreds of giant snow flakes falling. I started to get an uneasy feeling in my gut thinking about the day ending. I knew the time was coming, but I hadn't expected to get so close to Aaron and Dog.

I ignored everything except my thoughts and got started working on the food. Pop put the turkey in the oven, and I was well into making dough for the pie when Aaron interrupted me.

"What's wrong?" he asked. I looked up and saw Pop was sitting in the living room with Dog.

"I keep thinking about tonight," I replied.

"What about tonight?"

"It's snowing, Aaron. It's below freezing outside, and you and Dog have to sleep outside in it." I could feel the stinging in my nose from the emotion I was trying to hold down.

"Bentley, we're going to be fine. Tonight won't be the first time I've ever been out in the cold. It's not Dog's first time either. We manage to do okay, I promise."

"No, you're not fine. How am I supposed to sleep knowing you're out there?"

"You're making this much bigger than you need to."

"You've got to be kidding me. You're acting like it's not a big deal and I'm freaking out inside!"

"Okay, well do you want me to tell you it's a big deal and it sucks?"

"What? No! I want you to tell me you have somewhere to go."

"It is what it is, Bentley. I'll manage, and we will be okay. I don't want to talk about it anymore so let's drop it," he was getting frustrated, I knew he was, but I couldn't let it go. By then we had drawn the attention of Pop who was walking toward the kitchen.

"What's going on?" he asked.

"Nothing, Sir. We were just having a conversation."

"Bentley?" Pop looked at me. Aaron looked at me. Even Dog

was watching at me.

"I just," Aaron's eyes narrowed. "Aaron and Dog don't have anywhere to go this winter."

Aaron slammed the pot on the counter, walked to the living room to grab his backpack, and went to the restroom. When I heard the shower turn on, I turned to Pop and saw a disapproving look on his face.

"What did I do?" I asked.

"Why are you afraid to drive?" he asked. I felt my stomach plummet at the question.

"That has nothing to do with this," I said, getting angry that he would even bring it up.

"I'm trying to make you look at this differently. You went through something that forever changed you. There were circumstances out of your control that affected your life, so maybe you should think about that. Maybe something is going on, but Aaron would rather not sit and hash it out with you. Stop pestering him about it."

"Okay, I guess you're right, but I can't help it that I worry about him."

"Worrying about him is one thing, totally emasculating him is another."

"How did I emasculate him?" I almost yelled.

"Bentley, I saw his face. He didn't want you saying anything, but you took it upon yourself to tell me about it anyway. He's got enough problems to deal with without worrying about you telling everyone in creation about his problems. He's more than just a homeless guy. You throw him more pity parties than he's probably ever thrown for himself."

"He's said the same thing to me before," I whispered.

I placed the dough in the pie pan and poured the filling in. Pop was right; I needed to stop looking at Aaron like he was my poor pitiful friend.

When Aaron walked back into the room, an idea struck me.

"Move in with me," I said.

"What?" Aaron and Pop yelled at the same time. Their eyes mirrored each other in size and shock, and I would have laughed if I hadn't been entirely serious.

"For the winter months, move in with me," I tried again.

"No! Absolutely not, Bentley. I can't believe you would even suggest something so stupid," Aaron said shaking his head. He started back toward the living room so I followed. He walked over to his shoes and sat down to put them on.

"No, you're not leaving Aaron. I'm dead serious. You're my friend! You're my best friend." He stopped tying his shoes and looked up into my eyes. With hardly a foot separating us I watched the war in his eyes. "Please?"

"Be reasonable! You don't know me well enough to invite me to move into your home."

"I may not know everything about you, but that doesn't mean anything. I trust you." He went back to tying his shoes, and I started to panic. "What if it was me? What if I was the one that was going to be in the cold?"

"That isn't fair," he said, rubbing his hands over his face.

"How isn't it fair? It's a very serious question!"

"I'm not answering that question. It's ridiculous."

"It isn't ridiculous. Please talk to me. Don't just shut it down," I begged.

"No, it's not an option!" He pulled his backpack on and stepped out onto the porch. I followed. I could feel my face heating up with embarrassment and dread. I was either going to change his mind or lose him forever. I knew there was no in between.

"Get back inside, Bentley. You don't even have socks on, and it's snowing."

"I don't care. I don't want you to leave, Aaron."

"Well, that's too bad. Look, I'm sorry that you don't understand why I'm angry and maybe someday you will. I can't deal with this right now. I have too much to deal with already!"

"Then let me help you! I can be there for you. Just let me take one of your worries away."

"What are you talking about?" he asked, running his hands over his face in frustration.

"I'm not asking you to marry me, Aaron. I'm simply asking you to let me be your friend, let me take away one of your worries. Please?" I asked. I couldn't stop the lone tear that ran down my cheek, and I wasn't able to hide it from his eyes. "Wouldn't you do the same for me?"

I watched his shoulders sag in defeat as he watched the tear make its way to my chin. He reached out and wiped it away with his thumb and then shoved his hands into his coat pockets.

"Yes. If you were out in the cold, I would ask you to stay with me." He looked over my shoulder to where I guessed Pop was now standing. "Can you help me out here and tell your daughter that she's crazy?"

"Bentley, you're crazy," he said immediately, and Aaron looked relieved. "But I'm not going to tell you what to do."

"What?" Aaron asked with a shaky voice.

"She's twenty-two, son. I don't think I can tell her what to do anymore."

"Oh, you've got to be kidding me." Aaron laughed

humorlessly. "You're the size of a tree, I bet you would do alright."

"Yeah, I guess I do have a lot in common with a California Redwood," Pop said.

"Is that a tree?" I asked incredulously. "Why are we talking about trees? Aaron, please?"

He let his head fall backward and looked into the sky. "I have a few conditions."

"Anything!" I immediately agreed.

"One, this is the last thing you do for me. Two, I'm paying rent and pitching in with groceries. No, let me finish," Aaron said when I started to interrupt. "The third and final condition is the most important. When the snow is gone, you can't ask me to stay, no matter what."

I felt like that would come back to bite me in the butt, but I couldn't do anything but agree with him.

"Deal," I finally said.

"Deal," he added.

We shook hands, and he looked at Pop like he betrayed him. I laughed and made my way back to the kitchen. My feet were so cold I thought they might fall off, but I couldn't imagine a better reason.

After hours of preparing pies, potatoes, turkey, and food

galore, we ate our Thanksgiving lunch. We spent the rest of the day playing cards, eating leftovers and listening to Pop talk about weird things I was into as a kid. I didn't say a word to either of them about it, but it was by far the greatest Thanksgiving I had ever had.

CHAPTER TEN

When I first moved in, I decided I wanted the spare bedroom furnished in case Pop wanted to stay over. He had only stayed over twice, once when the weather was bad and a few weeks prior when I hit my head.

With Aaron and Dog moving in, I was thankful I'd thought to fix it up.

The room had a queen-size bed with a basic black comforter, a nightstand with a lamp and a dresser with a small television sitting on top. We walked into the room, and I could feel Aaron's tension.

"Feel free to put your things away. Some of your shirts are already hanging in the closet," I said pointing to what he'd left with me for work.

"Listen, I'm sorry I got so frustrated earlier," he said.

"It's okay. I shouldn't have kept pushing you; I should be the one apologizing."

" I reacted horribly, but I was serious about those conditions, Bentley."

"I know you were." I moved to leave but stopped and faced him. "I'm glad you're here."

"I am too," he said.

Before I could talk myself out of it, I walked toward him and wrapped my arms around him. My cheek rested against his chest, and I squeezed so tight I could feel his heartbeat. After a few seconds, Aaron's arms came up and pulled me even closer to him. I had to clear my throat before I could speak. We released each other, and I backed away.

"I forgot to tell you, Sam and I are going shopping in the city. I'll probably be leaving after breakfast, but I'll be home around 5:00 P.M., tomorrow."

"Is there anything you want me to do tomorrow while you're gone? Like, laundry or something?"

"Well," I said. "You could put up some of the Christmas decorations if you want."

"Christmas? It's still November!" he said laughing.

"I know, but if I put them up now, I can enjoy them throughout December and then put it all away on New Year's Eve.

That's what I always do."

"If that's what you want me to do then I'll do it. Just show me where everything is before you leave. Are you sure you don't have specific places for everything?"

"Nope, you can put it anywhere, and I won't care. Pulling everything out is my least favorite part, so this is perfect."

"Alright, well, goodnight Bentley. If you hear me moving around, it's just me taking Dog out so don't get scared."

"Okay. Goodnight Aaron. Goodnight Dog," I said.

I sent Sam a text telling her I'd be ready to go at 9:00 A.M., and I set my alarm before getting in bed. I was so thankful for the blessings I had received that year. I started thinking about Sylvia from Bucking Bandits and felt a twinge of guilt since I'd not been over there for a few days. I fell asleep thinking about how I could convince Pop to close Cooper's for lunch one day, so everyone could eat there.

When I woke up, I went to the restroom, showered and then got dressed in my most comfortable leggings, teal sweater dress, and boots. I curled my hair, put on a dash of makeup, and I was ready to go.

Aaron was sitting at the kitchen table with a coffee cup, watching the news while Dog was eating food out of his bowl in the foyer. I smiled to myself and let the new feeling wash over me.

"Let me grab you a cup of coffee," Aaron said as he stood and went to the kitchen.

"Thank you," I called out to him. I walked to the closet in the foyer and started pulling boxes out. It was the only place I had room for my Christmas decorations, and since it was the only holiday I decorated for, I had quite a bit of stuff. I heard Aaron laugh and turned to find him leaning his back against the wall with his arms crossed over his chest.

He was still in what I assumed were the clothes he slept in, due to all the wrinkles. His oversized sweatpants, black t-shirt, and mix-matched socks paired with his messy man bun were a sight to see.

"You're wearing two different colored socks, Aaron," I laughed.

"Am I?" he asked looking down at his feet. "It was pretty dark when I put them on this morning."

He pushed off the wall and walked toward the closet that I was now standing in. "So, uh, does this closet go all the way to your room, or is there an end to all these boxes?"

"There's an end!" I laughed.

"Come on then, and get out of the closet," he said in a British accent.

"You're in a good mood today," I said, stepping over boxes on my way out.

"I'm pretty happy, other than the fact that I woke up to hear you snoring more than once last night, I had a pretty good night's sleep." I gasped.

"I do not snore!" My face was probably as red as a tomato because the truth was, I sometimes did.

"It was just a little bit, I promise, and if there's a cute snore, it'd be what you do."

"That is mortifying," I said. "Let's pretend I don't snore and change the subject." Aaron laughed and looked into the closet like he couldn't believe all I had fit in there.

"Okay, there's enough stuff to keep me busy all day. I have to run out, and I don't have a key, so I may have to wait until you're back to finish everything."

"I'll give you the spare key so you won't get locked out. What do you have to do today?"

"Bentley," he said in a way that I knew the conversation was shut down before it even began.

"Sorry," I said and then started dragging boxes into the living room.

We spent the next hour getting boxes out of the closet and pulling the Christmas tree branches apart. Pop let me have my childhood tree when I moved, so we had to separate the branches by color and fan out all the pieces. By the time Sam knocked on the door, we had been in two bow fights, and Aaron had one stuck to his head. I was laughing when I pulled the door open, and I lunged to hug her.

"Sammy!" I said in a sing-song voice.

"Oh no, you don't. You go right ahead and change that nickname before you get attached to it," she laughed, hugging me back.

"Come see what Aaron's doing today!" I threw my arm over her shoulder and dragged her into the living room.

"It looks like Kris Kringle threw up in your house, Bee," Sam shuddered. Apparently, she wasn't into red and green.

"I'm almost positive Bentley and old Saint Nick are best friends, there are more boxes in the hallway," Aaron said. He was sitting on the floor in the middle of the mess.

"You know you have a bow in your hair, pretty boy?" she asked laughing. He smiled despite his eye roll.

"If you don't want to do all this alone just wait for me. I feel awful now that I'm leaving you with all of it," I told Aaron.

"It's not a big deal. How about I just get as much done as I can. If there's more, we can work on it tonight."

"Okay, I guess I'll see you later then." I walked over and gave him a quick hug then went to Dog and did the same. Dog whined when I left, and I heard Aaron call him a flirt under his breath. Smiling, Sam and I headed toward the door.

"Don't forget your coat," Aaron called out. I grabbed my coat and purse, waved goodbye and shut the door behind me. I was halfway to the stairs when I remembered I forgot to give him the key. I told Sam to wait in the car, and rushed back to the apartment and pushed open the door.

Aaron was standing in the middle of the living room with his shirt hanging in one of his hands. My eyes widened, and I felt my neck and face catch on fire. So, I concluded right then and there; Aaron was seriously attractive, and he found some way to work out.

"It got really hot in here," he said, lamely.

"Uh, yeah. Make yourself at home," I squeaked out. "I forgot to give you the key, so uh, it's here on this hook." I pointed to the key holder by the door to the only key left hanging. He nodded in acknowledgment, and I turned and ran out of the room, slamming the door behind me. I ran down the stairs, and when I got into the car, Sam looked at me like I was crazy.

"What happened to you?" she asked.

"I just had an encounter with Aaron's abs." Sam burst out

laughing and pulled away from the curb heading toward the

highway.

CHAPTER ELEVEN

For the entire hour drive, Sam and I listened to every song we could think of. Her taste was a lot like Pop's work out mix. She loved bands I couldn't name and had no desire to listen to.

"I couldn't even understand any of the words to that last one," I said about a song she had just played.

"If you hadn't been banging your head so hard you probably would have heard them. I think you might have gotten brain damage," she giggled.

"But I thought that was what you were supposed to do? That's what Pop sometimes does."

"Your dad is weird. Hot, but weird."

"Ew!" I mock gagged on my finger. "Aaron is amazed by his muscles," I added, laughing.

"Speaking of Aaron," she nudged me with her elbow over the

console.

"What about him?"

"You guys seemed pretty chummy today."

"Yeah, the bow fight really brought us closer." I rolled my eyes. "He moved in last night. He'll be there for a few months, and then, maybe I can help him find a place once he saves some money. I haven't talked to him about it because he was so reluctant to agree to stay with me, but I think it will all be okay."

"Does he know you care about him?"

"Of course he knows. I mean he knows I care about his friendship. I'm not sure if he knows that I'm starting to care about him though."

We made it to the mall, and I started getting giddy. I usually saved all year-long so that I could get gifts for Pop, and the guys that worked at Cooper's. My list seemed much longer this year, though, and I had only added a few names.

Store after store, I added more and more bags. I chose a scarf, some candles and eye shadow for Sylvia. I bought a few shirts for Jerry and the guys at the shop as well as a small, home toolset for all the men in the office. Pop and Sam ended up with the same gift, which proved to be a challenge since I had to sneak away so Sam wouldn't see me buy it. They were so alike;

it was crazy and I knew they'd both love it.

It was harder to pick something out for Aaron. I wanted to buy him unreasonable amounts of clothes, but I had a feeling it would have upset him. I settled for two outfits, a few board games, and a pocket knife.

I ended up buying Dog a bed so he wouldn't have to sleep on the floor anymore, and I couldn't wait to get home and see if he liked it.

After what seemed like thirty trips to the car, and special maneuvering to fit all our bags in the backseat and the trunk, we walked across the parking lot to a small restaurant for lunch.

"I'm surprised you didn't spend more on your dad," sam said once we sat down.

"I would have if there was anything he actually needed or wanted. I swear he is the hardest person to buy for. If he needs or wants something, he just goes out and buys it."

"My dad waits for the holidays and starts dropping hints to my mom. It's kind of hilarious because he gets impatient sometimes and acts like he's going to buy something just to see if she bought it already." We were both laughing when the waiter came to ask for our drink order.

"The same for me, please," I said after Sam ordered water.

"No problem, I'll be right back with that," he said, smiling down at me. I smiled back and looked at Sam, who was wagging her eyebrows at me.

"What?" I asked.

"He didn't even notice anyone else at the table with how much he was drooling over you."

"I didn't really notice, but I can assure you, you're hard to miss. If it's not the obvious beauty that lures people in, then it's the pink hair and giant piece of metal in your face." She laughed and threw her napkin at me.

"Whatever, maybe there wasn't actual drool, but he definitely checked you out."

"I'm sitting down and slouching, so I probably look frumpy."

Sam laughed and said, "I wasn't going to say anything, but you do have a frumpy look right now." The waiter came back with our drinks and sat them down.

"Ready to order?" he asked me. I fought the urge to snort a laugh and looked at Sam.

"Go ahead, Samantha."

"I'll take a grilled chicken salad and fries."

"We don't serve fries here," he said, giving her a strange look.

"Right, well how about a baked potato?"

"Sure, and you?" he asked, cutting his blue eyes back to me.

"Same," I said. I kicking Sam under the table in response to her wide, telling grin.

"Alright, I'll get this out to you as quickly as I can, ladies."

"He's probably putting a rush on the order," she said when he walked away.

"Oh yeah I bet he is, so he can hurry up and get a couple of weirdos out of here."

"You're probably right," she laughed. "So, what did your dad say about Aaron moving in?"

"It was kind of funny, actually, because Aaron expected him to freak out and refuse to allow it, but he just said I was crazy and told Aaron I was an adult. The look on his face was hilarious."

"But," she said, encouraging me to say more.

"But, what?"

"But how did he really feel about it?" I shook my head. She hadn't been around long, but she knew Pop pretty well already.

"I had three texts from him when I woke up this morning," I said smiling. "He asked me if I knew what I was doing in two of them and then told me he supported me in the last one. He added that I shouldn't be surprised by random visits by him in that one, too."

"What's funny is, he's probably already at your place."

"Oh my gosh, I hadn't even thought of that, but you're probably right!" Our food was brought out, and we immediately started eating. Shopping had made us ravenous.

We were leaving the table when our waiter walked up to us. His short blonde hair added to his boyish charm, but before I could help it, I was comparing him to Aaron.

"Hi, sorry to be this forward, but I was wondering if I could have your number," he said. Sam made a gesture like she scored a touchdown and walked out the door, leaving me with Peter, or at least his name tag said that was his name.

"Oh, wow, I'm really flattered, but I don't think so," I said, and he turned red.

"I don't think anyone has ever turned me down that fast," he said, scratching his neck. "Are you seeing someone?"

"Not that it's any of your business, but no, I'm not."

"I didn't mean to be rude. I was just curious I guess. Okay, well now that I've made things awkward, I hope you have a good day."

I laughed and said goodbye, meeting Sam outside the door.

"You are a jerk, Sam. A very big jerk." She laughed all the way to the car, and I wondered how severe the damage would be if I punched her in the kidney. Probably too much, so I settled for enjoying the image in my head.

The ride home was as loud and obnoxious as the ride there had been. We rocked out to more music and debated opening a restaurant in Taylorsville since the diner was the only food place other than one fast-food restaurant. Then we realized the extent of our talent was what I made for Thanksgiving and figured it would turn out awful.

Sam had easily fit into my life. I spent so many years being afraid of letting people in because of what I had gone through, that I missed out on all of this. The singing and goofing off in the car with a buddy and the meals with your best friend. I chose to forfeit all of it out of fear of getting hurt. I was starting to regret my decision to build a wall around my heart.

I know there were times when I wore my emotions on my sleeve, like when it came to caring about Aaron. Before that day with Sam, I believed anyone in my life, other than Pop, would one day abandon me. Sam's friendship helped rid my mind of that thought. I trusted that if we were ever to move away from each other, we'd still be very present in each other's lives. I

couldn't imagine not having her as a friend now. I felt saddened
by the fact that for so many years, I'd resolved myself to
thinking that no one would ever want to stick around. No one
would ever choose to stay with me after they got to know me.

The person that was supposed to love me and want me no
matter what abandoned me, so why on earth would someone choose
to be a part of my life? My logic had been so twisted for years.
Since the age of five when I watched her walk out the door, I
began struggling with my self-worth. Pop was the one who got me
through. When I was around twenty years old, he really broke
through some ice.

I had been throwing another pity party for myself because
"she" didn't want me and he'd finally had enough. He began
telling me all of his favorite memories from my childhood, the
things we had done together, him and I. The softball games,
teaching me how to ride a bike, riding my first horse on a farm
in Tennessee, and playing paintball with some of the men he'd
served with. The memories went on forever and ever. He had given
me such a full life that I realized I didn't need her love to
make me a whole person. I was already whole because Pop had
given me enough of himself to fill the void caused by her.

I looked over at Sam and smiled to myself. She was singing
and banging her head enough that her hair was bouncing around,

almost hitting her in the eyes. For the first time in such a long time, I felt like my heart was relaxed. I wasn't scared of losing Sam, Aaron, Dog, or even Pop. I felt relaxed enough to be content.

CHAPTER TWELVE

"Wow!" Sam and I both said when I opened the door to the apartment.

"How about I bring your stuff to you Monday after work or something?" she asked.

"Okay, that sounds great."

Everything looked amazing. Aaron had put all the decorations out, and there were a few candles lit throughout the living room. It smelled like a mixture of pine trees and food. I gave Sam a huge grin as she waved and backed out of the doorway into the hall. I took off my shoes and went on a search for Aaron.

When I walked into the kitchen, he was standing at the stove, so I leaned against the fridge and watched. From the tortillas on the counter, I assumed we were having some form of

a taco. My favorite, which he knew from a previous conversation
we had on one of our walks to work.

"I'm home," I finally said so I wouldn't scare him.

"I was wondering how long you were going to stand there
like a creep," he said turning around to grin at me. I laughed
and walked to the stove to see what he had.

"You knew I was standing there?"

"Yeah, I'm pretty good at knowing what's going on around
me."

"You're like a ninja," I said, and he laughed. "So, tacos?"

"Oh, definitely. It's probably the only food that can be
sketchy and good all at the same time."

"Yeah?"

"Yeah. That and this is the only thing I felt confident
enough to cook. And not even that confident, to be honest."

"I'm sure it'll be great!" I said grabbing the applesauce
out of the fridge.

"What's that for?" he asked.

I looked down at my hands and thought about what I should
do. Did I tell him or just put the applesauce away? I chose to
tell him and prepared myself for the inevitable response.

"Okay, well, I have this thing with tacos, spaghetti, uh,
basically all foods when I'm home. I just kinda throw applesauce

on whatever I'm eating."

"You mean you like to eat it on the side?"

"No, you'll see."

We filled our plates, and Aaron poured lemonade for both of us. Making our way to the table in the dining room, I stepped over a sleeping Dog.

"He sleeps a lot," I said as we both sat down. "Are you sure he's only three?"

"I got him when he was about a year old, so he's going on five now. I think he's used to sleeping during the day since we've been doing that for so long."

"When will you have to do a night shift for whatever it is you do?" I asked, hoping he would give me something.

"I think I can go out Thursday nights for the next couple of months. It's cold, so traffic is slower than usual."

"Traffic for what?"

"Come on Bentley," he said smiling. "You know I'm not going to answer that."

"Just thought I'd try." I opened the applesauce and began pouring it over my taco meat. I folded up the tortilla and took a huge bite. Amazing. I glanced up to see a horrified expression on Aaron's face.

"What in the world? No. No, that can't be a thing," he said

shaking his head back and forth.

"It's a thing, has been since I was, like, in the womb. Freaks the crap out of Pop though so I can't eat it at his house. Wanna try it?" I asked, offering him my jar of applesauce.

"No, I don't want to try it! I'd puke."

"Oh, wow you big drama queen," I said laughing. I took another bite, and he cringed.

"One bite?" I tried again. He sat back in his chair, and his grimace turned into a wide grin. It was infectious.

"Only one bite, even though I'm positive I'm going to throw up." He poured a small amount onto his taco and took a bite. The second he gagged, I lost it. I laughed as he stood, running into the kitchen to spit it into the trash can.

"What in the world was that?" he yelled. His eyes were huge, and he was looking at me like I was psychotic. "That's the most disgusting thing I've ever eaten, and I've eaten some weird crap, Bentley."

"It's not disgusting! It is a little weird, but I like it."

"Something is wrong with you," he said, sitting back down.

"Aaron?" I asked after a few minutes of silently enjoying our meal.

"You don't have to say my name every time you want to tell

or ask me something," he joked.

"I'm curious, what's going on tonight?"

"What do you mean?"

"I mean you're so," I paused, trying to find the right word.

"Talkative?" he asked.

"Yes, talkative, happy, smiling. You let yourself almost puke on purpose."

"To be honest, I made a decision today," he admitted.

"What did you decide?"

"I guess I chose to leave my issues outside the door. I don't want any problems to exist in here, with us."

I smiled. "I like that."

We finished eating and cleaned up our dishes together. I was wiping down the stove, making fun of him for almost getting sick when a giant clump of bubbles landed in my hair.

"You did not just do that!" I laughed so hard I snorted. "It probably has something gross in it."

"Oh well, you can wash your hair," he said. I walked over to the sink and grabbed the sprayer attachment. I pointed it in his direction and squeezed the handle. Faster than I could have imagined, he lunged forward and grabbed the hose away from me, turning it in preparation to spray me in the face.

"Surrender," he said, leaning toward me.

"Okay, okay! I surrender!" He put the sprayer back and folded the towel over the sink.

"Do you want to watch a movie?" he asked.

"Yes!" I ran to the living room and picked up a DVD.

"Let me guess who's in that movie," he rolled his eyes.

"My future husband, of course,"

"He's so old!"

"Yeah, but I have hope. He keeps going younger and younger with his wives, so I'm thinking by the time I meet him I'll have a fighting chance."

"I'm picking the movie," he laughed.

"Fine! Nothing sappy though."

"I thought we could go for a good cry." He said with a straight face that only lasted a moment before he broke out in a grin. His smile was so amazing. He had his beard trimmed down to only a few weeks worth of length, and his hair was in a regular ponytail. Everything about him was relaxed and at home, and I was surprised with how fast he was able to be this relaxed. I was happy he was comfortable, but I was scared he might be putting on a show for my sake.

We had had plenty of conversations and learned pretty basic things about each other over the weeks he had been working for

Cooper's. Things like his favorite color was blue; mine was black. He loved country music. His favorite food was chicken pot pie. He hated that he didn't have a huge beard; it had taken him two years to get it as long as it had been but he wanted to clean up for his new job. So many small things that I would try my hardest to remember, but nothing too personal. Nothing that would tell me how he got to where he was or how he became the man he was. I decided to try again.

"I have an idea! Let's play Rummy," I said.

"You like Rummy?" he asked, shocked.

"I love it! I had a babysitter when I was little that loved the game and taught me how to play it. She was a little older than Pop at the time."

"Okay, I haven't played in so long."

I ran and grabbed the cards out of my bedroom and met him at the dining room table. I dealt the cards, and we started the game. He went first, laying down three twos. He was getting a good start because I had absolutely nothing in my hands. I was okay with that, though since I had a plan up my sleeve.

"Let's play for something, like betting but not with money."

"What would we use?" he asked, concentrating on his hand.

"How about, whoever gets the most points during the hand

gets to ask a question and the other person must answer. So, if you win this hand, you can ask me whatever you want, and I'll answer honestly."

He stared at me for a moment. "You can't ask me questions about work," he said sternly. His tone told me I shouldn't even try if I did win, so I nodded.

"Deal. I can't ask you questions about work, and you can't ask me about the woman that gave birth to me."

"I agree to those terms." His lighthearted humor was back in place. I wanted it to stay forever.

We buckled down and focused on our game. We were both in it to win it, and I suspected for very different reasons. I'm sure Aaron had questions about me, but he was probably trying to prevent me from being able to ask anything about his life. He quickly won the first game.

"What's your question, Mr. Ninety Points?" I asked, writing down our scores on a piece of paper I pulled out of a notebook.

"Easy. What's your favorite book?"

"There's no such thing for me," I said. "I have so many favorites, but they're all so different. All romance, of course, but some take place in alternate universes, one is about a caveman, there are a few werewolves, vampires, and aliens. You name it; I've probably read it."

"Aliens? You think one would make a good boyfriend?"

"Ew, no!" I laughed. "There are a few authors out there that can write a good science-fiction. I mean, for instance, two of the greatest sci-fi hits in the world take place in space."

"What about werewolves and vampires? I can understand the alien thing, barely, but, animals?"

"I grew up on good vampire stories," I laughed. "Not just that though, I guess I like the doors that books open. Who wants to be a boring old human when you can be a wolf or a dragon?"

"I think I'll stick with the human race," he said, and I smiled.

"It's your deal."

He dealt the cards and we got back to business. I meant for the night to be fun and exciting and it was turning into a real competition. We both had a motive, and I was determined to win. Unfortunately, I lost again, sixty-five to twenty. I let my head fall to the table in defeat.

"Why didn't you go to college?" he asked.

"I did go to college," I answered, my head still laying on the table.

"Oh, I guess I assumed you didn't since you work for your dad."

"I went online, didn't even attend my graduation ceremony

since it was a two-hour drive from here."

"I bet your dad didn't like that at all."

"He said he didn't mind, but I think it bothered him. I feel bad now since I'm his only kid and he didn't get to see it. I thought about getting a bachelor's degree so that I could invite him to my graduation."

"What would you go for?" I lifted my head and smiled.

"Nice try, buddy. Hand over the cards," I reached across the table and took the cards, shuffling them and dealing. He won again.

"Oh my gosh! What's the point of this stupid game if I find out nothing about you?" I asked and ignored his chuckle.

"If you could go to college for anything, what would it be?"

"Well, I went for business since I'm going to own Cooper's one day. If that fell through, I don't really know what I'd do. It's literally the only thing I've ever wanted to do. So, I guess I'd get a bachelor's degree in business."

"There's nothing wrong with that. At least you have a plan."

"What would you go for?" I quickly asked.

"Ah, I don't think so. Just because you're such a bad player doesn't mean I'll take pity on you."

"Fine!"

He shuffled and dealt while I thought of the question I would ask if I did, in fact, win this round. And win I did! It was like the cards knew I needed a good hand because I had three aces my first turn. I beat his fifty-five points by a whopping thirty.

"Okay! Can you tell me anything about your family?" I asked excited at the prospect.

"I can share a little I guess," he paused. "I was adopted when I was sixteen. They were absolutely amazing, too."

"Were?" I asked quietly.

"They were," he answered with a sad smile.

"I'm sorry."

"Yeah, me too. Do you want to play another hand?"

"Yeah, if you want to."

"Sure, one more hand." I had a feeling Aaron was going to win that one, and I was right. I was too focused on the thought of him being without the parents that he hadn't received until he was a teenager. It broke my heart.

"Your hand, what's your question?" I asked.

"Can I think about it and ask tomorrow?"

"Yeah, I guess that would be okay."

"I want to think of a really good one."

"Okay," I smiled. "I think I'm going to bed now," I said after a moment.

"Sounds good. I'm beat since some lady had me decorate her entire apartment today."

"Our apartment," I corrected, wiping the smile off his face.

"Just for the time being," he said. Like he had to remind me.

"Right, well, goodnight, Aaron," I said. I left him and walked to my bedroom.

I changed into my pajamas and turned on my television to play in the background. I lied in bed going over my day and wondering if Aaron was happy. Thinking of the fact that he no longer had his parents broke my heart and I felt bad for going to bed early but I couldn't wrap my head around it. Losing Pop would be the worst thing in the world. It's something I hoped not to have to go through until I was old and senile enough not to know what was going on. I needed to change the road my mind was going down, so I fell asleep thinking about what I wanted to make for dinner the next day.

CHAPTER THIRTEEN

Someone was knocking on my bedroom door. At 7:00 A.M., if there wasn't an emergency, there was going to be a problem. I opened the door to Aaron in his grease stained jeans and coat holding a plate of bacon, eggs, and toast. I guess I could forgive him this time.

"Good morning," he offered me the plate.

"What's this for?" I asked, quickly forgetting my annoyance.

"I have to head to work, and I thought I'd make you breakfast before I left." I took the plate and ate a piece of the bacon.

"Thank you!" I said. "It sucks you have to go in today. I might come in later to do some paperwork, but I'm going to try to do it here on my laptop."

"You should just stay here."

"That's the plan if I have all the numbers I need." I laughed. We headed to the dining room, and I sat down to eat.

"I hate to think of you walking there all by yourself, though. Maybe I should leave Dog with you, in case you have to go in?" he pulled out the chair beside me. He sat facing me, and I immediately felt embarrassed. He was sitting so close, and I hadn't brushed my teeth yet.

"I've walked to work alone for over two years now. I'll be fine."

"But, it's different now."

"How is it any different?" I asked.

"You have me." I tried to ignore the smile that wanted to appear.

"I can take care of myself, I promise," I laughed. Looking over at Aaron I immediately noticed he didn't think it was as funny as I did. "I promise I'll be fine."

"I need to get a phone, so you can call me if you need me."

"You're overreacting."

"There are dangerous people out there, Bentley."

I didn't know what to say. I was glad that Aaron cared enough about me to worry, but Pop had always made sure I was comfortable when I was alone. It was one of those things that he kind of forced on me; I was going to know how to take care of myself even if it killed my old man.

"Listen, I appreciate that you're worried about me, but I really do know how to take care of myself. I can carry my gun if it makes you more comfortable though."

"Gun? Do you even have a permit?" he asked incredulously.

"Who are you, the gun police?" I asked, and Aaron narrowed his eyes a little. "Kidding. I have my permit."

"What time are you coming to work? That way I can watch for you."

I stood and carried my empty plate to the sink. After rinsing it off, I walked back to my room and turned to find Aaron hot on my trail.

"Thank you for making me breakfast. I appreciate it. You should probably get a move on though before you're late for work." I shut the door and locked it, smiling when I heard, what I assumed, was his forehead hitting the door.

"Please be careful. I'll see you later."

"See ya!" I chirped. I heard the front door shut, and I climbed back in bed. There was no point in staying awake if I didn't need to. After reading a few chapters of my latest find, I fell asleep.

There was banging on my door again. This time I was going

to break someone's knuckles, even if said knuckles were attached
to an adorable man with a bun! I opened the door and heard the
knocking coming from down the hall. The front door. I ran to the
door and looked out the peephole to see Aaron. A very angry
looking Aaron.

"Dude, what is your problem?" I asked when I opened the
door.

"You've got to be kidding me. I had your dad call your cell
phone to see when you were coming in, Bentley. Ten times! You
said you were coming in and we couldn't get ahold of you." He
had walked past me and started searching the apartment. I
started to get a little freaked out by his behavior.

"What are you looking for?" I asked, following him to my
room.

"For the reason that would prohibit you from answering your
phone, or a reason you couldn't come to work, like someone
breaking in. You scared the crap out of me, and I just need to
know that you're safe." He had found my phone and turned the
volume up. Making his way back to the living room after
determining the place was safe, he sat on the sofa and placed
his head in his hands. I walked to him and sat only a few inches
away.

"I don't understand what's going on," I admitted.

"I was just scared that something happened to you," he said. He sounded exhausted.

"I know there are bad people out there, and bad things do happen, but we can't live in fear of what might happen."

He leaned back and looked at the ceiling. I followed suit. My cell phone beeped a few times, and Aaron handed it to me so I could text Pop back and let him know I wasn't dead. He immediately responded that he got a kick out of seeing Aaron worry and I rolled my eyes. We sat there, both of us thinking, I suppose. I tried to put logic to the situation, but nothing made absolute sense.

On one hand, maybe Aaron was worried about me because he cared about me. I worried enough about him to understand that. The only thing that didn't add up was the fact that this wouldn't have been the first time I walked alone to work since he started working at Cooper's. On the other hand, it was possible he was one of those guys that liked to control women. That thought immediately fled my mind though. I believed to my core that he was a genuinely good person.

The only thing that seemed to fit the most was that he was in trouble with someone. If someone were after him, that would make sense that he wouldn't want me to leave the apartment alone. The question I had to ask myself was, was he the kind of person to get involved in something bad? Drugs? Did he owe

someone money?

"I need to know what's going on. Am I in danger because you

live here?" My voice, a whisper, was loud enough to make him

jump. His eyes met mine.

"One day I'm going to sit down with you and tell you

everything you want to know. Anything and everything, no limits.

That can't happen right now, not yet. You aren't in danger with

me here, but if you want me to leave because I scared you, I

will." He sounded so sad like the outcome was already decided.

"Can you at least explain to me what happened? Why you got

so panicky?"

"I've seen so many horrible things in my life, Bentley," he

said after a moment. "I've watched people get hurt. Heard the

neighbor beating his wife, saw the wife aiming a gun, heard

screams after the gun fired. I've seen kids get neglected while

their parents get high in another room. I've been in places

where I had to wear shoes all the time because if I didn't,

there was a chance I could step on a needle. I'm thirty-two, and

I'm finally getting to the point where I've experienced mostly

good for more than half my life, and I guess I got scared.

You're important to me; you're my closest friend. My only

friend, and I was so scared. So much good has been happening

that I was prepared to come home to find something bad had
caught up with me."

I could barely speak through the pain of emotion that
clogged my throat.

"You have a fear of driving, and I have a fear of something
happening to you," he added.

"I don't want you to leave," I said.

"Really?" he asked.

"Of course not, but I want you to promise me something."

"What's that?" he sounded nervous.

"I just want you to promise me that you won't act like that
again. If you can't get ahold of me, be calm and rational about
it instead of coming home and scaring the crap out of me. I
always keep the door locked, I have a gun, and the most
important thing is that I have enough faith in my ability to
protect myself that I'm not afraid of being alone. Not only
that, but I don't want to be scared of something that might
happen. I already deal with an irrational fear of driving; I
don't want to add anything to that list."

We watched each other for a few minutes before Aaron gave
me a small smile.

"I have faith in you, too. I'm sorry I got a little crazy
today, and I promise you, it won't happen again. I'll just

disable the ability to turn your phone on silent." His expression gave away the fact that he was joking and I laughed.

"Very funny," I said.

"What are your plans for the day?"

"I thought about doing nothing, actually. Want to join me?"

"Absolutely," he said.

We spent the rest of the day eating junk food and watching Law and Order. We talked about weird things like his obsession with cop shows and my aversion to birds. He laughed while I told him the story of when I was a child and a mother bird attacked me for getting too close to her nest, and the time I looked up in the sky only to have a bird poop in my eye.

Aaron shared a few things too. He told me from the time he was adopted to the time he lost his parents his mom would make him a blueberry pie every single Friday and how he missed things like that. I decided I wanted to make him one. It obviously wouldn't be anything like his mothers, but I could try. If it would make him happy, I realized I'd do just about anything.

CHAPTER FOURTEEN

On Sunday, we both took advantage of being able to sleep in, thank God. Feeling my bed dip, I opened my eyes to see Dog sitting beside me staring down into my eyes.

"Hi, buddy. I'm going to ignore the fact that you're on my bed, only because I feel like I haven't been paying much attention to you." He inched closer until he was snuggled close to me. He sat his head on my belly and closed his eyes.

I picked the book up off my nightstand and read while scratching Dog's ears. Aaron appeared in the doorway a little while later.

"Good morning. I see you have company," he said.

"Yeah, I think I hurt his feelings since I haven't spent any time with him lately. Maybe we could go for a walk or something today."

"That's a great idea. Did you want to go this morning?"

"What time is it?" I asked.

"A little after nine. Maybe we can go to breakfast."

"Okay! I'll get ready and be out in a few minutes."

Once we dressed, we headed to Bucking Bandits. I was excited to see the gang. As soon as we walked in Dog ran to the back and sat in a booth. He was ready to eat some human food again since he'd been on a strict diet.

"Hey Sylv," Aaron called out.

"Aaron! It's good to see you again. Where have you been honey?" she asked, hugging him. She moved to me and squeezed me. "We've missed you around here, Bentley."

"I know, I'm sorry I haven't been here in a few weeks," I said. Aaron walked over to talk to Pete and Rick, Sylvia's brother and their only cook. I grinned at Sylvia.

"Aaron moved in," I whispered. Her eyes widened.

"Really? How does ol' Pop feel about that?" she asked.

"It was weird. I don't think he liked the idea, but he said I was an adult and could make that decision on my own.

"He sounds like a smart man," she said. I nodded in agreement. "Honey, you know we love that boy. If I'd had a daughter, I'd have wanted her to be just like you. Unfortunately, Pete only gave me a few rowdy boys that think

it's fun to burp the alphabet." We laughed and headed toward the
bar seats.

Rick whipped up the works for all of us, then we ate and
caught up with each other. Nothing new had happened to them, so
Aaron and I did most of the talking. It felt like the first time
he had breakfast with me all over again. I don't think they knew
what to think of his open features and talkative attitude.

After breakfast, we decided to head out for our walk after
saying our goodbyes. Sylvia made me promise to come back soon,
and since they had refused payment for the food, I was even more
excited about convincing Pop to let the Cooper's employees have
an extended lunch break the next day.

"Where do you want to walk?" I asked Aaron once we were
outside. It was freezing, but I knew Dog needed some fresh air
and a chance to run around.

"There's an empty field a few minutes walk behind your
apartment if you want to head out there."

"That's fine. I've never been out there. Well, I don't ever
walk for pleasure so that could be why."

"You mean once spring comes you won't want to start jogging
with me?" he asked.

"You don't jog!" I said. I ignored the pang in my heart at
his mention of spring, knowing he wouldn't be living with me

anymore.

"I do."

"I guess that shouldn't surprise me. You have the body of someone that works out."

"Bentley? Have you been checking me out?" he asked. I rolled my eyes.

"You flaunt it enough! I may have noticed once or twice." I felt my cheeks heat.

"I've probably checked you out a couple of times, too," he said.

"Nice," I stated with a nod. Aaron laughed loudly enough to cause Dog to stop in his tracks.

"It's okay bud," Aaron said to him. "Bentley's just ridiculously funny sometimes."

"I beg your pardon; I am funny all the time."

"I'll give you seventy-five percent of the time."

"Oh, whatever. What do you know? You don't even like my favorite comedian."

"He's just not funny," he said. We made it to the field, and Aaron picked up a stick and threw it. Dog ran for it, missed, and just kept running. He ran the field like it was a race track, passing us every couple of minutes. Poor mutt probably was going to hate going back inside after this.

"He is funny, by the way," I said getting back to the topic. "He's made me laugh so hard I almost peed numerous times if you must know the truth."

"Maybe the video you showed me wasn't the best one."

"That one was my favorite," I said in defeat and Aaron took pity on me. He threw an arm over my shoulder and pulled me into a side hug. I wrapped my arms around his stomach, and we stood there watching his dorky dog run around. We noticed that it was snowing and Aaron made the call to go back inside.

Dog went off to mope in Aaron's bedroom, and Aaron took a shower while I called Pop to talk to him about Bucking Bandits. He agreed to shut the shop down for an hour and a half so everyone could enjoy lunch at the diner.

Aaron found me in the kitchen putting dishes away when he finished.

"I feel like you're always doing dishes," he said, putting the plates in the cabinet.

"It's my biggest pet peeve. I can't stand having dirty dishes; it irritates me."

We finished the dishes, and I walked back to the sofa. I noticed Aaron wasn't following.

"You okay?" I asked.

"I had to run to the store to get a few things for dinner

the other day while you were gone. I got something else, too,"
he admitted.

"Ice cream?" I asked, excited.

"Well, I got that, too. Just follow me."

When we reached the place where my door was on one side,
and his was on the other, he stopped and turned to face me.

"What did you get? It's not another dog, is it?" I asked,
looking down the hall to where Dog was now chewing on the
biggest bone I'd ever seen. He shook his head.

"No dog. Uh," he suddenly seemed nervous. "This might be
one of the dumbest things I've ever done." He took a deep
breath, looked into my eyes and pointed to the ceiling.

I looked up and stopped breathing. We were standing under a
mistletoe. Aaron had gone to the store and bought a mistletoe,
and I knew that for a fact because I'd never purchased one.

"I'll take it down if you want me to," he said, bringing me
back to what was happening. I shook my head no but didn't say
anything.

"Okay, well, I want my question from winning the last hand
the other day to be, can I kiss you?" he asked, and his eyebrows
drew together in confusion. "Are you breathing?"

"Eh, a little," I replied barely above a whisper. He smiled
at me, and I couldn't believe this was real.

"Do you want to think about it?"

"No, I don't need to think about it. My answer is yes."

Aaron took a step closer, erasing the few inches that separated us and he placed his hands on both sides of my face.

"Wait," I said.

"I'm sorry." He pulled his hands away from my face. "I've wanted to do this for so long that I couldn't resist the mistletoe."

"No, that's not it. I'm nervous about something," I admitted.

"What is it?"

"I read a lot of books." His eyes crinkled in the corners. "Don't laugh at my books."

"I'm sorry, it's just funny. You need a bookshelf."

"I know," I sighed thinking about my giant pile of books on the floor.

"Okay, you read a lot of books. Why does that make you nervous?"

"Well, the guys in these books, they all seem to suffer from the same disorder."

"And what disorder is that?"

"They all claim that they can't stop once they start kissing." Aaron was quiet for what seemed like forever.

"I'm kind of confused right now, Bent."

I took a deep breath.

"Book guys seem to be unable to stop with just a kiss. It's like a given, that once they get the girl, they develop this syndrome where they supposedly can't control themselves enough to stop."

"Are you kidding me?" Aaron looked disgusted. "I hope men don't say that in real life because if anyone ever tells you that they can't stop with what you're willing to offer, they aren't a man. I have no intention of anything more than kissing you, but only if you want me to. If you said you didn't want this, I'd take down that weird little plant and throw it in the trash can. I promise with all my heart that's what I'd do." I smiled in response.

"It's not that I don't trust you, it's just that I have a really important goal and I don't want to mess it up," I said.

"I promise I'll end the kiss before you ever start to worry."

"Well, I mean, you don't have to rush it," I said shrugging my shoulders.

Aaron laughed loudly pushed his fingers through the hair on the back of my head. His eyes were shining with happiness as he brought his mouth down to mine and his soft lips sent a surge of electricity through my entire body.

Everything seemed to fade into the background at that moment. My heartbeat raged in my chest against his, as if they were at war with each other. He grasped my shaking hands, pulling them up around his neck and wrapped his arms around my back. After a couple of minutes, Aaron pulled away, and it was over.

"That's it?" I asked, breathlessly. He placed a chaste kiss on my lips before stepping away.

What just happened?

"Let's go eat some ice cream."

"Yeah, I guess ice cream sounds okay," I said.

Aaron grabbed my hand and pulled me along toward the kitchen. I heard his chuckle and hid my smile behind his back. My mind was racing with questions that I couldn't calm myself down enough to think over. I'd need to reflect on it later if I wanted to be able to focus.

"Why'd you kiss me?" I asked once we were sitting at the table.

"Today, I saw the stone I gave you." I grabbed my chest, where the stone was safely tucked away. I had turned it into a necklace so I wouldn't ever have to take it off and I forgot about it sitting on my nightstand this morning when Aaron was in my room.

"I saw it, and I felt something. The truth is, I've wanted to kiss you for a few weeks, but it didn't seem right. It still isn't right to kiss you because I need to talk to you about something really important."

"Okay, go on."

"I want you to know that I like you. I don't know exactly when it happened. Maybe the first time you brought me something to eat or the first time you sat beside me and started talking about all the random things in your life. It could have been the first time we had a conversation, I don't know, but it happened. The thing is, I'm not at a point in my life where I can be with anyone. Someday soon, I pray I can be the man you deserve to have, but until then I can only offer you this friendship. I wanted to kiss you for two reasons. One, because I wanted to know for sure that this feeling I have is real. And two, because I needed to know what it was like to kiss you at least once. I wanted something to hold on to that would make me want to work harder at becoming what you deserve."

I wanted to be sarcastic and ask how he knew if I even liked him back, but I knew I had been wearing my feelings for him on my sleeve. Maybe I wasn't completely obvious, but I wasn't subtle either. I had to appreciate that he respected me enough to want to change his life before he offered me anything. It hurt that it couldn't be at that moment, though. I wanted so badly to tell him it didn't matter where he was in his life, but that was a lie. I couldn't hand my heart over completely to someone I didn't fully know, and while we were getting to know each other more and more, there were things he wouldn't open up about which scared me. There were things I wasn't even ready to tell him.

"Bentley?" I looked into his eyes and realized I hadn't replied. I smiled and said, "I like you, too, but I'm sure you know that. I'm happy to be friends until your ready to be more."

CHAPTER FIFTEEN

I made my way around Cooper's to let everyone know what was happening at lunch almost as soon as we arrived. I changed the answering machine to reflect the lunch hour as well. Come noon; we'd all be making our way to Bucking Bandits. I couldn't wait to see the look on Sylvia's face when she realizes she'll be waiting on that many people. Aaron and I seemed to be their only customers, and I was curious as to how they could afford to keep the diner open for so long.

The men were excited to shut down for an hour and a half, and since it wasn't something Pop was likely to do again, they were repeatedly thanking him when he walked by. I think he was getting annoyed by it though. It wasn't long before I was proven correct in my theory because when Jimmy walked over to thank him, he finally flipped out.

"If I hear another one of you thank me, I'm going to cancel today! Get back to work and quit sucking up. It looks bad on all of you." He stormed off and once his office door slammed everyone that was in hearing distance started laughing.

"Stop laughing and get to work!" Pop yelled through the door. I couldn't stop the laughter from bubbling out all the way to the shop. I walked in to find Aaron and Sam bent over a car looking at something.

"Hey guys," I said. They both looked up and smiled.

"What's up?" Sam asked.

"Nothing, Pop just freaked out because people won't stop thanking him. It was awesome."

"I thought I saw a vein in his forehead starting to grow a little," she laughed.

"So, what are you guys working on?" I asked. They both looked down into the engine.

"There was a sensor that went out, and we're replacing it, but we dropped a bolt. We're trying to find it," Aaron said.

"We have one to replace it, but we were trying to prevent that," Sam added.

"Alright, let me know if you need something."

"Will do, Boss," Sam said giving me a thumbs up.

"Have I told you how beautiful you are today?" Aaron asked,

shocking both Sam and me into silence.

"Yes," I said blushing. "You told me already."

"Ah, right. I did, didn't I? Well, maybe you should hear it again, because you look very beautiful, as usual."

"Dang, I need to get me one of those," Sam said under her breath, even her cheeks tinged with pink.

"Thank you," I said, he only smiled in response.

"What is it about this week?" Sam asked laughing. "First the waiter and now Aaron."

"The waiter?" Aaron asked. I cringed.

"Yeah, this young boy asked Bee here for her number this weekend." Sam shook her head like she couldn't believe it. Honestly, I couldn't either. Sure, I had been on a few dates in high school, and a couple of guys had randomly asked me out, but I wasn't in high demand. I'd never been interested enough in anyone to go on more than a couple of dates. No one until Aaron, and we weren't even dating.

I was too nervous to look at Aaron's reaction at first, and when I finally did, I saw his huge grin, which was surprising.

"Of course someone asked for her number, look at her," he laughed. "I'm surprised someone didn't ask for yours too, Sam."

"Oh, shut up," she said, getting flustered.

"I'm serious. You know you're a beautiful girl, don't you?"

he asked.

"Aaron, if you say one more word, I will take this wrench and whack you upside the head with it." Her face resembled a tomato by that point. I couldn't hold in my laughter.

"Sam-," I said before she cut me off by pointing the tool at me.

"The same goes for you, too." I raised my hands in surrender.

"Okay, okay! I'll let you kids get back to work," I said walking away from the shop.

By lunchtime, everyone was excited and ready to get to the diner. I was surprised only a few of the guys knew where Bucking Bandits was since it was only a few minutes drive from Cooper's. A few had seen the place but never went inside, and the rest of the guys accused me of making it up.

"What kind of food do they serve?" Jason, one of the mechanics, and Simon, one of the salesmen, had been following me around for five minutes asking about the food. I laughed because they weren't the first ones to ask.

"It's just like any diner, I suppose. What do you like?" I asked.

"Hamburgers. The works," Simon answered. "You think they have fresh veggies and such?"

"I've had their burgers, and they're fantastic," I assured him.

"What about breakfast?" Jason shouldered his way in between Simon and me and threw his arm over my shoulders. "Do you think they'd serve breakfast for lunch? I could go for biscuits and gravy."

"I think if you used even a fraction of your charm on Sylvia, she'd have Rick cook about anything for you."

He shot me his lopsided smile and ran to tell the other guys that breakfast might be an option.

I met Aaron at Sam's car and we all followed Pop to the diner.

When we pulled in, I got out and rushed inside. Sylvia jumped when I threw the door open and smiled at her.

"What's up Sylv?" I asked.

"Bentley, what's going on?" she asked looking scared. She looked behind me and watched as the three other vehicles pulled into the parking lot.

"I brought some people with me for lunch. Eleven people, including myself, to be exact." Her eyes widened in shock and excitement.

"Oh, my word, girly! You should have called and warned me!" she laughed.

"No way! I wanted to see your face." She walked over and hugged me just as Aaron, Pop, and Sam were walking in. I introduced them.

"It's a pleasure to finally meet you, honey," she said to Pop, hugging him like she already knew him.

"You too, ma'am. Bentley's told me so much about this place and begged me to bring the men."

"Well, everybody take a seat," she yelled over the chatter that now filled the diner. We all walked to the tables, spreading out all over the place. Even spread out, we were pretty close to filling up the tables.

Sylvia walked around taking orders and bringing drinks. I looked up to find Pop and Jerry talking to Pete at the register, laughing. Everyone seemed to be laughing about something.

"It was nice of you to convince your dad to do this today," Aaron said after we sat in the booth where we had our first breakfast together.

"I felt bad for not coming here these last few weeks," I replied.

"Yeah, I've been feeling guilty, too. I've missed their company."

"How often did you guys come here?" Sam asked, breaking into the conversation as she sat beside me in the booth.

"Well," I said, Aaron and I shared a knowing smile. "It all started earlier this year." Sylvia made it to our table and sat down beside Aaron.

"I don't remember the last time we had so many people in here," she said wiping her brow.

"The guys are going to want to come here all the time after this," I said and Aaron nodded in response.

"You're such sweet kids," Sylvia said. "What can I get ya'll to eat?"

After we ordered we watched Sylvia walk back and forth for a while making sure she had taken everyone's orders. She may have acted like she was working up a sweat, but I knew. I knew Sylvia was secretly enjoying every single minute of it. She loved to fuss over people. We laughed every time she thought she was sneaky, pulling food out of her apron pocket and giving it to Dog. She knew he was on a strict diet now and, "hated it for the poor baby," she said.

After everyone finished eating, we began to make our way to the door to leave. As Sylvia walked through the group hugging and saying goodbye to the men, Pop walked up and pulled me aside.

"Why don't you stay and help them clean up?" he asked.

"I can do that," I smiled. "I didn't even think about all

the dishes and stuff."

"That's my girl," he said, before hugging me and walking out to his truck. I saw Aaron's expression and instantly knew why he looked like he was a mixture of sick and worried. I slowly walked closer to him and offered up a smile.

"You have to trust that I can take care of myself," I whispered. I expected him to argue or even try to talk my dad into leaving him there with me, but he didn't. I wasn't expecting him to close the distance between us and pull me into his arms.

"I trust you, babe. I just worry about you being alone, I'm sorry," he said. I wrapped my arms around him and smiled into his chest.

"I know, it's okay to worry. I've done quite a bit of that for a really long time."

"Be careful," he said in a lower voice. "I'll see you when you get back to Cooper's." He let go and walked to Pop's truck. I watched them all drive away and turned to see Sylvia's questioning look.

"Oh, hey," I laughed. "I'm going to stay and help you guys clean up."

"Thank God!" Rick yelled from the back and we all laughed.

CHAPTER SIXTEEN

The next few weeks flew by and Thursdays, when Aaron would
disappear for the entire night, I would lay awake for hours.
Even though he came back every night unharmed, it did nothing
but further frustrate me. It wasn't that I didn't trust him
because I did. I didn't understand why it was such a huge
secret. I thought about following him sometimes but that could,
and most likely would wreck our friendship forever.

Before I knew it, Christmas was only a few days away.
Cooper's closed down from Christmas Eve until the day after New
Years every year. One of the great things about owning your own
business was, you could make decisions like that.

The day before Christmas Eve, Sam helped me deliver gifts
to all the guys at work. I opened a few things they'd given me
and laughed when I opened a book with directions for changing

your oil. I'd practiced changing the oil on one of Pop's junk cars during the summer, and forgot to put in a filter. It wasn't funny at the time, but all the guys thought they were hilarious.

Pop was excited about his gift and immediately went to his office to start looking for new songs to download. When Sam opened hers, she hugged me so tight I thought I might need to go to the hospital for a broken rib. Her scream almost caused my ears to bleed, but I got her back when I opened my card and saw what she'd written inside.

"Hey Bee,

Tell me when you're ready, and your first tattoo is on me.

Love your favorite friend,

Sam"

Pop wasn't too thrilled and begged me not to get one, saying something like his heart couldn't take the stress of his daughter getting ink. I knew he had a couple, so I brought them up.

"The only things I ever had the guts to put on my body permanently were the two things I'm most proud of in my life; what I did for my country and my only child's birthday," he stated as if that was the end of the discussion. All I could do was smile and walk away.

The work day ended, and Aaron and I made our way to Bucking

Bandits to hand out the items we'd picked out for them. The gang thanked us and then we headed home. I was nervous and excited about spending the next few days alone with Aaron since Pop and I didn't make a big Christmas dinner as we did for Thanksgiving and Easter.

Aaron and I were setting up a card game when my phone began to ring. I glanced at it to see another unknown number and ignored it.

"Who was that?" Aaron asked.

"I don't know. I've been getting calls from an unknown number for a while now, but they never leave a message."

"You should just answer it next time," he suggested.

"Nah, they'll stop calling eventually."

"How long have you been getting them?"

"I seriously can't even remember. It's not a big deal."

"Alright well, are you ready to get your butt kicked tonight?" he asked, dealing out the first hand of Rummy.

"I'm sorry to be the bearer of such bad news, but, you're going down!" I said looking over my awesome hand.

"Let's play with questions," he added smiling.

"Yes!" I agreed immediately. "There's no other way to play."

"Agreed."

I won the first hand after only a few turns and giggled when Aaron threw his remaining cards in the air.

"How are you going to count your points now?" I asked.

"Just ask your question, you little cheater," he said as he picked up his mess.

"I definitely didn't cheat, but my first question is," I paused and watched him settle back into his chair. "What do you want to do with all our time off?"

"I want to relax and have fun together."

I smiled. "I can't wait."

The next hand went on for so long that we were down to only a few cards in the deck. When I played the last card, we counted our points, and Aaron gloated about his ten-point victory.

"What's your question?" I laughed. He waited a moment before answering.

"Can I kiss you?" he asked.

"What kind of kiss?"

"How about I surprise you?"

"Okay," I whispered.

Aaron stood, walked around the table and grabbed my hands when he got to me. After pulling me up, his hands lifted and made their way into my hair and he gently pulled my face toward his.

Our lips met in a soft, sweet kiss and I gripped his shirt in my hands. Butterflies erupted in my stomach when he deepened the kiss. I felt like my heart was going to give out at any second if I didn't back away, but I didn't want this ever to end.

One of his hands slip forward to cup my cheek and I noticed a slight tremble. He was just as affected by this moment as I was.

When he pulled away, he didn't speak immediately. His thumb moved back and forth across my cheek and after what seemed like forever, he smiled.

"Wow!" I said.

"I know I don't have it all together right now, but I just want you to know that I want to be in the running to win your heart."

I smiled and moved close enough to wrap my arms around him. "You're the only one in the race," I whispered.

Aaron sat back in his seat and we continued our game. There was a change in the air, and I didn't think I was the only one that felt it because neither of us could stop smiling.

"Did you play sports in school?" I asked after my third win.

"I didn't," he answered. "I got moved around a lot, so I

never stayed in one place long enough. Then, once my parents adopted me, my mom decided to homeschool me. What about you?"

"I played softball for a couple of years. It wasn't my favorite, so when Pop told me I could quit, I did."

We played a few more hands, and Aaron ended up finding out more about me than I had about him.

"I think you cheat," I said, crossing my arms over my chest.

"I promise you; I do not cheat. You just stink." Aaron laughed when I threw the empty card box at him.

"Yeah right."

"Think whatever you want, but I don't cheat. Either way, it's my win so my question. It's kind of personal, I think."

"You think?" I asked.

"Yeah, I guess it depends on the answer but I have a feeling it's personal, so if you don't want to, you don't have to respond to this one."

"Okay, that's fair."

"I've been wondering for a while now what you meant when you said you had a goal before we kissed the first time." I felt my face heat under embarrassment. Not because of the goal itself, but because I was going to say it out loud to Aaron.

"It is personal, but I don't care to answer it."

"Then why are you so red?"

"Because it isn't something I talk about with anyone," I laughed nervously. "I want to tell you though."

He remained silent, waiting for my explanation and I took a deep breath before I started.

"Well, to simply put it, I'm saving myself for marriage. I know it's not very common anymore but, that level of intimacy is something I only want to share with my husband one day."

He smiled. "I think that's a terrific goal to have, Bentley."

"I think so too." There was an awkward silence, and I felt embarrassed again.

"Do you want to watch a movie?" he asked.

"Sure!" I went to my room to change into my pajamas and met Aaron back on the sofa. He picked a DVD out of the entertainment center cabinet and put it in. The credits gave it away.

"Nice choice, this is," I said in my best impression. Aaron laughed, and we were transported into space.

I cooked dinner when the movie was over, we ate hamburgers and coleslaw and headed to our bedrooms. I had been lying in bed for over an hour when there was a knock on my door.

I wonder who that could be. I thought to myself and laughed under my breath. I opened the door to find Aaron dressed in his shoes and coat.

"Does Dog need to go out?" I asked.

"No, I'm so sorry, but I've gotta run out tonight." His expression told me exactly what I needed to know and I had the sudden urge to shut the door in his face. My heart started aching which only served to irritate me more. I cared too much about this man that had too many secrets, and it was tearing me up inside.

"Okay," I said, moving to shut the door.

He stopped the door with his hand, and I looked up into his eyes as I felt mine fill with tears.

"Please don't cry." Aaron stepped forward and pulled me into a hug. "I'm sorry," he said. "I promise these secrets won't always be hidden. One day I'm going to be able to answer your questions, I just need you to trust me."

Trust is earned, and I tried to tell myself that it wasn't possible for me to trust him so completely yet, but the truth was, I did. From the moment I invited him into my home for the first time all those weeks ago, I knew I could hand over the key to my apartment, and he wouldn't hurt me. It was a gut instinct.

"I trust that you won't ever hurt me, Aaron. I don't know if I can be okay with whatever you do at night though. It scares me," I said.

"I can't do anything about that right now. All I can do is promise you this isn't going to last forever. I'll be able to leave all of it behind one day, and you'll never have to worry about it again. Okay?"

"Okay," I said. "I can deal with that for now." He leaned down and placed a soft kiss on my lips before leaving with Dog. I stood in the hall and waited until I heard the front door lock click into place.

I stood staring at Aaron's door for what felt like an eternity. The need to walk into that room felt like a physical attack against me.

"I can't do this to him," I said to myself. The fact that going through his things was even a thought in my head made angry at myself. I finally convinced myself that it was the worst idea I'd ever had, worse than patting him down to try and find an ID. I walked back into my bedroom and climbed into bed.

It was well after four in the morning when I heard Aaron finally come back in. I jumped out of bed and ran into the living room to ask what had taken so long. He was almost always in before midnight when he had to leave and when I rounded the corner to the foyer, I stopped. Aaron's shirt was off and he was looking at his ribs that were covered in bruises.

"Aaron!" I cried. "What happened to you?"

He must not have heard when I got up because when he saw me standing there, he paled.

"Go back to bed," he demanded.

"Absolutely not! You need an ambulance," I started back toward my room to get my phone, but Aaron ran and grabbed my arm.

"Listen to me very carefully, Bentley, you can't call anyone."

"Yes, I can, and I will."

"Nothing happened," he grabbed my shoulders and begged me to believe him with his eyes. "I fell and I know I'll be okay because nothing is broken."

"But you need to see a doctor," I said.

"I don't want to leave, Bentley, but if this is something you can't trust me on, I'll have to."

My heart plummeted and I wondered if he would lie about something like this. Did he fall, or did someone hurt him? I had no idea what he was involved in so I couldn't even be sure he interacted with people when he wasn't with me. I wanted to believe him, and I knew it made me stupid and weak.

"You fell?" I asked.

He closed his eyes and exhaled slowly. "I fell."

"Are you sure nothing is broken?"

"I would be having a terrible time breathing if anything was fractured. I just need to ice it and I'll be as good as new tomorrow."

I stepped out of his hands and walked to the freezer to get a bag of frozen veggies.

"Can you handle this?" he asked from behind me. I looked down at the bag in my hands and nodded. "Look at me."

I looked up and ignored the hand he had placed over his side.

"You fell," I repeated. "I can handle you falling, as long as you get back up."

"Can we pretend tonight didn't happen?" he asked.

"Sure," I lied. I handed him the bag and told him to sit down while I got painkillers. Between the two of us, it looked like we'd be going through my medicine pretty quickly.

I fed him two pills and left him with the veggies and a glass of water. He was an adult perfectly capable of knowing if he needed a hospital so I went back to my bedroom and climbed into bed.

I stared at the ceiling as I fought the urge to scream. Later, I heard a light tap on my door and quickly stood to opened it.

"Are you okay?" I asked Aaron. He was leaning against the

frame, but he didn't look like he was in too much pain.

"I am, I just wanted to make sure you were."

"Why wouldn't I be okay?"

He leaned forward to kiss me and I backed up a step.

"That's what I thought," he said before taking a deep breath. "I'm promising you that I'm fine, okay? I swear to you that I am okay and if there was something broken, I would let you take me to the hospital. I'd go willingly, but nothing is wrong."

I felt better knowing he'd be willing to go to the hospital if he was in more pain. His reaction to me calling had scared me almost as much as the bruises, but maybe he was just afraid of doctors, like a lot of people were.

"Okay," I said, and he smiled.

"Can I kiss you now?" he asked. I nodded and he placed a finger under my chin, tilted my head back, and placed his lips over mine.

He took a step back, breaking the kiss and smiled. "Goodnight, Sweetheart."

"Goodnight, Aaron," I replied.

CHAPTER SEVENTEEN

I had my phone alarm set to vibrate early on Christmas morning. I wanted to get an early start making the blueberry pie I had hidden. I wasn't the greatest cook, but I would try my best.

I thought about the night before and wondered how he'd be feeling today. I didn't want to bring it up and have him get upset with me, so I decided I wouldn't talk about it. If he had a concern or if he was in pain, he was capable of asking for help.

By the time Aaron emerged from his bedroom I was putting the pie into the oven.

"Happy Birthday, Beautiful," he said walking up behind me and placing a kiss on the top of my head.

"You remembered?"

"Of course I did. I couldn't forget something like that."

"I'm glad I get to spend the day with you," I said.

"I figured your dad would want to see you today. It's Christmas and your birthday, so it's a pretty special day."

"Yeah it is, but we're together almost every single day, so it's not a big deal, and plus, he already gave me my gifts. He'll probably call later though."

"You should invite him over for lunch or something. I bet he'd like that."

"Okay, I'll go call him." I made my way toward my bedroom when my phone started ringing. I saw it was Pop when I glanced at the screen, so I quickly answered.

"Merry Christmas, old man!" I chirped.

"Happy Birthday, squirt."

"Thanks! Do you want to come over for lunch today?" I asked.

"Uh," he paused. "Actually Bentley, I have some plans today. I only made them because we already had our thing at the house."

"What possible plans could you have on Christmas?"

"This is kind of awkward," he said taking a deep breath. "One of our customers lives far away from her family. We got to talking the other day when she was getting her car worked on and

I slightly asked her to go to dinner with me."

"You slightly asked her to dinner?" I asked. I couldn't stop the smile that was forming on my face.

"More than slightly I guess, I asked her out, and she said she'd love to. Her closest family is a son that lives in Georgia, so I felt really bad for her."

"Is she hot?" I asked.

"Obviously," he answered, and I laughed.

"There it is."

"Shut up. Listen, I wanted to call you and say Happy Birthday, but I've got to get going. I need to shave and crap."

"You're so charming. I hope you have a nice time, for real though, Pop. I love you."

"I love you, too. I'll let you know how it goes."

"You better."

I hung up the phone and sat down on my bed. My father was going on a date. He hadn't dated the entire time I was growing up, and I was appreciative that I didn't have to watch women come in and out of our lives. No matter how I felt, I just wanted him to be happy. He, more than anyone, deserved it.

"Was that your dad?" Aaron asked from the doorway of my room.

"Yeah, he has plans tonight."

"Who makes plans on Christmas?" he asked.

"I know, right?" I laughed. "He has a date. I guess the lady doesn't have a lot of family around here."

"I see," Aaron smiled. "I'm surprised women aren't too scared of him to show interest."

"No one is actually scared of him."

"Speak for yourself," he said. "So, I found what was in the oven." That got my attention.

"Yeah?"

"Yeah. It smells amazing."

"It won't taste anything like your mom's, I'm sure, but I wanted to give you something special for Christmas."

"I can't believe you remembered."

"Of course I did. I couldn't forget something like that." Aaron smiled down at me in response to hearing me use his own words from earlier.

"I wanted to get you something special, too," he said.

"Really? What would that be?"

"Follow me." He turned and walked to his bedroom. When he opened the door, I saw a pile of wood beside a box. The cover of the box showed a beautiful bookshelf. I could feel my excitement in the tips of my toes.

"Oh my gosh, Aaron! What is this?"

"I decided you needed a bookshelf for your bedroom," he laughed

"I can't believe you bought this! Where did you get it? How did you even get it up here?"

"Sam actually helped quite a bit. She picked it up for me, and Drake and your dad helped carry everything up while you were sleeping one night last week."

"You're so sneaky!"

"Yeah, that was the plan. I couldn't have you trying to guess anything. You do know that's how surprises work, right?"

"Hilarious. I'm not good at being surprised," I mocked. In truth, I wasn't good at receiving surprises, but this was something that I was going to remember for the rest of my life.

"I figured we could put it together tomorrow if you want. I'd like to make sure we have it built by the end of the year."

"Yes! That sounds exciting."

"I'm glad you like it."

"Do you want to open up your gifts?" I asked.

"Sure. I have a few things for you under the tree, too."

"I noticed there were more gifts under the tree than I had put there."

"I bought Dog a few things, too."

"Oh my gosh! I forgot to pick up something for him for

today. I already gave him the bed."

"Seriously? Don't beat yourself up. He's the most spoiled dog I've ever seen."

"I still feel bad. Maybe he can have some human food tonight," I said. Dog was curled up in the corner of the living room sleeping, and as if he knew he was being talked about, he had gas, and the smell immediately filled the room.

"That's disgusting," Aaron laughed.

"Okay, maybe no human food for him then."

We made our way to the living room and sat down on the floor beside the tree. Once there, we decided Aaron would open his first since I was so excited about it. Every gift he opened made him smile, and that's something that I loved about him. It didn't matter if it was a shirt or something silly like the space themed clock I bought him. He loved it all.

When it came to opening my gifts, I was so nervous my heart was pounding in my chest. It was one of those moments where you just know something monumental is happening in your life. I opened my first gift and squealed a little. A box set of movies that starred my favorite actor, how did he know? A beautiful scarf, a pair of matching gloves, a figurine of a dad and a daughter, and a framed picture of Sam and me followed.

His gifts meant so much to me. The figurine of the dad

holding his little girl was pretty special. Pop meant a lot to
me and the fact that Aaron captured that in a gift was
priceless.

By the time we were done throwing the wrapping paper away,
and putting our things into our rooms, the timer on the oven
started beeping.

We made our way to the kitchen to get the pie and Aaron
almost immediately dug in. I had barely convinced him to cut it
and put it on a plate before he ate it. I couldn't control my
laughter.

Since I had extra ingredients leftover from the pie crust,
it was pretty easy to figure out what I'd be making for dinner.
Chicken pot pie was his favorite, and I couldn't wait to
experiment with a recipe I'd found in an old cookbook. Together
we made a mess of the kitchen and spent time talking about his
mom and dad.

Since he hadn't been adopted until he was sixteen, he
seemed to have more bad memories than good. His childhood didn't
sound encouraging, and he'd never had a voice telling him he was
worth it. That was, I guess until his mom and dad came into his
life.

"When I became a teenager, it was like I'd finally given up
hope that someone would swoop in and save me. Even after I moved

into my parents home and felt their love, it took a while for me to open up. Just like that day when I barged in here and freaked out because I was so scared something bad had happened to you, I felt like something was just going to rip the rug right out from under me. I lived there the first couple weeks, expecting it all to vanish.

"My dad finally broke through to me one day. He took me out for a drive, and I was convinced he was taking me to drop me back off with my caseworker. I thought someone was giving up on me again, but that wasn't the case. That's the day he told me that they wanted to adopt me. That was, by far, the best day of my life."

I didn't say it aloud, but I couldn't get past feeling sad that I'd never gotten to meet these amazing people. I started to wonder if his parents' death was the reason he was on the street or if it was just purely unforeseen circumstances that placed him there.

"They sound like amazing people," I said.

"It's hard to talk about them sometimes."

"We can change the subject if you want," I offered.

"I'd like that," he smiled in response. "Can you tell me something about you that I don't know yet?"

The question startled me a bit. There was already so much I

had told him, and I only had a couple of things I kept close to my vest. I knew I was pretty much an open book for the most part, but those couple of things were something I didn't talk about with anyone but Pop. To be honest, we hadn't discussed them in years. I didn't think Pop liked to talk about it, and I felt even less comfortable with it, so it became a mutual understanding. We would never talk about her, and we would never talk about what happened.

"That's a hard question," I laughed. "You've known me for such a long time. I think I may have told you everything."

"I know that's a lie, Bentley," he gave me a sad smile.

What was I going to tell him? Other than the topic of my mother, I had told him everything.

"Okay, if you weren't going to run your father's business what would you do?"

"You've already asked me that."

"No, I asked you about college. What I'm talking about is a career path. What would your dream job be if Cooper's wasn't an option?"

I sat in silence for a few minutes. I had never asked myself that question because from the time I could walk, I was at Cooper's with Pop. That was where I'd learned everything I know about being a good leader; it was where I learned I wanted to be a leader. It's where I went when the first date I ever went on went wrong because he was boring, it's also where my father told me if any man hurt me he would go to prison for me. Many of the guys agreed with him.

I had never thought about any other options. I knew that things could go wrong and maybe Cooper's wouldn't be there one day, but for some reason, I completely chose to ignore that possibility. Cooper's was one of the things in my life I completely relied on. Not just because it was my job, and it provided for me growing up because it was my father's business, but there was more to it. I guessed when things happened with my mother I started to question commitment. Even at a young age, I questioned it, so the things that were left in my life became stable establishments in my mind. I hadn't had close friends because I couldn't risk them leaving. In hindsight, I suppose it's why I'd never seriously dated anyone. It was that moment sitting on the sofa with Aaron that I realized I had built two more pillars.

All my life, Pop, Cooper's and the employees made up this safe place in my mind. This permanent place and without realizing what was happening, I had added two more people. Sam and Aaron. It was a scary revelation in a sense because what if one of those pillars fell? What would happen to whatever they were holding up?

It was a silly question, but I could almost feel the importance of the answer to Aaron's question vibrating through me. I needed to have an answer.

"I don't know. I've never thought twice about my life's plan," I admitted to him.

"You should."

I should have felt angry that he was questioning my plan, but I think if I had said I was interested in something other than taking my family business over, he would have nodded and moved on in the conversation. I don't think he was suggesting that I throw the blueprints of my life out the window and start over, but that's kind of what I felt like doing.

I still wanted to take Pop's place one day, that would never change, but what if there was something I was missing out on? What if there was a passion waiting for me around a corner I refused to take for so long? I was still young enough to think about what I wanted to be when I grew up, and there was no harm in looking.

If I never found something I'd be interested in, I would take it as a sign that I was where I needed to be. If I did find something, well, I didn't know what I would do. I'd probably have to talk to Pop about it and see what he said.

After dinner, we played a new board game Aaron had received for Christmas, and I was proud that I wiped the floor with him.

It was during the new episode of New Girl that my phone rang and an unknown number popped up. I ignored it, and after the ringing stopped, it started up again. The call was from the same unknown number, and Aaron shifted beside me.

"What?" I asked, already knowing what was coming.

"I think you should answer the phone."

"I'm not answering it. If they don't want to leave a message, then they apparently don't think getting ahold of me is that important."

Right after I uttered the words, my voicemail notification went off, and I stared blankly at the phone.

"Well that's never happened before," I mumbled.

I picked it up and played the message. I'd like to say that the three seconds of empty silence surprised me, but it didn't. Whoever this person was, they were cowardly.

"See, it's nothing."

I put my phone on silent and tucked it under my leg. I resumed the show and tried to pay attention to it, but I could feel Aaron's tension. He continued to glance at me throughout the entire time we sat there and an hour later I'd finally had enough.

"Aaron, if you don't stop looking like you're trying to figure this out I'm going to go to bed."

"No, you're not," he said shrugging off my comment.

I stood and walked to my room, shutting my door behind me. I wasn't someone who bluffed often. I walked to my bookshelf and picked up a book I hadn't read yet.

Well into chapter two, I reached for my phone on my nightstand only to realize it wasn't there. I had left it on the sofa. I got up and walked into the living room. Aaron was sitting in the same place, arms crossed over his chest, looking at my phone that sat two feet away from him.

"Have you been staring at it this whole time?" I asked.

"Yeah," he replied. He finally lifted his eyes to meet mine. "Why won't you answer it?"

"Because I don't know who it is," I answered.

"How do you know? What if it is someone you know?"

"Aaron, why do you care?" I was getting frustrated.

"I just think it's weird you're getting phone calls from people you won't answer."

"I'm not answering because I don't know them."

"Does your dad know you're getting strange phone calls?"

I could feel myself getting angrier. I tried not to glare, but I felt it nonetheless.

"If you so much as utter one word to him I will," I didn't finish my sentence.

"You'll what?" he asked with a goofy smirk. "Fire me? Kick me out? Break up with me?"

I felt my heart stop at the last one.

"Break up with you?" I asked.

"You know what I meant," he corrected. "You wouldn't want to be friends or something."

My face broke into a smile and just like that the phone call was forgotten by us both.

"I wouldn't break up with you," I teased. He narrowed his eyes and stood from the sofa.

"I'm going to bed," he said. He sounded grumpy, and I couldn't help but laugh. I decided not to tease him any further because I truly did respect his stance on what he could offer regarding a relationship at this point.

"Goodnight, Aaron. I had fun today." He stopped and walked back over to me, pulling me into a hug.

"Me, too. Thank you for today," he said before he turned and walked into his room.

I fell asleep quickly, thoughts of the night before completely gone from my mind.

CHAPTER EIGHTEEN

"I have a surprise for you," Aaron said from my doorway. I was sitting at my desk looking through some emails on my computer.

"You do?" I asked. "What is it?"

"You really are bad at surprises," he laughed.

"We've been over that already. What's the surprise?"

"If you put on some warm clothes and meet me downstairs, I'll show you."

He walked out of my room, and I heard him shut the door to the apartment. I got dressed as quickly as I could and pulled my hair back into a long braid. I shoved my head into my hat and locked the door before heading down.

Pop and Sam were waiting on the sidewalk with Aaron when I arrived.

"What's going on?" I asked.

"I asked your dad to take Dog for the day, and Sam's here to drive us somewhere I think you'll really like."

"Which would be?" I tried again.

"Not a chance," Sam laughed. "Get in the car Bee."

I hugged Pop and watched as he drove away with Dog sitting in the front seat. We all loaded into Sam's car, and she drove us toward the city.

Aaron was sitting in the front seat so he could give her directions to wherever we were going, and I sat in the back. The way they acted with each other made them seem like brother and sister, and it was the weirdest thing. He was eleven years older than her, yet they bonded. I leaned my head back and closed my eyes. I was excited to be going back to the city so soon and for whatever Aaron had planned for us.

About an hour later we were pulling into a building that I'd never seen before.

"Where are we?" I asked.

"This is the skating rink!" Sam replied. She was obviously excited.

"Skating rink? I've never been skating before though," I said.

"Me either!" Sam chimed in.

"That's alright. I can help you both, and you can hold onto the railing. You'll get the hang of it pretty quickly." Aaron climbed out of the car and opened my door.

We walked in, and Aaron paid for all our skates. He helped us lace them up and told us to practice walking in them while he got his own on. I felt like I was walking a tightrope.

"You doing okay?" Aaron asked from behind me.

"Yeah, I guess so. This is really hard!"

"I think you're doing great," he encouraged. "Let's get out on the ice."

"Oh no," I muttered to myself. I looked at Sam and could see she was now thinking the same thing.

"Bet you regret agreeing to this, don't you?" I asked her as I wobbled past.

"You have no idea." I laughed at her shaking voice.

When we got to the ice, I was sweating. Wiping out was in my future, I could feel it.

"You ever been here before?" I heard a male's voice coming from behind me. I turned to look in their direction and saw this guy talking to Sam. He looked to be around our age. He had black hair that fell into his eyes, and his ear gages were about the size of the tip pinky.

"I think we lost Sam," I said pointing my finger in her

direction.

"Who is he?" he asked.

"No idea. Probably her future husband, if Sam has anything to say about it." We both laughed, and Aaron grabbed my hands and helped me onto the ice.

"Okay, keep ahold of one of my hands and hold the rail with the other."

We started out moving slow, and with each minute, I was getting more and more stable on my feet.

"I'm assuming you've done this a few times," I said after a few minutes.

"Quite a bit actually. My mom was really into ice skating when she was growing up, so it was the very first thing we did as a family. It was something we did at least a few times a month from then on."

"That's a lot of ice skating."

"Yeah, it is. How weird is it that I've missed it? Not very manly."

"It's really special to you, of course you'd miss it. Plus, there are more men out here than women." Aaron looked around and smiled.

"I guess you're right."

"Girls should definitely come here to meet guys. They're

all pretty attractive." He narrowed his eyes at me, still smiling.

"You already met a guy."

I decided not to say anything else on the matter. I had met a guy, an amazing one at that. I won't lie, it did frustrate me at times. He was very adamant about us not being in a relationship, and I respected him for it, but then there were things like this. I'd been holding his hand for half an hour and, for me, I felt this moment in my soul. He was sharing a very special part of himself with me, how could I not fall a little more for him because of it?

"You're really quiet."

"I'm just trying not to fall," I said.

"I wish it could be today, but it can't."

"I know. I'm okay with waiting." We shared a smile and continued to skate.

I looked around trying to find Sam and spotted her and the mystery guy. He had both of her hands and was pulling her while he skated backward. It looked to be going well until her foot moved weirdly, and before long they were both laying on the ice. I heard their laughter from across the rink and over all the other noise.

"She looks like she's having fun," Aaron said.

"She is. She's totally digging him."

"Do you want to go a little faster?"

"Not yet, sorry."

"It's not a big deal. Just take your time."

"I have a question for you," I said. "It's a bit personal, I guess, but I just want to get to know you."

"You can ask me anything you want; I just can't promise I'll answer."

"Okay, well, I was kind of wondering what you see for yourself in the future. Like, do you want to get married and have kids?" In a way, I was asking because I wanted to think if he felt this connection like I did, there was the possibility of a future for us. In all honesty, I was curious, too.

"Definitely. I'd love to get married and have a family. I want a lot of kids," he laughed.

"Really? You don't look like the type."

"I guess it's got a lot to do with not having any brothers or sisters. I'd love to have a sibling right now."

"How many kids do you want?"

"I'm not really sure yet. It depends on who I marry, too. I'd love to have at least five, but I really need to adopt to."

"You need to?" I asked. I'd never heard anyone phrase it like that.

"Yeah, I can't explain it. Some people want to adopt, but it's ingrained in who I am. Adopting is much more than what I want, it's what I need to do."

"That's really beautiful Aaron."

Out of the corner of my eye, I saw him flinch. I figured the conversation was getting too deep so I decided to change the subject.

"We can go a little faster now. Just don't let go of me."

"Never," he whispered, and I hoped beyond all hope that he meant it.

I pushed off the wall and squeezed his hand.

Around and around the rink we skated, bumping into Sam and her new friend, Matt.

"Do you guys want to get something to eat?" I asked them once we were all sitting back on the benches. After skating for over two hours, I never would have thought I'd be that tired.

"Yes! Oh my gosh, I think I'm dying," Sam said. She was now laying on the disgusting floor while Matt was taking her skates off. Aaron rolled his eyes at her antics and took our skates back to the woman at the counter.

"Get off the floor, Sam," I giggled. Matt smiled down at her and pulled her up by her hands before returning their skates.

We left and headed to the closest fast food restaurant. We all learned that Matt was one of five kids, to which Aaron and I shared a secretive smile. He was only three years older than Sam and had been a nurse at a local hospital for two years.

Matt and Sam seemed to hit it off, and I think I saw them exchange numbers while Aaron and I waited in the car.

"Thank you for today, Aaron," I said. I was so exhausted I felt like I could fall asleep in the back.

"You're welcome. I'm happy you had a good time."

"We should do this again sometime."

"I'd love that," he said. Sam got into the driver's seat and waved goodbye to Matt one last time.

"That dude was hot," she said when we pulled away. Aaron looked in her direction and smirked.

"Did you get his number?" he asked.

"Well, duh," she said. She looked at me in the rearview mirror and smiled. "He said he'd call me in a couple of hours."

I raised my eyebrows in shock.

"Way to go Sammy!"

"Agh! You just killed a small part of me."

"Sammy and Matty," I laughed.

Aaron and I teased Sam for most of the ride home, and when we reached Taylorsville, I called Pop to let him know he could bring Dog home.

"Thank God! This creature needs to go to the vet. He smells almost as bad as death itself."

"I'm pretty sure that's just his natural odor," I replied. Aaron laughed, obviously guessing what I was talking about.

"Alright well, I'll meet you at the apartment. What are you doing?" he yelled. "That's not-. Dang it, Bentley! I gotta go. The dog just ran off with my steak."

I hung up the phone and told Aaron what happened. I decided I needed to think about getting Pop a dog for Christmas the next year. It was just too funny of an image to pass up.

CHAPTER NINETEEN

The days we'd had together were spent at the apartment, except for when we had to check the mail and walk Dog. Every moment we spent at home was spent being consumed with each other.

Christmas melted into New Year's Eve, and before we knew it, we were counting down until midnight and watching the ball drop. When we got to one, Aaron grabbed my face in his hands and kissed me. The kiss felt so different than the few others we'd had. It was almost as if he was at peace. Before, he kissed me like he was saying goodbye every single time, but that night in my living room it felt like he was saying he'd never leave me.

I was standing in my living room, listening to cheers and screams coming from the television, being kissed by a man that had completely captured my heart when the realization hit me.

Somewhere along the way, I had fallen in love.

I wanted to be giddy and tell him the moment I felt it
bubbling up in my chest, but I remembered his promise. He was
working on things, I knew he was, and I was so excited and proud
of him. I couldn't tell him that I was in love with him and risk
ruining his vision for his life.

When we finally separated to go to our rooms, I couldn't
sleep. I stared at the ceiling asking myself if it was possible
to feel this way so quickly. What did love even mean to me? How
could you fall for someone you didn't know inside and out?

I knew for a fact that I could commit myself to a
relationship with him if there were no secrets between us. I
made a promise to myself that I would tell him about my mother.
If I expected truth from him, I had to give it, and I was caught
off guard by the need to tell Aaron everything.

I thought about times when Pop would tell me he'd die for
me if it ever came down to it, and beyond a shadow of a doubt, I
knew I'd do the same for Aaron. I wanted a better life for him,
and I wanted him to be proud of himself.

With the comfort of knowing he was in the next room, I
drifted off to sleep.

The next morning, I was walking out of the kitchen when
Aaron came out of the restroom.

"I have to get something off my chest," he said.

"Okay," I answered. Nervous wasn't the right word for what I felt about what he might say.

"I just want to make sure we're on the same page. We can't be an official item yet, and I hate it. I so badly want to say that I can give you all the answers you want, but I can't. I can't be the man you deserve yet. I feel like I'm so close, Bentley. I promise you I am so close to being where I should be."

"How do you know you're close?" I asked.

"I can feel it. Do you trust me?" I took a sip of my coffee to hide my smile.

"I trust you, and I want you to know something," I paused giving him a moment to let it sink in that I did, in fact, trust him. "I want you to know that I don't care if it takes weeks or months or even a year, I'm going to wait for you because you mean so much to me."

I had barely gotten the last few words out when Aaron took the coffee cup out of my hand and set it on the table. He wrapped his arms so tightly around me, it was hard to breathe, but I relished the feeling. Maybe it wasn't the right time to tell him that I was in love with him, but I needed him to know that this was something more to me.

After what seemed like the world's longest hug we grabbed
our coats and headed to Cooper's. You could clearly hear how
happy I was in my voice, and the smile on my face wasn't going
anywhere. The time we had spent trapped in the apartment
together had done so much more than the month of friendship we'd
had.

I wasn't sure what the remainder of our strictly friendship
relationship would look like; honestly, I didn't care. All I
knew was, we were in the place we wanted to be.

About an hour before lunch, I was walking into my office
when I was shoved from behind. I heard the door slam, and I
whirled around to see Sam standing there with a huge grin on her
face.

"What in the world is wrong with you?" I yelled. "I'm
probably going to need to see a chiropractor now."

"What happened between you and Mr. Dreamy?" She demanded.

"Shut up! My dad is across the hall!" I laughed.

"You can't stop smiling. Aaron can't stop smiling! He made
a joke today Bentley. He actually made a joke and I missed the
punchline because I was too shocked to hear it. You know how I
love a good joke."

"I do know." I couldn't help the giggle that escaped.
Seeing Sam bent out of shape was nice.

"Well? Are you going to tell me?"

"I promise nothing happened. We talked a lot, I mean, I feel like we got a lot closer but he still doesn't want a relationship yet."

"Yeah, I understand that."

"So that's where we are. I'm waiting for him to be the person he wants to be and I don't want to expect anything before he's ready."

"That's smart. I just worry about you getting your hopes up," she admitted.

"I've thought about that, too. I keep asking myself what I'll do if he doesn't change or he doesn't open up to me."

"But you can't be too hard on him about not being open. You're not that open either."

"I know," I sighed. "I already decided to talk to him about her."

"You did?" Sam's eyes grew in shock. She may not have known anything about my mother but she knew it was something I didn't talk to anyone about. She knew this was a big deal. "Have you told your dad you're going to tell him?"

"No, I didn't think I needed to. Do you?"

"No, I guess not. I just think that it's as big a part of him as it is you. Plus, if he doesn't know Aaron knows and then

Aaron asks him a question one day, he might feel awkward."

"I didn't even think about that. I doubt Aaron would talk to Pop about anything we talked about but I'll tell him just to be safe."

"Good idea."

"It was your idea."

"I know. I was talking to myself," she laughed. I rolled my eyes and opened the door to let her out.

I headed to Pop's office to tell him about the plan. I couldn't remember the last time I'd been nervous about my father's reaction to something I needed to tell him. Well, probably when I got my period and he had to take me to The Market, but this felt different.

"Hi," I said walking to a chair to sit down. Pop raised his eyebrows when he saw me.

"Why do you look like you're about to puke?" he asked. He nudged his trash can toward me with his foot and then scooted back in his chair until he hit the wall behind him.

"I have something really important to tell you and I guess I'm just scared."

"I swear if you tell me you're pregnant I will walk out to that shop and ring that boy's neck," he said.

"What? Why would you think that? You know me so much better

than that!" It hurt my feelings that he thought I would be that irresponsible with my life. Sure people could be good parents at any age, but I wasn't ready for that.

"You're right. I'm sorry, I just keep seeing his stupid smiling face and it was starting to tick me off."

"Wow. Well, I'm glad I know how you'll react when I do come to you because I'm pregnant."

"I'll be dead by then because you're going to wait until I'm dead to have a serious boyfriend."

"Or husband," I offered.

"Yeah, I like that better."

"Wait a second!" I said when I realized what he'd said. "I'm not waiting until you're dead to get married and have kids."

"I can't take the stress, Bentley."

"You're so dramatic!" I yelled.

"Be a dad and then come tell me how excited you are when your daughter starts talking about marrying someone and having babies."

"I'm not getting married! No husband, no babies, not even a boyfriend!" He was so ridiculous and I couldn't stop laughing at him.

"I'm not going to lie right now, kid. That's a relief." He

wiped his bald head with a tissue. "So, what's going on?"

"Well," I started. "Although I was being truthful about not having a boyfriend, I do care about Aaron."

"That's not news to me."

"One of my issues is that we have secrets between us. I want to open up to him though, Pop. I want him to know about her."

The few minutes of silence that followed felt like much, much more. I watched for any sign that he'd actually heard what I said and got nothing. He sat in stony silence.

"Pop? I asked.

"You want to tell him about your mother," he clarified.

"Yeah," I swallowed the lump in my throat. It was so strange hearing him say those words. He sighed and rubbed his hands over his face in frustration.

"Don't be afraid to come to me about anything ever again Bentley. I'm your father, not a stranger. I have always been here for you and you know that's never going to change."

"I know. It's just that we don't talk about her. I hate talking about the whole situation but I wanted to tell you before I told Aaron."

"I appreciate the warning, but if you want to tell people, that's up to you. I never meant to make you feel like you couldn't."

"You didn't, I promise. I honestly hate it. I haven't even said her name in years."

"It's been eighteen years," he said looking down at his hands. I stood and walked over to hug him.

"I don't care what she did or said; I couldn't have hand picked a better dad."

"I couldn't have picked a better daughter," he said, returning my hug.

I left his office and headed to the shop to see if Aaron wanted to go to get a few things for dinner from The Market during lunch.

"How will we keep everything cold?" he asked on our way over.

"We can use the mini-fridge in the break room."

"What sounds good?"

"I was thinking, stir-fry and ice cream," I answered.

"Oreo?" he asked, grabbing my hand while we jogged across the road.

"For sure," I answered.

CHAPTER TWENTY

We walked through the aisles and filled our basket with goodies. In the end, there was no order to the things we'd picked out, and I looked forward to Ramen Noodles, cream corn and garlic bread with my favorite ice cream for dessert.

"Let's get some pop," he said while we were standing in the check out line.

"Yes! Good idea. That way we'll both have the urge to belch all night, and the apartment will smell disgusting."

"That sounds like a plan!" he laughed. I picked my favorite, and he chose the competing brand. It was the only thing that made me second-guess my gut feeling about the guy.

We paid and were walking out of the store when I heard someone yell my name. Thinking it was one of our shop customers I turned with a smile and my world stopped.

The woman was trying to push through the line at a register, and no one was letting her squeeze through. I couldn't remember ever seeing her in real life, and I only had one picture of her, but this was a person I'd recognize in a heartbeat.

Amelia Kay Duncan.

My mother.

"No, no, no. This cannot be happening," I whispered.

"What's wrong?" I heard Aaron. I couldn't focus on anything else he said, and when she turned to go through another lane, I grabbed his hand and started pulling him behind me.

"Aaron, I need you just to trust me and walk as fast as you can. I cannot believe this is happening! Eighteen years, Aaron! I was five, and she just left me!" I could feel the tears streaming down my face, and I was angry that I allowed myself to react that way.

I couldn't tell if I was crying because I'd not only seen my mom for the first time since I was five, but I'd heard her voice and somehow remembered it, or if I was crying because I was angry that she'd had the courage to contact me.

I felt like my skin was on fire and I could feel the scars on my heart ripping open as if they were physical. It was a breathtaking experience in the worst way imaginable.

By the time we got to my apartment, I looked at Aaron and
noticed something was wrong. He looked like he'd seen a ghost.

CHAPTER TWENTY-ONE

Aaron

"Bentley?" I heard a woman's voice call out behind us and
Bentley turned to look. I watched the worlds most beautiful
smile turn into shock and then pain.

"No, no, no. This cannot be happening," she only spoke loud
enough for me to hear.

"What's wrong?" I turned to look behind us and didn't
notice anyone trying to get her attention before I looked back
at her. "Who is it?"

"Bentley!" The woman yelled out again, and that time when I
turned, I looked at a face I hadn't seen since I was a child.

Amelia Duncan hadn't changed one bit in all this time. Her
blonde hair was so perfectly styled that not a hair was out of

place. She looked like she was on her way to a fancy dinner.

There were too many people in front of her in the line she was in so she turned and took off, trying to cut through another line. For some reason, this piece of my past was trying to get to the woman holding my hand.

I felt Bentley start to pull me out of the store and I didn't try to stop her. I could hear her voice in the background of my thoughts, but I was too concerned with the wind tunnel that seemed to be sounding in my ears. Before I could stop what was happening, I was thrown back in time by my memory to a night that forever changed my life. A time when I went by Brennan, not Aaron.

Fifteen years old

"Come on Brennan! We've got to go!" I heard Will yelling from the living room. I grabbed my giant coat and pulled it on, running through the house.

"Can I drive tonight, Will?" I asked, hoping he'd forget I was only fifteen and let me.

"Listen," he said, pulling my jacket open and shoving the little bags into my hidden pocket. "If we weren't crunched for time, I'd be okay with you driving tonight. Even though you're only fifteen." He zipped the pocket and then zipped up my coat.

Ruffling my hair, he smiled down at me, and I felt on top of the world.

We climbed into his dad's truck and pulled onto the main road. I remember thinking how creepy the town seemed. There were houses with windows blacked out and stoplights that didn't always work. There wasn't a single street light on, despite it being almost eleven at night. The January snow was pouring down on us, making us that much later. I could tell Will was nervous about the time and every glance I made toward the speedometer made my stomach twist in a knot. He was going way too fast; even if it hadn't been snowing, I would have been scared.

One minute I was watching Will as he chewed his fingernails and the next I heard him let out a string of curses before he slammed his foot on the break. I could feel that we were still moving at a speed that was far too fast and the truck started to spin. I had a moment where I was able to glance out the windshield, and I watched the driver's side of the small car catch the corner of the front end of the truck. My head slammed into the window, and everything went black.

When I woke up, I was freezing. There were lights all around, and a man was kneeling over me as I lied there on the ground in the snow. He was shining a flashlight into my eyes and when noticing both eyes were now open, he yelled for someone to

come over to us. I turned my head to the right and saw a woman
in a uniform, like the man beside me, sitting beside a girl's
body. She was halfway zipped up into a large bag, and when the
woman was finished writing something on her clipboard, she
finished zipping it up. I began to hyperventilate. I didn't see
Will anywhere, and the man above me started talking.

"Calm down, son. You need to calm down. Look at me; I need
you to stop moving around so much, okay? You hit your head
pretty hard. We've got to get you to the hospital and stitch you
up," he said.

"Where's my brother?" I asked, using that term for the
first time, ever. The man sighed and looked over to the left of
us. I followed his gaze and saw Will was talking to a police
officer. His hands were held behind his back by handcuffs, and
he was placed in the backseat of the car. I remember thinking
how he must be worried about me since I was knocked unconscious
and I called out to him. He spoke to the officer while
maintaining eye contact with me. I didn't understand what was
happening, why he was getting arrested when we were in an
accident. The cop looked over in my direction and nodded his
head before walking over.

"Young man, do you have any drugs on you?" he asked,
glancing at my coat. He knew. There was no denying that he knew

and I was trapped. Everything went by in a blur. My coat was taken, my rights were read to me, and I was placed in an ambulance and taken to the hospital with my police escort. An officer sat with me through the entire ordeal. I had five stitches in my eyebrow, and after I was cleared with no signs of a concussion, I was released into the custody of the officer.

The next image I remembered was in the courtroom when I was being sentenced. I heard crying from behind me and saw the woman with a young man in the back.

Present

When my mind allowed me to come back to the present, I noticed we were in Bentley's apartment. I was sitting on the couch watching her pace back and forth. She had tears running down her face, and I felt like the worst person in the world because I couldn't allow my questions to go unanswered.

"Who was that Bentley?" I asked. She let out a sob, and I forced my muscles to stay still. I couldn't get up and go to her.

"That was my mother," she cried. I felt fire somewhere inside me. It was like my worst nightmare was coming into play at that moment and I couldn't stop it.

"Why don't you talk about her?" I was getting angry.

"Because she doesn't deserve to be talked about," she spit out.

"What happened?" I yelled. She jumped at my tone, but I couldn't control my voice. I was experiencing more fear than I'd felt in a very long time.

"When I was five," she started. She wiped some tears away and sat on the floor across from me. "That's not really where it starts I guess. It was more like when she met my father. Amelia met Pop when he got back from California. He'd been living there since he joined the Marines but decided to come back to his hometown when he didn't reenlist again. She already had two kids and didn't want anymore, and Pop was okay with that. He said she married him for security and I guess she didn't want any attachments to him. She didn't even change her last name. So, she got pregnant with me, and just kind of threw me at him. Said he could name me and raise me. I don't have a lot of memories of her, but the one that sticks out the most is the one that hurts so bad. I was five, and her daughter was in a car accident. She was only sixteen, but she died. Amelia went kind of crazy I guess. Said she couldn't deal with this town anymore and she left with her son. I don't have many memories of my siblings either. How weird is that? To remember nothing?"

She still had tears running down her face and neck. She

continued to talk. "Pop said she left only a few days after Erica died. I guess she buried her a few hours away from here."

I was so confused. How had I not known that Bentley was related to her? How had I been involved with this family for so long without noticing something that could have warned me about who they were?

I was becoming too relaxed in life. I was so in love with this girl that I'd forgot what was important. I didn't have any room for errors like this.

"I have to go," I said. I stood and walked to my room. I heard Bentley following me.

"Where are you going?" she asked. She sounded so scared, and I wanted to turn and comfort her. I wanted to take her in my arms and tell her how much I loved her. I wanted to hold on to her for the rest of my life, but I couldn't do that. My mind didn't have enough space for something so big. I was a part of killing Bentley's sister. I was part of the reason her mother abandoned her. I was part of the reason this beautiful, beautiful woman was deprived of something so important.

"I'm leaving," I said through my pain.

"But why?" she asked.

"I can't do this anymore; I have to go."

"Are you coming back?" I shut my eyes and inhaled through

my nose.

"No," I said. I grabbed my bags from underneath my bed and began to pack everything up. I was careful only to take the things I had bought and left the gifts from her in the closet.

"Why are you doing this?" she asked. She was crying in earnest. "I just told you the one thing I've held so close to me. I just saw my mother for the first time in eighteen years, the woman who left me because I wasn't good enough and now you're leaving too?"

"I told you, I just can't deal with being in a relationship right now." There would be no coming back from this moment.

"But we aren't in one! Isn't that what you said this morning? That this couldn't be a relationship? I said I was okay with that! I told you I'd wait."

"Bentley you have to listen to me." I had my bags packed and on my back. I looked her in the eyes. If I was getting out of this apartment, I was going to have to say something I'd regret. "I do not want to be here anymore! It's time for me to move on."

How was it possible for just a few words to visibly crush someone? I watched the last little bit of hope vanish from her eyes. She stepped out of the way, and I walked past her. I whistled for Dog and headed for the front door. I didn't want to look back, but I loved her. I loved her so much it physically

hurt to be doing this to her but it was for the best. I made her

a promise, and I intended to keep it. One day, I'd tell her

everything, and there would be no secrets separating us. To do

that, I had to do this, and so with the willpower I didn't know

I had, I opened the front door and walked out.

When I got to the sidewalk, I turned right and made my way

past Bucking Bandits. I continued for about an hour and

eventually arrived at the run-down storefront that had a covered

porch. No one lived in these houses; I had already known that.

This was where I spent most nights. The nights Bentley worried

so much about.

"Hey, Aaron!" I heard the familiar voice yell from across

the street.

I looked up and saw Theo walking toward me.

"Hey man," I said. Dog let out a low growl, and I patted

his head.

"You got anything for me?" he asked. The look of excitement

was evident in his features. I opened my bag and pulled out a

small box.

"What are you after?"

"You got any nose candy?"

I opened the box and pulled out a baggie.

"Where's my money?" I asked, looking him in the eye. He reached into his pocket and pulled out a small wad of cash. After handing me some bills, I gave him the bag, and he walked away with it.

Even after all the time I'd spent selling cocaine, I still had a pang in my gut every time I sold it.

CHAPTER TWENTY-TWO

A few days later

I lost track of how many days I'd been lying in bed. Sam, Pop, and the unknown number I finally figured out was my mother, continued to call me.

I hadn't heard from Aaron.

The day he left I sat down on my sofa and cried for hours. I'd texted Pop and told him I wasn't feeling well so I wasn't coming back in and he said to tell Aaron to take good care of me.

That made my chest hurt.

Aaron wouldn't be taking care of me. Aaron wouldn't be anything to me ever again, and I had no idea why.

I was in my bed when someone knocked on my door. Pop and

Sam had called a few times to check on me, but no one had come over until now.

I made my way to the door and opened it to see Sam standing there with a backpack.

"Hi," I said.

"What's going on Bentley?" she asked. She looked scared. I didn't know what I looked like, but obviously, it was bad enough to frighten her.

I sucked in a breath and started crying again. I was so overwhelmed with my feelings and the thoughts floating around in my head. Sam walked into the apartment and shut the door behind her.

"What happened?" she whispered. She grabbed my hand and pulled me to the sofa.

"I don't even know Sam."

"Well, tell me what you do know because I'm tempted to go get your dad."

"No, I'm not ready to tell him yet." I took a deep breath. "I ran into my mom a few days ago at the store. It was so weird and messed up because when we got home I was freaking out and so was Aaron. By the time I finished telling him who she was, he flipped out and just left me."

"Why did he leave?" she asked, shocked.

"I honestly don't know. That's what I'm trying to tell you, I have no idea what happened, but he left, and now I'm just-,"

"Heartbroken?" she offered.

"Yeah. Heartbroken."

Sam turned the television on and went to get the comforter off my bed. She tucked me in on the sofa and went to the dining room. I heard her cleaning up the few bags I'd left where Aaron dropped them.

While she cleaned the kitchen, I watched a show on television and tried to laugh when the audience did. I couldn't get Aaron and my mother off my mind though.

I was so angry at myself for allowing Aaron into my heart. Not only had I grown to rely on his friendship but I'd brought him onto the Cooper's family. I wasn't the only one who relied on him.

No matter how bad my heart hurt when I thought about him leaving, I still worried about him. It was still so cold outside, and the snow was piling up. I told myself I was a complete idiot for caring, but that was just who I was. I cared about people. Not only had he taken his companionship away from me but he took Dog, too. I didn't think I'd ever been the kind of person to love an animal so much, but I missed his quiet presence.

I was also angry at my mother. Why would she choose such a fantastic time in my life to come in and ruin it? She'd gone so long without me I figured I'd never hear from her again. It brought too many emotions to the surface for me. I thought that I had gotten past the pain of not having a mom, but she completely took away that illusion.

Now I was sitting in my living room wondering why I wasn't enough to make her stay. I couldn't imagine losing a child the way she did, but she had me there.

"Sam, I want to tell you about my mom," I said. She walked over and sat beside me, handing me a cup of coffee. I smiled as best I could through my sadness in thanks.

"Pop had just returned from California when he met my mom," I began the story. I told her about my mom's other kids and her marriage to Pop. About how when I was five my half-sister was involved in a car accident, and after her death, my mom took my half brother and left Pop and me. Sam cried with me when I talked about my insecurities.

We alternated between talking, crying, watching TV and sleeping throughout the rest of the day. At one point Sam went to the store and purchased all the cliché things that were supposed to heal a woman's heart after a breakup. It may not have been an official break-up, but it sure felt like it.

When Sam came back, we watched a cheesy romance movie and ate Oreo ice cream. It did not do what it was supposed to do. I felt a little better and even laughed a few times, but when I went to sleep that night, my thoughts returned to my mother and Aaron.

Two days later I was again disturbed by someone at my door. According to Sam, it had been three days since I'd last shown up to work.

I opened the door to my father and stepped aside so he could come in. I'd been dreading this moment.

"I talked to Sam today," he said. He looked angry, and I wasn't sure who he was mad at; me, my mother or Aaron.

"So, she told you everything?"

"Yeah and I want you to know, I called Amelia."

"What?" I was completely shocked. "How did you have her number?"

"She called and left a message, asking me to call her."

"How did she get my number?" I asked.

He sighed. "I honestly have no idea. I'm so sorry."

"It's not your fault, Pop. So," I took a deep breath. "What did you do?"

"I called her and told her to stop trying to contact you. She lost the right to barge into your life unannounced when she left you. She asked me to have you contact her when you were ready."

"I'm not ready," I whispered.

"I know squirt." He put one arm under my legs and the other behind my back and sat me on his lap. I laughed at the sudden change but laid my head on his shoulder. I don't think I'd sat on my father's lap since I was seven years old.

"How are you, really?" he asked after a while. I immediately felt my eyes start to water.

"I'm just confused," I confessed. "He just left me, Pop. Just like she did. People just leave me."

"Bentley, you've had five days to wallow in self-pity, and for a good reason, but it's time to buck up, babe." I reared my head back and looked at him like he was crazy. Did he not know the trauma my heart just went through?

"Don't look at me like that. You can't act as if everyone leaves you because two people in your life left."

"I didn't have very many people in my life to begin with!"

"Who cares if you have ten or ten thousand. The important thing is that you have people that would do anything for you. You have me, and if I thought it'd make you smile, I'd find Aaron and put the boy in the hospital. I would have taken your mom to court and made her pay child support or something since

she abandoned you, but I chose not to raise you that way. I
never wanted you to want retribution or vengeance against
people. That's no better than drinking poison."

"It's not that I want vengeance, I just want an
explanation."

"I know, but it doesn't look like you'll be getting one. At
least not from Aaron. Maybe you're not ready now, but one day
you could benefit from getting closure with Amelia. If you don't
forgive her now, you need to take a moment when you're a mom to
try to understand that she went through something that forever
messed her up. I don't know if I'd ever come back from losing
you if anything ever happened."

"Let's not talk about losing each other. It makes me
nauseous," I said, and Pop nodded.

"Did you forgive her?" I asked.

"I forgave her for leaving me the minute she filed for
divorce. It was never a love connection for us, and I was okay
with that. What I don't know if I'll ever be able to forgive her
for is leaving you behind. I would have fought until my last
breath if she'd tried to take you with her, you have to
understand, you're my kid, Bentley. But sometimes I hate her for
hurting you. You have a mark on your heart from that woman
that'll always be there, and I wish I could take it away and

carry it for you."

I nodded my head in understanding and stood to walk to the kitchen. I made myself a sandwich and grabbed sodas for both of us.

"We still haven't talked about one of the biggest pieces of this story," he said after taking a drink. I fidgeted in my new spot on the sofa. I was unsure why I all a sudden felt uncomfortable talking about it.

"I don't know what to say," I said.

"You had a sister die, and you have a brother you haven't seen since you were five. I think it's something you should deal with. It's a big part of your life."

"But, I don't want it to be part of my life. I was so young when it happened, and you shielded me from everything along the way. I barely remember them to be honest, so I don't understand why they have to be a part of who I am today. Plus, he's never tried to contact me so why should I care?"

"When Amelia left, Jackson didn't want to leave you behind," he said, and it stunned me into silence. He'd never told me that before.

"Why didn't you tell me?" I asked.

"How would I have explained to you that your mom didn't want you but your brother did? I think knowing that would have made letting go of your mom harder for you. You would have tried to contact him, and I didn't know if Amelia would have allowed that. What if you'd tried calling him and she told you not to call again or something? I drove myself crazy just thinking about the possibilities."

"I can understand that I guess," I said, taking a bite of my food. "Still would have been nice knowing someone else wanted to be a part of my life."

"Yeah I bet it would have, but you still had more than a lot of kids from broken homes. At least you were loved and fed and taken care of. Some children don't get that. Broken homes can put these kids in the middle of fights that result in the police being called or long custody battles where they don't want to win because of their children but because they want to beat their ex."

"You're right." I had plenty of years to mope about my mom not being around and I was using her as an excuse to feel pity for myself because Aaron left.

"Now, I hate to be that guy, Bentley, because you know how much I think that guy sucks, but I'm about to be him. You have got to stop calling off work because of Aaron. You have an entire company that relies on you. You calling off has forced a couple of people to have to pick up your slack, and that isn't fair. I know I'm your dad, but I'm also still your boss, and if you miss another day of work I'm going to have to write you up."

"Write me up?" What was he talking about?

"It's a real thing, I checked."

"I know it exists; you just can't threaten to write me up over missing some days. I've never missed a day of work in my life!"

"You've left me with no other choice. Clean yourself up and get your act together. People are going to come and go, that doesn't mean we stop living, especially when you're the owner of a company. It makes you look weak."

"Sometimes I hate how brutally honest you are." I huffed.

"I'm never going to lie to you."

When he was finally ready to leave, I told him goodbye and thanked him for his advice. He may have had a horrible approach to the truth, but it was the truth.

CHAPTER TWENTY-THREE

Brennan (Aaron), sixteen years old

The moment my mother conceived me, she hadn't wanted me, or so I was told by my case worker. I always wondered what it was she did or didn't see when she looked at me that made the decision so easy for her.

From birth, I bounced from foster home to foster home, and I was currently with a family of seven. Other than Will, who was their biological son, I was the oldest and therefore I was Will's right-hand man.

Will had been a part of this process for almost an entire year, and since he turned eighteen a few weeks before, he needed me. If the police caught him with this, it would be his third offense, and he feared the judge wouldn't go as easy on him. I didn't realize then that Will was using me, I just knew that for the first time in a long time, someone needed and wanted me around, so I was there.

At only fifteen years old I had been involved in an accident that took the life of a young girl. Since I was brought up on different charges than Will, I never got to be in court with him to see what happened but my lawyer said he was convicted of vehicular manslaughter and received fifteen years in prison. When he tried to throw me under the bus, it only served to hurt him since I didn't have any priors on my record.

I deserved more. I had nightmares every single night of the woman that came to my sentencing and sat in the back crying with a boy that looked to be the same age as Will beside her. I tried my hardest to pay attention to everything that was happening, everything the judge was telling me, but it was hard. I heard references to some drugs I had in my pocket, and he asked me questions about what my intentions had been that night. I was completely honest. I told him about Will asking me to help since he was considered an adult, and how I wanted to be an important member of the family, I was staying with. I told him about the two other times I had gone with Will and dropped off the same amount. I said the places changed every single time and we didn't know where to take it until the phone rang and someone

told us where to go. Every single detail I could remember of
what had happened those nights and where we went came tumbling
out of my mouth.

I became a rat, and I didn't even care. Will hadn't thought
about me when he told the cop to search me, so I didn't think
about him when I told them all I knew. The only difference
between us was, I wasn't malicious about it.

I remember my lawyer, after the final sentencing, telling
me I got off easy. I would spend six months in a Juvenile
Delinquent Center and then spend another six months on house
arrest, with whatever foster family would take me in.

Every time I felt like my life sucked, I would close my
eyes and think about the girl's life that ended. Maybe I wasn't
driving, but I was a part of that night. That night was a
permanent stain on my soul, and there was no washing it off.

When I was released, I was taken to a new foster home three
hours away from Taylorsville. The drive was long, and I slept
the entire way. We finally arrived at a small country house in
the middle of a huge field. I noticed the horses running along
with the car, and when I looked at the house again, I saw the
police cruiser. Really? I thought. They had to accompany me to
my foster home like the large black ankle bracelet wasn't enough
embarrassment.

"Why is there a cop here?" I asked.

"That's Phil's. He's your new guardian." Tabitha, my case worker, saw the horror on my face and quickly cut into my thoughts. "Brennan, they asked for you. They followed your story even after the news stopped, and they asked the state to consider placing you with them. It took almost two months to get it approved. They're excited for you to be here."

It sounded more like a nightmare to me. In my sixteen years, I came to realize people only wanted you if they knew they could get something out of you. It was easier to sit and wait for them to disappear than it was to get attached and have them walk away.

Ten weeks. I was there ten weeks before Phil finally broke through my wall. I was outside working in the stalls when he walked in and threw my coat at me.

"Come on, Brennan. I'm sick of your moping." He turned and stalked off to his car, and I felt dread fill my stomach. Maybe I didn't try with them, but that didn't mean I wanted to leave. It was the most stable home I'd been in so far. I got to eat three meals every day, I hadn't been hit, and I was catching up on all my school work I'd missed. Linda, Phil's wife, decided it would be best if I was homeschooled and she was the most nurturing teacher I'd ever had. She had so much patience with me

I was positive she was the definition of the word.

I put on my coat and took my time zipping it up. If he was
this upset, he probably already had my things in the trunk, so I
walked to the car and got in. Without a single word, he drove a
few miles down the road, to a heavily wooded area and pulled off
into the only section of land I'd seen for miles that didn't
have trees.

"What's going on?" I finally asked.

"I want you to understand something, and then I want you to
make a decision," he answered, staring out over the field. He
was twisting the gold band on his finger that stood out against
his dark, brown skin. "One day my wife and I were watching the
news. We saw a young boy was involved in a fatal car accident.
The news didn't follow your story like they did the young man
that was with you. You were just forgotten. I found out you'd
been in foster care since you were born and it was hard for us,
thinking about the pain you were going through. We were already
registered as a foster family, but we hadn't had anyone contact
us looking to place a child yet."

"Why did you decide to be a foster family?" I asked,
cutting him off. "You aren't too old to have your own family," I
added, and he sighed.

"About three years ago, Linda and I found out we were

expecting a baby. We had been trying from the moment we got married to start our family, and it took ten years for her to get pregnant. Everything seemed fine, and the doctors weren't concerned until one day when she started bleeding. She was only eleven weeks into her pregnancy, and she was losing the baby. She didn't want to try again after that. She said she had built up this image in her head of everything this baby would be to us and then it was taken away from her in an instant, without any warning. We had already started the nursery and one day I found her in there, lying on the blankets we bought just crying. I asked her what would help her heal and told her I'd do anything to make her happy again. She said she didn't want to try to get pregnant again, but she thought maybe she'd want to adopt one day. So, I waited. Almost a year later she came to me with a huge packet of paperwork and pamphlets about becoming a foster family. I was onboard almost immediately because she had that spark in her eyes again. The more we studied and read about it, the more excited I became about being a foster father.

"We went into it with the intention to adopt, and we were told we would most likely get a call within a few weeks since there's such a huge need for families. It didn't happen though. We waited and waited for the call to come, asking us to take in a child in need of a family. The call never came, and then right when we began to lose hope, and the light started going out of her eyes again, we saw that boy on the news. It was like we were on the same page instantly and I started making phone calls the next day at the station. I had the Chief pull strings to get me in contact with your case worker, and she came out and did a few home evaluations before telling us she'd submit her thoughts to her boss. She said she was rooting for us because she was so tired of seeing you hurt every time you had to move to another home and a couple of months later she called us with the greatest news we'd ever heard. We were approved to be the foster parents of Brennan Sanders, and he'd be moving in, in just a few months. Brennan, I know your life hasn't been the greatest, and you've gone through things that will probably haunt you forever, but I want to be there for you. I hope you know we care about you; we did even before you stepped foot into our home. We want to adopt you if you'd let us."

I was stunned into silence. I hadn't been open to them one bit since I'd been there. It felt like a dream. I opened my mouth to speak, but nothing came out, so we sat in silence for a few minutes. For the first time in my life, I felt like I was wanted and I couldn't respond because I was too scared I would cry. I looked at Phil, and he was watching me quietly. All I could manage was a nod of my head, and Phil lunged across the seat and pulled me into a hug.

Here I was, a sixteen-year old man, in my own eyes, and I was about to cry. I fought as hard as I could against the tears, but I didn't win. I knew he and Linda truly wanted me, I had heard the emotion at the very surface as he told me his story but I don't think they knew what they were taking away from me.

Hunger, pain, sleepless nights, cold, fear, trauma, stress, the weight of the world, anxiety, helplessness. Feelings of betrayal, abandonment, heartache, resentment, bitterness, anger, disappointment and restlessness. They were filling the void with love, redemption, joy, beauty, family, patience, rest, forgiveness, honesty, faith, strength, peace, friendship, kindness, sympathy, and hope.

I cried because I was thankful, I cried because I was happy and I cried because I didn't know what to do with myself now that I didn't feel the weight of my own life on my shoulders. Phil held onto me as if he was willing to take all the pain away and when I finally sat up, I saw the tears in his eyes as well.

"So, why did you bring me out here to tell me all of that?" I asked after a while.

"This land used to belong to Linda's father. When he passed away, he left it to her, and she didn't know what to do with it until now. This is yours, Brennan. When you turn eighteen, this is going to belong to you."

"What would you have done if I'd said no?" I asked.

"I was hoping I wouldn't find out because I didn't have a plan for that," he laughed.

We drove back to the house, and Phil told Linda I'd agreed to let them adopt me. She cried more than I had. They assured me I didn't need to feel pressured to call them mom and dad or change my name and they shocked me again when they told me they already filed the papers for the adoption.

Within a few months, I was legally adopted, and I willingly went from being Brennan Sanders to Brennan Murphy. Phil and Linda became Mom and Dad long before we received the birth certificate that reflected who they were to me.

Present

Caleb was starting to grate on my nerves. I knew I was getting closer and closer to ending this madness that was my life, and the one person that could get me there was the guy I couldn't stand. He was my only hope of ever moving forward, so I suffered through the torture.

"You have a girl?" he asked for the eighth time that evening.

"No, Caleb, I don't have a girl."

"You disappeared there for a while, man. I thought you got smart and found a nice girl to take you in."

He was dangerously close to the truth. I knew I'd covered my tracks every night when I made my way back to Bentley's apartment. Plus, I was confident that he wasn't smart enough to follow me. I didn't know who I worked for, but I was surprised he hadn't killed Caleb already. The guy was an idiot.

"No girl, I just found an empty building." I answered.

We sat in silence for a while before a car drove up to the abandoned building down the road. We patiently watched a man get out of the car with something about the size of a pizza box, and walk into the building.

Dog growled so I placed my hand on his head.

"Your mutt's gonna get shot one of these days," Caleb whispered. I didn't know why he was whispering, but I also knew he was right. I thought back to the night I'd come back to Bentley's with bruised ribs. Dog had gotten me into trouble with one of the guys we delivered cash to.

His need to bark or growl at anyone he didn't like ended up making someone angry enough to hold a gun on his head. I took the beating for the mutt after I begged for his life.

I didn't care that he was a dog, he was the only companion

I'd had for two years before Bentley came along.

"I've never seen somebody do as good as you," Caleb said, pulling me out of my thoughts.

"What's that supposed to mean?" I asked.

"You showed up one day and kinda took over. It's no wonder Link is doing so well now."

"Link?" I asked. I could feel my heart rate drastically change.

"You haven't met Link? Well, he's your employer, boy."

"Haven't had the pleasure," I said trying to keep my cool.

"He's up at the old Billard Estate. Somehow came into the inheritance or some nonsense."

The Billard Estate was miles out of town sitting in the middle of dense woods. With no neighbors and having come into the house legally, it was the perfect place to set up shop and hide in plain sight.

When the car pulled away and drove out of sight, we made our way over to the building and picked up the new shipment of cocaine. I think Dog felt my urgency, because as soon as I lost Caleb, I was running to the nearest payphone.

CHAPTER TWENTY-FOUR

Spring

I couldn't regret the changes I'd made in my life following Aaron's vanishing act. After a few weeks of thinking about what I'd do if I didn't have Cooper's, I began to research careers. Once I ruled out teaching and professional figure skating, I decided it was time to talk to pop.

I spent every day making sure I was keeping my priorities straight. Currently, in my life, I was a boss first. I was running a business with my father, and I couldn't let him down. I couldn't let any of my employees down. So, I did what Pop told me to do, and I put my feelings to the side until I was alone.

Every night I would think about the decisions I had to make, like if I was going to let what happened with Aaron dictate my level of trust I have for others in the future. I also had to consider hearing Amelia's side of the story. I may not ever understand how she could do what she did, but I had to give her a chance to explain.

One day in March, I went to pop and told him that I'd started questioning my career choice. I was scared it was going to be a devastatingly emotional moment, but I should have known better because Isaac Cooper is a realist. He told me that it didn't matter what I wanted to do in my future. He said if it wasn't Cooper's it was going to be okay because he had complete faith in me.

When I told him I wasn't sure about the career path I should take, he dedicated his lunch hour to help me decide.

"What kind of things do you like to do? That's the first question you have to ask yourself."

"Well, I'd like to help people, and humor is a big part of my personality. I thought about teaching, but I don't think that's it. I guess I'm pretty friendly. I like being a boss, but I think it's because I like leading people. I don't think my future career is going to be in business, so I just don't know."

"So, look into counseling."

"I don't need counseling for this. I would really like to decide this on my own."

"Bentley," he said, his voice sounded strained. "I mean go to school to be a therapist or something. Help people by counseling them."

"Oh," I said, and he laughed. "Got it. I hadn't thought about that."

I took out my notepad and wrote it down so I could search it later.

"What happens if I really do go down another road? What will happen to this place?"

"You'll still own it, squirt," he said through a bite of his taco. I looked down at my applesauce covered taco and remembered Aaron trying it out. I smiled despite the sadness.

"How can I own it if my work takes me away from Taylorsville?"

"Did you know we're some of the only owners that work at the business they run? Most people just hire a manager to take care of day to day things."

"A manager. I like it! Who would you choose?"

"Oh, that's your job when the time comes. I'm not planning to retire for another ten years or so, so when I do, and you take over you can make those calls if you need to. I always hoped you'd stay and run the place like I have but that wasn't a fair dream for me to have. You have to figure out your own life."

"Cooper's is always going to be a part of my life, you
know? I can't begin to describe how I feel knowing one day I'm
going to own this place, even if it turns out that I won't be
here to run it."

As close as we were, the weeks that passed brought us
closer. Pop really helped me narrow down my ideas and when I got
an acceptance letter to an online school and started classes,
this dream I didn't know I had, became a reality.

After the snow had melted away, Pop and Sam cornered me in
the break room at work and started hammering me about driving.
Sam quickly put together that my fears stemmed from my sister's
death, and she said she couldn't stand by and let fear consume
me.

I almost regretted giving her the full-time position in the
shop, but this was also why she was my best friend. People only
made you face your fears when they really cared about you.

Every single day one or the other would take me out for a
quick drive around town (it started out in the parking lot of
The Market, after hours). Before I knew it, I was driving the
back roads in the country of Taylorsville, and I eventually saw
the dead-end sign that signaled I needed to turn around.

I don't know why but having the ability to drive only

furthered my desperation to get my degree and explore new
places. I had confidence because I would never have to bum rides
from my father again.

Speaking of the old man, after their Christmas date, Pop
and Maria started exclusively dating. She was a catch! Attorney
at Law, forty-six, great hair and a physique that said she
worked out like a madman. I wasn't exactly pumped about how
obsessed she was with running, as it hadn't been my strong suit.
Ever.

One morning in mid-May I woke up with the determination to
call my mother and see what she had to say. I called Pop to get
the number and contacted Amelia to set up a place to meet. The
moment she answered the phone I blurted out where and when and
that I would be there if she wanted to talk. I hung up almost
immediately. It was better than the trial run I'd done in my
living room, talking to my wall.

The next day I was sitting in a booth at Bucking Bandits,
waiting for this woman I didn't know to come and meet me for
coffee. I'd arrived early so I could fill Sylvia in on all that
had happened and begged her not to talk about Aaron. Her eyes
reflected her sadness at the request, but she complied.

I didn't dare ask if they'd seen him because I didn't want
to know. I tried to convince myself I didn't care and that I

didn't love him, but I knew I was fighting a battle that had already been won. I did love him, and that was why the betrayal still hurt.

I could have been facing my mom with him by my side today, but I wasn't. I was doing it alone. Pop offered to come with me, but I decided it wasn't a good idea for him to see her again, especially when I had so much to say to her.

When the door opened, Amelia walked through and searched the diner for me. When she laid eyes on me, she smiled, and I felt bile rise in my throat. Forgive, remember, grow, move on. I repeated Pop's words from our last-minute phone call in my head as she approached.

"Hello! Oh my, you've grown so much!" she said. She looked like she was going to go in for a hug and I held up my hand to stop her.

"Eighteen years do that to ya," I said. She only allowed her expression to slip for a second before her mask was put back in place.

"I've been trying to get in touch with you for so long! I suppose you're quite the busy gal." Why did this feel like I was her long-lost friend?

"I've had quite a bit on my plate lately. Trying to run a business and all."

"Oh Bentley," she clicked her tongue and shook her head. "You're such a beautiful girl; you should be doing something far better than trying to run a business in this rat hole of a town." She eyed the diner like it could, in fact, be infested with rats.

The combination of her nonchalant attitude, and her disgust for one of my favorite places on earth made something in me rise up. I had felt like I owed her this moment to redeem herself as a mother but in a split-second, I realized I didn't need to hear a single word.

"Listen," I started after Sylvia sat our coffees down. "I only agreed to this meeting because I wanted to listen what you had to say but I don't think I need to. See, for the past eighteen years of my life, I was being raised by the most incredible parent a girl could ever ask for. His parenting went far and beyond what was expected of him. He molded me into the woman I am today, the woman I'm proud to be. You had something tragic happen to you but seemed to forget that something tragic happened to me too. Instead of losing a sibling and being comforted by my parents, I lost a sibling to death, lost a mom to abandonment and lost a brother because she took him with her. I didn't get a choice in any of the things that you decided for me. You decided I would grow up without a mom; you decided a single father would raise me, you decided I wasn't worthy enough to be your daughter. I don't think I'm going to let you decide anything else for me. I want you to know that I forgive you for leaving. I forgive you for being overcome with grief and thinking there was no other way. I need you to know something though. I may forgive you, but I don't need you. I've lived my life without you, and I can live the rest just the same. You were the one that chose to walk away, and I really resent the fact that I feel like you think I should be the one to beg you to stay now."

I didn't wait for a response. I felt this moment entirely. I didn't need a relationship with Amelia to help me heal. I grabbed my emotional sewing kit and closed up the holes in my heart on my own.

I walked home from the diner after handing Pete money for the coffee. Once I was in my room I looked in the corner where my bookshelf stood, and I remembered the night Aaron and I put it together.

It took hours, but every single minute was so much fun. I had a sudden urge to knock it over, still riding my high from being honest with myself about how I felt about Amelia, but I didn't. It meant too much to me, as silly as it was.

Now, I had to continue to live with the knowledge that I

loved a man that didn't love me back. I loved a man I didn't even know how to find.

I forced myself to change direction and started my next week's assignment early. I poured my energy into my schoolwork. Sam called me close to 8:00 P.M., to tell me how her date with Matt had gone that day. I was happy that she was happy.

When we hung up, I picked a book off my bookshelf and got lost in another world.

CHAPTER TWENTY-FIVE

Brennan (Aaron), three years ago

After I graduated, I enrolled in the local community
college for criminal justice and then transferred to a
university. The night of my graduation, I got to surprise my dad
with my acceptance letter to the police academy.

At twenty-three years old, I landed a job with my dad's
station, and I started building my dream home on the land my mom
gave me on my eighteenth birthday. I poured every single dream I
had for my future family into that place, and I spilled more
blood and sweat over that property than I thought possible.

I had been living on my own in my new home for three years,
approaching my twenty-ninth birthday. I was on my way home from
work, and the station put out a call concerning a young man

walking around town without shoes, and they needed a responder.
I was off the clock but didn't hesitate in turning around and
heading back into town.

Evin Scott was in his early twenties and was in a scary
state when I arrived. His breathing was erratic, and he kept
saying he bought weed and that's all it was, but this wasn't a
typical reaction to marijuana. When we got to the hospital, the
doctor gave him a shot of whatever medication they use to bring
down someone's heart rate, because it was getting dangerously
close to two hundred beats per minute. Another shot and nothing
was happening. They took a blood and urine sample and rushed it
off to do tests, trying to figure out what this kid was on so
they could save his life. I sat there and watched the monitor
above his bed that showed his vitals and I started sweating.
Within twenty minutes the results came back, and he didn't have
a trace of anything. It was obvious what happened at that point,
and I felt at a loss as I watched the doctor administer yet
another dose into the boy's system.

Synthetic marijuana had recently become a huge hit in so
many communities. It succeeded in getting you high, and it
couldn't be found in urine or a blood sample. Laced with spice,
the combination was deadly, and the doctor was trying his
hardest to prevent that outcome. Sitting in the critical room of

the Emergency Room I prepared myself to watch the death of a young man.

The monitor started beeping again, and the numbers scared me. The screen went from green to red and showed his heart rate had picked up speed again. One-hundred and ninety-five beats per minute. The doctor ran in with another dose which brought the number down twenty beats. It stayed there for a while until they came and administered another dose.

After a few hours, Evin's heartbeat stayed at one-hundred thirty-five beats per minute. His rambling were finally coherent. He was paranoid and nervous about what was going to happen to him. Honestly, I could have gone home at that point, but I kept having flashbacks to when I was a young kid. The life that illegal marijuana took that night and the life it almost took tonight.

It started bothering me, the fact that I hadn't been punished enough for what I was involved in as a kid. When the boy was in the clear and my paperwork was done I went home and started questioning what I was doing. I enjoyed being a cop, I did, but I didn't feel like I'd done anything noteworthy in my career.

I started thinking about what I wanted to accomplish in my career, and I thought about the boy I almost watched die. There

was always a need for Narcotic Detectives, so I began the
process of the change.

Within the year I was our station's only Narcotic
Detective, and I was tasked with was seemed to be an impossible
workload. I was supposed to get as many drugs as I could, off
the street.

I had barely been working my new job for six months, when
the Chief was contacted by the precinct near Taylorsville, Ohio.
They needed a man to go undercover, so I drove to meet them
immediately.

"We've been trying to find this guy for over twenty years,
but he's a ghost. We know you were a part of this specific drug
ring when you were a kid, and we were wondering if you'd be the
man for the job," Richard, the Chief from Hillview, Ohio said.
Hillview was the town beside Taylorsville; it was the town I
lived in when I was fourteen and fifteen years old.

"I wasn't involved for very long at all. Wouldn't it be a
risk for me to go back since I spilled some of the information?"
I asked.

"We'd be sending you undercover. It might take some time, a
few years even. This guy isn't a rookie anymore. He's had time
to weed out all of the bad ideas, and now he thinks he's
untouchable."

"I see. So, I'm going undercover as a drug dealer?"

"No, you'll become Aaron Fitzpatrick. You'll have no ties to anyone alive, and you'll be homeless. I need a clean slate, Brennan and this is the only way we can assure no one finds any connection to you. You need to find a way in and start climbing the ladder. Your job is to find the leader and take him out."

"How do I keep you in the loop if I'm homeless?"

"Send a postcard every few months addressed to 'Simon Denbar' with 'need more juice' as the message. We'll know you're fine and things are going well."

"Simon's registered as a dealer?" I asked thinking Richard had done his homework.

"Of course," I laughed. I didn't know any junkies that sent postcards to their dealers, but I'd do what I needed to do. If they had this avenue thought out, I could trust them to keep me safe.

"This here is Charlie," he said pointing. I looked down the hall to see a german shepherd walking toward me with another officer. "He's going to be your partner for the next, well, however long this takes. That is if you take the case."

I stared at the dog with the horrible name and tried to feel anything inside telling me not to take this job. I'd have no contact with my parents or my friends back home, but that was the only negative I could think of. This was something that truly needed to be done.

"I'll do it. I need to call my parents so they can take care of the house and the animals, but I'll take the job." The Chief stood and took my hand in his grasp.

"Thank you, Brennan! We would have sent one of our guys in, but they all have young families and couldn't give up the possibility of a few years of their life for this. I didn't want to have to go out of house to handle this, but I have faith in you. I think we can take this guy down.

"I appreciate it, sir."

I left to call my dad and tell him what was going on. We'd have no contact for a long time and my mother was devastated. She cried for a while on the phone with me, and I tried as hard as I could to reassure her that this was important. People in these small towns had every chance to become addicts and not enough people fighting to save them from it. I wanted to be one of those people.

I thought about the young girl whose life was taken away from her at no fault of her own. It was taken away because I wanted to make money for a family that didn't want me.

This will be my payment. I said to myself. Nothing will ever take away what I did, but I can use this moment to right my wrongs. Payment for my involvement.

Two weeks later I was sitting in the parking lot of a diner with a dog that looked like he had better things to do. This was to be my life.

I gave myself a few weeks to get a feel for what the town was like now. It had been sixteen years since I'd been around this area and while the looks hadn't changed, the street did. I quickly found my way in and started climbing.

Present

Including myself, there were thirty officers surrounding the Billard Estate. Even though I'd known where this guy was for the past peek, I was still in shock that he'd been hiding in plain sight for over twenty years.

The urge to find out who this man was, was overwhelming. The access he had to new recruits that kept his secrets and did his dirty work was unbelievable. It was like he had arms stretched so far and wide, and I was ready to cut those arms off at the body. We all were.

I checked my radio right as the Chief gave the signal, and all the men made their way to the designated spots against the huge home.

I was a part of the group at the front door, along with the Chief, Shawn, and Wes. I tried the handle and wasn't surprised to find it locked. That's where Wes came in, and he busted the door down with one hit.

Chaos broke loose when the door came down, and I counted three guys running toward the back of the house, but we had that exit covered.

"Get on the ground!" I shouted. My gun was out and aimed toward the group that was left in the living room. I could hear our guys yelling orders all over the place.

I saw a man move out of the corner of my eye and quickly turned to train my gun on him. I recognized Will as soon as he made eye contact.

So many thoughts started running through my mind. I knew he'd been released from prison right around the time I'd taken the undercover job, but his paperwork said he was living in northern Ohio, where he'd served his full sentence. How had he managed to trick his parole officer? How long had he been here in Hillview?How involved was he in this operation?

"Murphy!" Chief Collins yelled from across the room. "You got him?"

"Yeah, Chief, I've got this one."

"You don't recognize me," I stated. Will's eyebrows drew

together in confusion. "My name is Brennan Murphy, but I used to
go by Brennan Sanders."

Recognition came when I said my name and he went from
looking confused to enraged.

"You're the reason I ended up in prison for half my life!"
he screamed. "I should have killed you when I had the chance!"

"Yeah, well, it's a little too late for killing me."

"I see you never lost your high and mighty attitude," he
spit.

Now I was the one confused. "I never acted like that with
you, Will, and you know it. I looked up to you."

"Yeah right! You threw me in jail!"

"You killed a girl!" I yelled. "You convinced a fifteen-
year-old kid to sell drugs with you! It's your fault you were
there, and no one else's."

He flinched. "I never meant to kill anyone that night. The
truck got away from me and I couldn't control it."

"Why are you back here?" I asked. "Why'd you come back to
the very thing that took away so much of your life?"

"Was I supposed to go to some fancy school and become a cop
like you? Maybe even a teacher?" he laughed.

"You could have worked at a fast food joint and had more
dignity than you do now."

"I'm perfectly fine with where my life is!" he yelled. He reached into his coat and pulled out a knife. "Why don't you and I go outside right now and see who's left standing? Let's see who the real man is."

"Will," I said when he took a step toward me. "You need to drop the knife."

He took another step.

"Will!" I shouted. "Drop it, now!"

He was one step closer and I only had a few more feet separating us.

In an instant, Will lunged toward me and I heard two shots fire, one right after the other. I hadn't fired my weapon, so I was surprised to see my former foster brother on the floor at my feet.

I turned slowly and found Shawn on the floor in front of the couch and another officer holding down a kid that probably wasn't even thirteen years-old. He looked angry.

"Please, don't hurt my baby!" A woman yelled from the couch. "He's a stupid boy, just don't hurt him."

Shawn groaned and I ripped off my belt to wrap around his leg. He was losing blood, but not enough to scare me. Not near the amount that was soaking into the carpet from Will's body.

"I think he nicked the artery," he told me.

I smiled. "I think you're going to be alright, buddy."

"You knew that guy?"

"Yeah," I sighed. "He was my foster brother for a while when I was a kid."

"I'm sorry, I saw him lunge and I acted. I didn't know he was your brother."

"He wasn't my brother," I patted Shawn's shoulder. "I appreciate you having my back. You saved my life."

"And now I'm gonna die," he laughed.

"You're not dying," Rodney said. He had the hands of a man well into his sixties cuffed behind his back. I looked at Rod.

"Is that him, Link?" I asked.

"This is him," he said, before walking him out the door and to a cruiser.

"I did not expect him to have so many wrinkles," Shawn said in a low voice only I could hear.

"Tell me about it."

All together, our guys arrested seventeen men, including Link, whose real name was Denver Lincoln Grots. Will was pronounced dead at the scene and I watched as they zipped him up into a body bag. I tried to see it as poetic justice, but I couldn't. He'd only been in my life for a short time, but I couldn't dismiss that time. His influence changed me forever.

It took hours to do a final sweep of the property and it was approaching 2:00 A.M., when a guy walked up to me.

"I'm here for Charles," he said. "I'm Landon."

I shook Landon's hand and looked down at my feet, where Dog was lying.

"He goes by Dog, now," I said before leaning down and patting my companion on the head. "I'm gonna miss you, buddy."

Landon snapped a collar and leash onto Dog's neck and started walking away. I heard him whine and felt my heart break when he looked back at me. I waved and turned to find the Chief.

I gave him all the names of the people I'd met along the way and their positions. Then, for the first time in almost three years, I headed home.

I was going to be busy helping close up this case in the next couple weeks, and it almost angered me that I would be. I wanted to see her again. I wanted to hold her and kiss her. I wanted to wake up in the middle of the night and know she was in the same house.

It wasn't going to be easy. In fact, it would probably be the hardest thing I ever had to do; convincing her that she could trust me.

I'd left her in an extremely vulnerable state. I'd abandoned her when she needed me most, but it wasn't something I could help at the time.

I had to protect my years of work and the position I held in this ring. I couldn't risk who I was coming to light.

I was going to have to bare my soul to her and wait. I didn't care how long it took; I'd wait forever if she needed me to.

I'd wait an eternity to love her the way I wanted to.

CHAPTER TWENTY-SIX

July

It was finally time to visit Erica's grave. I'd spent the past few days mentally preparing myself for something I had never done, and I felt as ready as I could.

When Erica was killed, Amelia had her buried about three hours away, in their home town. Amelia didn't tell Pop when the funeral would be, so I didn't get to attend, but I don't think Pop would have wanted me to be there anyway since I was so young. It was a closed service, and no one other than their close family was invited.

None of Amelia's family liked Pop, so they didn't care that I wasn't there.

After Pop told me that Jackson had wanted me to go when

they left, I felt a weight I didn't know I had, lift off my shoulders. I'd spent a long time pushing the thoughts of siblings into the back of my mind. I may not have had any memories of them, but at least now I could think about them without feeling a raw pain.

As I made the long drive to the cemetery, I pulled my cell phone out and dialed the newest number on my favorites list, Jackson.

Shortly after my encounter with Amelia, I decided to try to get in contact with the only other living blood relative I was open to having a relationship with.

"Hello?" his deep voice came over the line.

"Good morning, sorry if I woke you," I cringed realizing the time.

"Well, since it's before eight, you can rest assured you woke me up."

"I'm so sorry!" I said.

"It's alright, Logan didn't wake up, so we're good," I heard Jackson's wife, Olivia, giggle in the background.

"What's up?" he asked.

"The reason I called was to see if you'd be willing to take me to Erica's grave. I've never gone, and I think it's time I go."

"Wow, yeah! I'd love to take you. I'm glad you asked me," his voice was laced with emotion.

"Oh, thank God. I was so scared you wouldn't want to go."

"Of course I want to go with you."

"I'm about an hour away now so do you want me to meet you at your house?"

"Sure. Once you get off the exit, there are only a few turns. I'll text the directions to you."

"Okay, I'll see you soon."

"Okay, sounds good."

After hanging up, I waited for the text alert and pulled over to a gas station to fill up and map out the rest of my drive.

When I pulled into the driveway of their modest two story home, I started getting nervous, like I always did when I was going to see Jackson. He and I had spoken over the phone often, learning all there was to know about each other. We hadn't spent much time together in person, so I was still nervous when I did get to see him.

I said hello to Olivia and baby Logan before we got into Jackson's SUV and he drove us to the cemetery.

"Are you okay?" he asked. We were parked on the road at the bottom of the hill, and he was waiting for me.

"I just feel so guilty," I whispered.

"There's no need for you to feel guilty, Bentley. You were only a kid when all that happened. All that matters is, you're here now." I looked into his eyes and could see he meant what he said. I didn't see any anger or resentment, so I took a deep breath and opened my door.

We walked up the hill and made our way through a small group of trees that were separated by a beautiful stone path. It was so peaceful there, and the caretaker took wonderful care of the place.

Erica's grave had flowers and balloons anywhere that would allow.

"Mom comes up here almost every other day to redecorate. She's relentless about it," Jackson said. I felt pity for Amelia and hoped for her broken heart to heal.

We sat on the ground by her headstone and Jackson told me stories about when I was little and even before I was born. We laughed and cried over the sibling we both missed. It had taken me so long to realize I missed her. Even though I couldn't remember her or Jackson clearly, I truly missed having siblings.

After a while, we decided it was time to head back to his house, and he walked to the path in the trees to give me a moment alone.

"Hi," I said. It felt so weird to talk to a headstone. "I just wanted to say that I'm sorry it took me so long to get here. I'll be back, though. I promise."

I touched the stone where her picture was and turned to leave.

"Who the heck is that?" Jackson whispered to himself when we walked out of the trees.

I looked up and saw a man with short brown hair standing in a police uniform. He was standing by his cruiser, and I wondered if Jackson had made some error in the way he'd parked.

We approached the officer, and I felt nervous for no reason at all. I was a law abiding citizen, but I always seemed to check myself when I was around cops. I laughed aloud at myself, and the man must have heard me because he turned around.

I smiled at him when he looked in our direction, but when we made eye-contact, I felt like my heart was going to catapult out of my chest. It was an out of body experience as recognition washed over me.

"Aaron?" my voice didn't sound right.

"You know him?" Jackson asked. He was looking between the two of us like that would give him some answer.

Aaron stared at me for the longest time.

"What are you doing here? How did you get here? Why are you

dressed like a cop?" The questions came pouring out, and I was incredibly proud of myself that I hadn't rushed to hug him or started crying. Inside I was jumping for joy knowing he hadn't been harmed or worse in all the time he was away, but I was still hurt and now, very confused.

"Bentley," he finally spoke. "There's so much I want to talk to you about."

"Who are you?" Jackson asked, irritated.

"I'm Brennan Murphy; it's a pleasure to meet you." They shook hands, and it took me a full ten seconds to grasp the words that had come out of Aaron's mouth.

"Brennan?" I asked. I didn't know if my brain could handle what was happening.

"Brennan," Jackson looked at Aaron or Brennan like he was trying to figure something out. "Why do you seem so familiar?"

"Brennan?" I asked again. "What's going on?"

"I'd like to speak to you about a few things, Bentley. If you'd let me I'd like to take you to dinner tonight."

"How did you know I'd be here?" I asked.

"I, uh, I spoke to Sam earlier this morning. Remember that promise I made you, that one day I'd tell you everything? That can be today."

"You can't just randomly show up with a different name and

expect me to go with you. I'm so confused." I started shaking
and couldn't stop, so I shoved my hands into my shorts pockets.

"There's a picnic table right over there. I can stay if you
want to talk for a bit," Jackson offered. I looked at him and
saw something in his eyes. He looked almost as confused as I
was.

"Are you sure you can be gone that long?" I asked.

"I'll give Liv a call," he said. I nodded, and he walked to
his car. Pulling out his phone, he pulled himself up onto the
hood of his car and waited.

"Bentley," I heard the man beside me say my name. That
familiar voice I'd missed for so long.

"Let's go talk." I walked past him and headed toward the
picnic table.

He followed, and we sat across from each other. I wrapped
my arms around my middle in an attempt to shield myself.

"So, I'm going to start at the beginning, if that's okay."

All I could do was nod.

"Baby, please look at me." His voice was laced with so much
pain that my eyes stung in response. I looked up to meet his
eyes and swallowed the knot that had risen in my throat.

"Just, tell me what's going on. Please?" I asked.

"Okay." He took a deep breath. "The moment I was born, I

was put up for adoption, but you already know that. I wasn't

adopted until I was sixteen so all the time before that I was in

foster care. When I was fifteen, I was with a family in

Hillview."

"You were so close to me," I whispered, shocked. He nodded.

"I had been there for a few months when my foster brother

asked me to do a run with him. He sold drugs and had been busted

too many times, so I was supposed to be the fall guy. I didn't

see it that way. I was so naive. I just wanted to be accepted

and loved by someone; I thought I was helping him out. The first

couple times went as planned but the third time we were in a car

accident." He stopped talking and ran his hands over his head.

"Bentley, there is no right way to say this, but I was in

the car that killed your sister. I was part of the reason she is

dead today. The driver was my foster brother."

All the air in my lungs escaped as if I'd been punched in

the gut. My mind couldn't form any thoughts other than Jackson.

I looked over at the car, and he was standing with his hands in

his pockets, staring in our direction.

"I don't know what to say." He didn't talk, giving me the

time I needed to absorb what he was saying. I stood and walked

in the opposite direction of Jackson.

When I'd made it to a small stream, I stopped and sat on a

rock. This place was beautiful, and I just wanted to focus on that instead of what he'd just told me.

I tried to remember everything I'd ever learned about Erica's accident. The only things I knew for a fact was that the man that had hit her had served time in prison and the other kid was innocent. That's what Pop had told me. There was a young guy in the car, and he was innocent.

"Bentley?" I heard him behind me. Brennan, not Aaron. He walked to the rock I was sitting on and crouched down in front of me. "I'm so sorry for what I've done to your family."

"Did you know the whole time?" I asked.

"No, I didn't realize who you were until your mom found you in the store that day."

"So then you just left me? Because, what, you couldn't handle telling me the truth?"

"I told you I was going to tell you everything today if you wanted me to."

"I do," I immediately replied.

"When I was sixteen I was adopted. It didn't matter that they didn't meet me until I was sixteen years old or that we didn't share the same DNA, they were just mom and dad, and it was so natural.

"My dad was an officer. After watching him be a hero to so

many people, it shaped who I wanted to be. I wanted to be just
like him, and I decided to be a police officer. It all clicked
into place for me. After a few years I transferred to the
narcotic department, and about two years later I was asked to go
undercover."

This all felt like a dream. His explanation was so perfect,
and I hated it. How could I be mad at a police officer for doing
his job?

"I was placed undercover in Hillview. They needed someone
without a history, so I was homeless. I needed to find this drug
dealer and almost two years into my investigation you came into
the picture. When I left you, Bentley, I had to go. I couldn't
afford to have my cover blown by your mom, not when I was so
close to the end."

"This can't be true. It's just too weird."

"I promise you, it's the truth, and I can prove whatever
you need me to."

"This is all just too much."

"How can I make this right?" he asked.

"I don't know if you can. I mean, it's so much more
complicated, now." I took a breath and stood. "There is nothing
to forgive when it comes to Erica's death. There was never a
second that I blamed the passenger in the other vehicle, and

when I was old enough, Pop told me most of the details. He went out of his way to explain to me that no matter what the situation was we needed to forgive because it was only going to make me unhappy. Even then I didn't think there was anything to forgive you for because you didn't do anything. You were only a kid."

I looked into his eyes and saw a tear running down his cheek.

"I can forgive you for leaving the moment you knew your cover could be blown. I'm not stupid, I know what you were doing had to be important if you were undercover for such a long time. I can respect that and even appreciate all you did to make Hillview safe. I love that you're the person that you are and I will never have to question your safety and health." By this time, I was crying. I wiped the tears off my face and powered on.

"But what I can't forgive, or even grasp is that every single emotion I've felt along the way has been for a man I thought I knew. He was homeless and hungry. I gave him a job and a place to live because my heart could not handle doing anything less. I worried until I was sick some nights because I didn't know if he was safe. Every morning I asked myself if that would be the morning he wasn't sleeping in his spot." I had to stop so

I could breathe. I gave myself a moment.

"Do you understand, I fell in love with him?" I whispered. "I cried myself to sleep for weeks after he left. I'd just opened my chest and shown this man the scars on my heart, and he just left me."

"I didn't want to leave you, Bentley. Please believe there were moments I wished I was Aaron again, for you. I wanted to be him for you."

"Of all the days you could have come back, why did you have to choose the day I decided I was ready to visit my sister's grave?" He swallowed roughly and looked at the ground. I didn't receive an answer. "I just need time. I need some time to take in all of this information."

"Okay. I'll wait as long as you want me to," he said.

Without responding, I turned and walked back to Jackson's SUV. I got in and rested my head on the window. Jackson got in and looked at me.

"You okay?" he asked.

"No," I admitted. "I need to talk to you when we get back to your house."

He nodded and pulled out of the cemetery.

CHAPTER TWENTY-SEVEN

I felt like I was processing too much at once. I was
drinking sweet tea with my older brother in his kitchen while he
was waiting for me to start talking. I hadn't said a word since
we'd sat at the table. Brennan being one of the people in the
accident that killed my sister was almost too vast to believe. I
didn't hold it against him, I hadn't lied, but it was still a
strange thing to grasp. Now, I had to explain to Jackson that
I'd fallen in love with Brennan.

The thing that was so hard for me to move beyond was the
fact that Aaron wasn't real. The man I'd fallen in love with had
been created in the imagination of a team of law enforcement
officers. I didn't hate Brennan for doing his duty as an officer
and finishing his job without telling me the truth. I wouldn't
have wanted it any other way. I guess I just wished I hadn't met

him until after he'd finished his job.

On top of everything, my heart was hurting. I'd gone six months without the piece of my heart I'd given to Aaron. Was I supposed to let him back in?

I couldn't do that. I was too scared.

Even if he had an explanation for everything over the past year, I couldn't hand my heart back over to him. I didn't even know Brennan. Maybe I knew pieces of him, but I didn't know for sure.

"The man you met today, Brennan," I started.

"Brennan Murphy. Do you know who he is?" I whipped my head toward Jackson.

"Do you?" I asked.

"He looked so familiar. He has a different last name, but I know who he is. How do you know him?"

I told him about how I'd met Brennan and quickly went through the course of the last year of my life. He sat patiently, listening to every detail and held my hand when I cried my way through watching the only guy I'd fallen in love with leave me. Then, I told him what Brennan had been doing the last three years.

"That's insane," he said. He sat back in his chair and shook his head. "What are the chances that he'd show up in your life?"

"From what I understand, he was only fifteen when the whole
thing happened. He wasn't at fault for any of it." Olivia said
from the doorway.

"I have to agree with her," Jackson said. "It's so weird,
but he wasn't the one at fault. Even the police officer that
testified at his trial said the boy he was with threw him under
the bus to try to get off easier."

"That guy was his foster brother," I said.

"Can you imagine what he's gone through though?" Olivia
asked. "I don't mean to dismiss what you guys have lost because
I can't imagine losing my sister, but he was a little boy and
probably carries a lot of guilt."

"I don't know what to tell you, Bentley. It's a crazy
situation, but I don't think Brennan should be blamed for
Erica's death." Jackson said.

"Why aren't you bitter?" The question came out before I'd
thought about why I was asking. Jackson and I were fine. I'd
grown up thinking he and Amelia didn't want anything to do with
me because they were bitter about Erica's death and while that
was true for Amelia, the same couldn't be said for my brother.

"I struggled a lot through my teen years. I hated the
entire world. When I was three, my dad decided the family life

wasn't for him. Then a few years later my older sister died, and my baby sister was forced to stay behind while I got to watch my mom suffer depression. By the time I got to high school, I was awful."

"He was our school's bad boy," Olivia smiled at him.

"Who knew spray paint could be so powerful?" he laughed. "So, my sophomore year we got a new student. Little miss goodie two shoes, she even wore her hair in braids. For some reason, my English teacher thought I needed help in her class, so I got paired with the little brat."

"The only points you had were the points you got for showing up to class! And, you didn't even have all of those!" she said, swatting him on the shoulder with the kitchen towel she'd grabbed off the island. He laughed and pulled her into his lap.

"Yeah, well I ended up showing up to class more often. And I even started getting better grades, although I'm not exactly sure why."

"It's because you thought your tutor was hot," she giggled.

"Heck yeah, I did." He paused to give her a quick kiss then looked back at me. "She contributed a lot to how I viewed myself. I started going to my school counselor a lot, too, which helped tremendously."

"I think joining the football team did you right too," Olivia said. Jackson rolled his eyes at her.

"She only liked the muscles."

"Did not!" she winked at me, and I laughed.

I looked down at my phone and was shocked to see it was nearing 7:00 P.M., and said, "wow, I didn't realize it was so late."

"Why don't you stay here tonight? You can wear some of my clothes to bed if you want," Olivia looked like she'd cry if I said no.

"Do you think you can get off work tomorrow?" Jackson asked.

"Let me call Pop, but I'm sure it won't be a big deal."

"Yay!" Olivia jumped up and ran into the other room to tell Logan his Auntie Bee was staying the night with him.

"Let's order some pizza for dinner." Jackson got up and called the pizza place while I called Pop to let him know I wouldn't be home until Monday evening if it was alright and he said he thought he could handle Cooper's in my absence.

We ate dinner and then watched a kids program before Olivia showed me to their guest room. Thankfully, they had an extra phone charger, and a few minutes after I was in bed with my eyes closed, my text alert went off.

I looked at the screen and didn't recognize the number, but opened it anyway.

_I know you need time, but I wanted to make sure you had my number. This is Brennan.

Me: How did you get my number?

Brennan: I remembered it.

Me: Oh, okay.

Brennan: Please don't think I'm a stalker.

Me: I don't. It's not a big deal.

Brennan: Well, I'll let you get back to whatever you've got going on.

I stared at the phone debating my answer.

Me: I'm just lying in bed. Nothing too crazy going on.

Brennan: Would you want to talk a while?

Me: Would it be okay if I asked you a few questions?

Brennan: Of course, ask me anything.

Me: How much of what you told me before was true?

Brennan: Every single thing, except my name, was true, Bentley. I never lied to you about myself.

Me: And the fact that you weren't homeless.

Brennan: I had a home three hours away, but I was technically homeless. I'd been living on the street for almost two years when you came along.

Me: So your parents are alive?"

Brennan: They are. I never said they were dead; I just didn't correct you. I couldn't have you trying to figure me out more than you already were. I did miss them, though.

Me: I told my brother who you are.

After a few minutes, Brennan finally sent me a reply.

Brennan: What did he say?"

Me: That he never blamed you, but it was crazy that you ended up in my life.

Instead of another message my phone started to ring.

"Hello?" I answered.

"Can we talk like this?" he asked.

"I guess that's okay for right now."

"So, your brother doesn't hate me?"

"You're a police officer, Brennan. If you were at a crime scene and a fifteen-year-old was in the passenger seat of a car that killed another driver, what would you tell them?"

"It's different. I had drugs on me, Bentley."

"It's not different. You were a kid. I don't understand why you think you should be held accountable for her death."

He was silent for a minute.

"You know, I wanted to drive that night."

"You weren't old enough."

"Will would have let me; he didn't care about my age. But we were in a hurry so I couldn't. Your sister probably wouldn't have died, and your mom wouldn't have left you."

"Brennan, I don't blame you. My brother doesn't blame you. So please, stop blaming yourself. It wasn't something you set out to do; it was an accident."

"I feel like this should be so much more challenging. I'd understand your anger, but I don't know how to handle your forgiveness. I've gone over this for the past six months, and this isn't the outcome I expected."

"I might not hold anything against you for Erica or even your investigation, but Brennan, I still don't know how to feel about you. I'm scared I don't know you."

"I have an idea to help you see I am who I've always been."

"What's that?"

"Do you think I could come back to work at Cooper's?" he asked.

"Can I text you later and let you know?"

"Yeah, I should probably let you go."

"Okay, I guess I'll talk to you later."

"Goodnight, Bentley."

"Goodnight."

I hung up the phone and thought about Brennan's suggestion.

Working for Cooper's again could help me get to know him as Brennan, but what if it was awkward?

I wanted to get to know him, I truly did. If I was in love wouldn't it make sense to give him another chance? I made up my mind and sent him a text.

Me: I think it would be a good idea for you to come back to Cooper's. But I'm leaving it up to you to convince Pop that it's a good idea. If you can get him on board, then I'll see you Tuesday.

CHAPTER TWENTY-EIGHT

Brennan

The morning after talking to Bentley, I left the hotel I
was staying at in the city and headed for Cooper's. By the time
I arrived, I had chastised myself for not telling someone what I
was doing that day because if there was one person I was
concerned about killing me, it was Isaac Cooper.

I climbed out of my cruiser and walked into the building.
Isaac was standing in the lobby watching my every move, and when
I was close enough, recognition hit him.

"Hello, Mr. Cooper. Can I have a word with you in private?"
I asked. I felt the sweat collecting on my palms and could feel
every single beat of my heart.

"Without a single word, he turned and walked to his office,

leaving the door open.

I haven't been punched yet, so that has to count for something. I thought.

I entered the office and sat in the chair in front of his desk. He was looking at me like he wanted to take me out back and bury me, but I was here because I loved this man's daughter. I didn't want to be a coward. I wanted to be what she deserved.

"I'm going to get straight to the point. My name is Brennan Murphy." I touched on everything I'd already told Bentley. It didn't matter how carefully I watched his expression; he didn't twitch. Even when I said the part I was most afraid to tell him, he didn't budge. It was almost like talking to a brick wall, except this brick wall had brick arms and could knock me out.

"So, I went undercover, and I was there almost two years when Bentley came along. I didn't have any idea who she was or how our pasts were connected, I swear on my life. I would have never let things progress with her. I didn't know my cover was so close to being blown," I said finishing my explanation.

Isaac continued to stare at me for nearly a minute. Finally, his eyes narrowed, and he sat forward, resting his arms on his desk.

"How long have you been in law enforcement?" he asked.

"Ten years."

"In your ten years of police work, did you always string along girls that made their way into your life?"

"No, Sir. Absolutely not. To tell you the truth, I haven't dated since my early twenties. I was too focused on my career."

"How am I supposed to believe that's true? You've been Aaron for nearly a year to my daughter and my team here. How do I trust anything you say from here on out?"

He didn't sound or look like he wanted to hit me anymore. It was almost like he was asking me my opinion on how I could regain his trust.

"I'm not sure at this point."

"Here's the thing; I can't blame you for what happened when you were younger. I can't even blame you for leaving when you figured out who she was and worried about your case being blown. I understand why you did what you did, but I had to watch my kid hurt. One day, you're probably going to have a daughter and the first guy that comes along and breaks her heart is going to be on your list. Right now, you're on my list, and that's a dangerous place to be, son. The problem I'm having is understanding why you allowed yourself to begin a relationship with someone when you were on an assignment. You got involved with someone when you should have been entirely focused on your work."

He was saying everything that had run through my head a million times.

"I know it makes me look weak, but I was beginning to struggle when Bentley showed up. I was going on two years of no human contact except dealing, and it was messing with my head. I was craving something, and I didn't even know what it was until this quirky, full of life woman just inserted herself in my life." I smiled, remembering the very first time she brought me breakfast. She'd checked my pulse that morning, and I forced the laugh down until she left. "Sir, I didn't mean to fall in love with your daughter. I did though, and now I just want to fix everything. I can't go back and change my job or how I met her. All I can do is beg for your forgiveness and try to gain her trust, as well as yours."

"So, what is it you plan on doing to get that trust back?"

"I've asked Bentley for my old job. She said if you approved of it then she would, too. I figured just being here is as good of a start as any. I just want her to know I'm not going anywhere unless she doesn't want me to be here. In that case, I'd go back home. I've spoken to my Chief, and for now, I'm going to go on leave and see what happens here."

"Bentley spent a lot of time out in the shop after you left. Well, when I finally got her to come back to work, that is. For days, I couldn't figure out why she was out there until it dawned on me; She was waiting for you. Finally, after she started school she was spending every free minute studying, but there were times she'd just stare off into space. She looked so sad for a while then she'd snap out of it and get back to work."

Hearing this was tearing my heart into pieces. I focused on my breathing, trying to keep in under control when all I wanted to do was smash my fists into a wall. Listening to someone recount your loved ones pain that was caused by you is pure torture.

"I'm giving you another chance," he continued. "I know she cares about you and even if she's upset, I know she'd want me to say yes. But let me make you a promise, Brennan. If I ever see tears in her eyes that are caused by you again, breaking your legs wouldn't be enough to satisfy my anger."

"Understood, Sir."

"I guess I'll see you bright and early in the morning then." He stood and walked to open his office door. I said goodbye and made my way to my car. I purposely avoided making eye contact with the other employees. I wasn't ready to tell anyone else what had been going on. Most of them probably hated me on Bentley's behalf anyway.

I didn't realize how draining this would be. I knew I

wasn't a young kid anymore, but talking about all of these feelings and failures was pulling the energy out of me.

After I shut my car door, I called the number I'd found for an apartment to rent across the street from Cooper's. I agreed to sign a contract and wouldn't be moving in until tomorrow, but that was okay. Building up to this moment had kept me up most nights, and I needed sleep. Even if it was in my car.

I sent a text to Bentley saying her father agreed and I'd see her Tuesday. I received her Okay reply an hour later. Texting and phone calls were going to be on her terms, so I placed my phone on the night stand and went to bed long before nightfall.

CHAPTER TWENTY-NINE

I was walking to my bedroom, ready for bed, when my phone
started ringing.

"Come open your door," Sam said over the line after I
answered. Confused, I went to the front door and opened it to
Pop and Sam.

"What are you guys doing here?" I ended the call with Sam
and moved to let them in.

"We decided to bombard you tonight." Sam was sitting on the
floor taking her laced up combat boots off.

"She thought it would be too awkward to do it tomorrow at
work," Pop explained. "So here we are. Hope you don't mind, but
Maria's coming over, too. She went to get some pizza first."

"Where is she getting pizza in Taylorsville?" I asked.

"The Market. It's frozen so turn your oven on," he

answered.

I rolled my eyes and pre-heated the oven.

"So, Brennan was at the office today," Pop said getting straight to the point. I looked at Sam.

"So, you know?"

"I know a lot more now than I did the other day when he showed up at my house. Freaked me out when he showed up as a cop, but I knew you would want the truth. I hope you aren't mad I told him where you were going to be yesterday," she said.

"No, I'm not mad at all. It was kind of weird hearing all this at the cemetery but I wanted to know the truth, and now I do."

"How do you feel now?" Pop asked. We'd moved to the living room, and I sat beside Pop while Sam stretched out on the floor.

"I feel weird. I want to be so angry with him but I can't. I want to give him another chance, but it's like my head keeps telling me it's way too soon just to forgive and forget. I have to remember what happened to my heart when he left. The biggest thing I have to ask myself is, is he the same guy that I fell in love with, I mean, I fell for Aaron but who is Brennan?"

"I think they are the same person, squirt." Pop said.

"Yeah and you have to realize, there isn't a rulebook, Bentley. This is your story, not someone else's. Just because

other people don't forgive so easily doesn't mean you can't.
Your ability to let go of things is what makes you who you are,"
Sam said.

"She's right," Pop said cutting in. "Hank ran over Sam's
foot three months ago pulling a stupid car into one of the bays,
and she still hasn't forgiven him."

"I thought it was broken!" she said, waving her foot in the
air. "I went to the hospital and everything."

"You guys are so ridiculous," I laughed. "But you're both
right. This is all my decision, and I guess the most important
thing is seeing who Brennan is for myself."

By the time Maria showed up with the pizza, I was starving.
Thankfully, she was brilliant and knew us enough to buy two
pizzas and a bag of chips. Pop ate almost an entire thing by
himself. No matter how many times I watch him eat a whole pizza
alone, it impresses every single time.

Sam and Maria left soon after dinner and Pop stood in my
kitchen while I cleaned up the mess.

"Feel free to help out, Pop," I laughed. He smirked at me
but started helping.

"So, I've been thinking about something I wanted your
opinion on," he said when we were done.

"What's up?"

"What would you think about having some kind of outreach program or something?"

"I love that! Did you have anything specific in mind?"

"I do. What if we did something for the homeless shelter in Hillview? I drove by it the other day, and it looked awful. I don't know if they just don't get funding or what's going on, but I was surprised people were living in it."

I don't think I'd ever been so on board with an idea in my life.

"What's the plan?"

We pulled out a notebook and worked together to come up with more ideas that could raise even more money for the shelter. I finally had to kick Pop out when I was yawning every other minute but promised him we'd finish talking the next day at work.

After locking the door, I looked at my phone and contemplated what I was about to do. It was well past midnight, but there was something I wanted to say to Brennan. Something that hadn't occurred to me until Sam had declined my invitation to spend the night; because she didn't want to sleep in the spare bedroom. She hadn't wanted to sleep in his bed. I picked up my phone and sent my thoughts.

Me: There's something I need to say. I don't know if this

will make sense at all, but here it goes. I feel like I'm

cheating on Aaron. I know you are Aaron and I'm sorry, I just

can't help but separate you from him. I'm willing to give you an

opportunity to show me you're him, but please be patient with

me.

It hadn't even been two minutes before I got a reply.

Brennan: I completely understand, and if I'm honest, I am

whole heartedly jealous that Aaron has your love and I don't.

But I promise you, as long as you allow me to fight for it, I

will.

Me: I know you will. Goodnight, Brennan. I'll see you

tomorrow.

Brennan: Goodnight, Beautiful.

I set my alarm and spent the next half hour staring at the

ceiling. I know it had only been a day since I'd found out but I

was already sick of my feelings going back and forth. I was a

woman who knew what she wanted. I wanted to graduate college in

a couple of years with a degree that would help me be a high

school counselor. I wanted to help my father run his business

and, more than anything, I wanted everything to work out with

Brennan.

CHAPTER THIRTY

Nothing I did helped settle my nerves. All morning, I paced my apartment until it was time to leave and I ended up walking to work for the first time in months just to get rid of some energy.

Even though I'd spoken to Brennan on a couple of occasions, I was still nervous about seeing him again, and when he walked into my office, my heart began to pick up its pace again.

"Good morning," he said, taking a seat in front of me.

"Hi," I answered breathlessly.

Without any words, he handed me his driver's license, and I turned toward my computer. Brennan Jacob Murphy, born on June thirteenth. His address was listed in a town nearly three hours away from Taylorsville, and his picture looked exactly like the man sitting in front of me; A man with short brown hair, warm brown eyes, and a polite smile.

"I guess I missed your birthday," I said. "Happy Belated Birthday."

"Thank you," he answered.

"So, thirty-three?"

"Yeah. I'm getting up there in age," he laughed.

I smiled but then remembered what had been bothering me.

"So, where's Dog?" I asked. I was upset with myself that I hadn't asked sooner. I looked at Brennan, and he looked sad.

"The station that I worked with were the ones that owned him. He hadn't been placed with an officer yet when they asked me to come to Hillview, but now he's with a guy named Scott. They kept your name for him, though. I went back a few weeks later, and they were there. Everyone was talking about, 'Dog, the dog.'" He laughed, and I joined in. I was sad to find out that I probably wouldn't get the chance ever to see him again but I was glad he was okay.

"You live pretty far away from here," I said, pointing to his license.

"That's where I grew up. I own a piece of land and a house there now."

"Where are you staying while you're here?"

"In the apartments across the street, by The Market."

"Oh, those are pretty nice! They didn't have any vacant apartments when I moved out, or I would have lived there."

"I'm glad they didn't," he said. "I would have never had the chance to meet you, otherwise."

I ducked my head and smiled.

I was still smiling when Pop came into my office an hour later. Brennan had finished filling me in on the changes I needed for his employee information, and he went to the shop to work. Before he left, he looked me in the eye and told me if he didn't make it due to Sam "accidentally" dropping a car on him, he loved me.

It was supposed to be funny, but I couldn't laugh. I know he meant the words because if there was one thing I knew about him, it was that he wouldn't casually say that.

He gave me a sad smile and walked away.

"What's up chipmunk?" Pop walked in and took a seat. He must not have liked the way the chairs were positioned because he stood and moved them around a bit. Then he looked at the small pot of flowers on the corner of my desk and moved it to a different spot.

When he noticed my expression, he shrugged his shoulders and sat down.

"It's all about feng shui these days, Bentley," he said.

"Feng shui?" I asked, trying to hold in my laughter.

"Maria made me watch a movie. She moved my couch, Bent. Said it gave the living room the wrong energy. How can the couch give off bad energy? It's a stupid couch!" His bald head was getting more and more red by the second. A giggle escaped me on accident, and he narrowed his eyes.

"Sorry," I said. "Tell me what's going on."

"I like her a heck of a lot more than I planned on liking her and I want to see how things go, but she keeps hinting that she's leaving soon. I asked her something about next week, and she said, "sure if I'm still here." I don't want her going anywhere."

"Did you tell her you wanted her to stay?"

"Well, no! I figured letting her rearrange my house was pretty obvious."

"Pop, women need words. You can't expect her to read your mind. In all honesty, I bet she keeps bringing up leaving because she doesn't want to."

"That doesn't make any sense. If she doesn't want to leave, she should just tell me instead of acting like I'm going to wake up one day and she won't be there."

"Women are weird creatures. Sometimes, even though we know in our hearts what we want, we think we need this huge sign to show us it's the right decision. She's probably scared to make that step." I looked down at my hands and thought about how I was doing the same thing. Knowing I wanted to be with Brennan but not being able to make that move because my mind was in the way of my heart moving.

"You're right. Women are weird. I'll call her in a bit. So, what's going on with you?"

"You were just at my house last night." I reminded him. "Not much has changed since then."

"Tell me." I rolled my eyes and laughed.

"I'm trying to convince myself it's okay to want to forgive Brennan already; then I think I'm just making myself try to forgive him because I want this to be easy. What if I make myself believe everything is okay and then later, when we've been together for a while, I start feeling like I did when he left. What if six months down the road I feel betrayed again?"

"Loving someone is always risky. It's a gamble. It doesn't matter how strongly you feel about someone; there's always a chance you'll get hurt. I can promise you forgiveness doesn't abide by the same rules, though. Forgiveness isn't for the person that wronged you; it's for you. If you want to walk around with a chip on your shoulder then, by all means, hold on to the times you've been hurt by people, but if you don't want someone to hold power over your emotions, you need to forgive them."

"It's easier said than done."

"No, it's not. That expression is an excuse people use when they don't want to work on something. It's an excuse to be able to throw yourself a pity party. If you don't want to hold on to pain, then let it go."

"I can't just turn off my fear," I said.

"No, you can't. You can learn from your experiences. It's possible to forgive Brennan and be cautious at the same time. Just because you forgive someone doesn't mean you hand them your heart right back. I've told you before; you are the keeper of your heart. You're responsible for protecting it."

"It's weird, isn't it? Referring to him as Brennan?"

"I won't lie, I've called him Aaron almost every time I've had to say his name."

"Me, too," I said, and we laughed.

"How do you feel about him?" I asked. "What do you think I should do?"

"Bentley, I'd love to tell you what you should and shouldn't do, believe me, it's a dream I've had since you were little."

"Wait," I said cutting off his thought. "What's been your

dream?"

"To be able to tell you what to do for the rest of your life," he answered with a straight face.

"Pop!" I laughed, and he smirked at me.

"I'm not joking. If I made your decisions for you, it would help prevent a lot of medical issues for me, I'm sure."

"I'm serious. Please tell me what you think I should do in this situation."

"I think, if it's something you want, you should give him the opportunity to prove himself to you."

"That's what I was hoping you'd say. I feel like I keep asking the same things over and over. I'm just trying to sort out my head."

"It's fine. That's what I'm here for, but we need to get back to work. We have a lot of planning to do if we're having an event next month."

"You're right. I thought we could have a barbecue. I know it's not very flashy but in my opinion, the simpler, the better. We could ask Darin if we could maybe rent The Market parking lot from him."

"All profits could go toward the donation."

"I like it. I'm thinking we need four or five grills going. Do you think the sales team could take care of that?"

"No problem. Let me know what the date and time is so that I can talk to Darin about the parking lot. Then you should figure out all the other details," he said, standing to leave.

"You will be helping me, old man."

"I hear ya, I hear ya. Let me know when it's time to get the food and I can cover that."

"You're hopeless."

"That's what I hear," he laughed.

When Pop left, I pulled out my notebook and started writing down my ideas. The only thing that made me nervous about the charity event was getting enough people there to make a difference.

"Hey Pop!" I yelled. I could hear him rummaging around in his office across the hall.

"Yeah?" he yelled back.

"What if for every dollar the community donates, we donate two?"

He popped his head in my office and thought about it.

"Sounds good," he said and walked away again.

"Thanks!" I yelled.

I didn't hear a response. I tried thinking of different ways we could get the word out. Not long after Pop left, Brennan walked in.

"I was going to come find you in a few minutes," I said.

"Good news or bad news?"

I told him about the event we were planning and asked if he could think of any other way to spread the word.

"I could get in contact with the Chief that I was working for. He and his men would probably come. They could hang the flyer up in a few stores around the station too," he offered.

"If you don't mind that would be awesome!"

"I don't mind at all. I'd love to help in any way I can. I think it's great that you're doing this. They've needed help for a long time."

"I just hope we can raise enough money to make a difference."

"Anything you do for good makes a difference," he said.

"Was there something you needed?" I asked.

"I was going to let you know I had to head out early today. I spoke to your dad and let him know, but I have to meet the landlord to sign a new lease."

"Why do you have to sign a new lease?" It wasn't my business, but I was too curious not to ask.

"They let me live there on a day-to-day basis while there wasn't an application in so that I could figure out everything between you and I. I called them this morning to let them know

I'd be staying for a while, so I'm signing a lease with them."

"Oh," was all I could say.

"Yeah," he smiled. "I'll see you tomorrow."

"See ya," I said.

Once he left and I got over the joy of knowing he was staying for a while, I got back to work.

CHAPTER THIRTY-ONE

August

An hour into our barbecue, things were going well. We had five grills going, and there were a few tables holding chips and a few different sides that wouldn't ruin in the heat.

There were people everywhere, and we'd already sold three cars, so I took that as a good sign. I glanced toward the shop and watched the guys.

In the weeks since Brennan had been back with Cooper's, we all finally stopped calling him Aaron. We all also found out that he was an extremely hard worker. I didn't know if it was because he felt like he had to prove something or if it was because it was his nature but he caught the shop back up in no time.

The first week he was back, I didn't get a lot of alone time with him. We did, however, have a date a few days later.

I'd been sitting in my office, and he asked if he could talk to me. I was so nervous because I'd been waiting for this moment and now that it was here I didn't feel like I was ready.

"Sure," I said. Brennan walked in and sat down, wiping his palms on his jeans.

"I was wondering if I could cook you dinner tomorrow night. I've got a brand-new deck of cards, too."

Despite my apprehension, I smiled, remembering the carefree fun that seemed always to accompany us.

"What time were you thinking?" I asked.

"I figured we could head over after work. I was planning to make chili. I'm going to start it in the morning in the crockpot."

"Okay, that sounds good," I said, and he looked at me in shock. "What?"

"I just didn't expect you to say yes to my first date proposal," he said.

"How am I supposed to give us a shot if I turn you down?"

"I don't know, but I'm glad you are."

"I know I should be nervous about having our first date, but I'm kind of excited now. Are we playing for answers?"

"Definitely," he said.

The next evening, after work, we walked across the street to Brennan's apartment. The building was two stories high, but he lived on the first floor.

We walked through the front door and immediately stood in the living room. With an open floor plan, I could see the kitchen, his bedroom, and the bathroom all with a glance around. It was the perfect size for a single person, and as much as I loved having an extra room, my apartment often felt too big for me.

"You don't have much furniture," I commented before I could stop myself.

"I wasn't sure how long I'd be here," he answered.

He served the chili, and we sat at the table to eat dinner.

"So, what happened to your hair?" I finally asked.

"I have to keep it short when I'm on duty so when I went back, I had to cut it."

"What are your plans? I mean, I know you're taking time off, but how long can you take off?"

"I have quite a bit of vacation time saved up so, for right now, that's what I'm on. I have another month left, but I'm not sure what I want to do anymore."

"You don't want to be a cop?" I was shocked.

"I don't think I'll ever be anything else, to be honest. I've put ten years in and even though the last few were rough, I'll never regret it. I don't think any other career field would make me happy, to be honest. I just meant when I left I was in narcotics, but I don't know that I want to stay there. I've thought about being part time since the station I work at offers it."

After dinner, Brennan got out the cards and shuffled them for us. I silently watched as he dealt the hand and couldn't stop the slow smile that spread across my face. I missed this so much.

"Why are you smiling?" he asked.

"I just really missed playing cards with you. Not even so much the cards as having fun. Having these moments, I guess."

"I missed it, too, Bentley. I hope you understand how much I thought of you while I was finishing the case. Every single night I wanted to walk back to your apartment and tell you what was going on, but I had to protect what I was doing."

"I understand that, and it's all in the past now. Let's just focus on now."

We played a few hands of Rummy and asked each other silly questions that didn't hold a lot of meaning. I learned that he hated when people popped their gum and he learned that I often did it on accident when I wasn't paying attention.

I didn't want to stay too late since we'd have to go to work the next morning. Not only that, but I wanted to date in a real way. I knew I could easily spend days at a time with him and it wouldn't be weird. When we lived together for over two months, our friendship had been so natural, but this was different. I wanted to be with him, and he wanted to be with me. It's not that I wanted to treat this as if I'd just met him because I didn't want to lose what we already had, but I didn't want just to assume I knew all of him already.

"I'm glad you're driving now," he said when we arrived at my car.

"Me, too. No more creepy walks home," I laughed.

"Will you text me when you get inside, so I know you're safe?" he asked.

"Sure, if I remember," he frowned. "I'm just kidding. I'll text you."

"I had fun tonight." He leaned forward and placed a chaste kiss on my forehead.

"I did, too."

After a quick hug, I climbed into my car and drove home. I kept my word and sent him a message letting him know I was inside safely and going to bed. His reply was his usual,

"Goodnight, Beautiful."

"How do you think it's going?" Pop asked, pulling me out of my thoughts.

"I'd say pretty well considering we only opened an hour ago."

"True. So, I want to go ahead and make the announcement," Pop said. He was ringing his hands together, and his nerves made me want to laugh.

The announcement he was referring to was a proposal. He'd finally talked to Maria and told her he wanted her to stay. According to Pop she said she loved him, and it was about time he picked up on her hints, but he didn't say the words back. She was upset, but he'd simply explained that he would only ever tell his wife that he loved her. Little did she know he wanted her to be that woman.

"Well, go do it then." He made a face that convinced me he was scared out of his wits and I laughed. Probably wasn't the smartest thing to do but I couldn't help it. This guy feared very little and watching him sweat out his pre-proposal was oddly satisfying.

"Sometimes I regret not being so scary when you were growing up," he said before he walked toward the front of the lot. I giggled and scooted myself closer.

"Can I have everybody's attention?" Pop called out over the crowd. Everyone quieted their conversations to see what he had to say and even the shop seemed to pause.

"I'd like to thank everyone for coming out today in support of Hillview's homeless shelter. About five years ago they suffered severe water damage in a few rooms and the basement and since have struggled to get back on their feet. I think it's great when a community can come together and make such an incredible effort to help those that aren't quite able to help themselves. So in the spirit of that, I'd like to ask my girl, Maria to come up here."

Everyone whispered to each other and waited. Instead of her natural light brown skin, it was now furiously red with embarrassment. She sent an awkward smile to the people gathered around, and when she got to Pop, she gave him a look that said she wasn't going to forgive him for this.

"Two weeks ago, I told you the only woman other than my daughter I'd ever love would be my wife."

My mouth dropped open in shock. What kind of woman stuck around after a guy said something like that? No wonder she'd given him the cold shoulder after declaring her love! He'd basically insulted her. I started laughing, along with everyone around me and prayed that he would learn how to romance this woman better than he was.

"Shut up everybody, I know it sounded awful, but I'm a straight forward man. I don't sugarcoat anything. Anyway, back to my point. I was trying to say that one day I'm going to tell my wife I love her, and I want that to be you." He got down on one knee and held up a small black box. Maria smiled down at him.

"Will you marry me, Maria?" he asked, and she nodded her head yes through the tears that were sliding down her cheeks.

He slipped the ring on her finger and grabbed her waist, pulling her in for a kiss. Everyone whooped and hollered their congratulations to them before getting back to whatever they'd been doing when Pop interrupted them.

I walked over to where they were now standing and Maria was already on the phone.

"Horrible speech, Pop," I said, hugging him.

"I was sweating so bad. I'm surprised I didn't say something even worse than I did."

"The only thing worse than that would have been demanding the marriage," I laughed.

"I was thinking about it," he said. Maria hung her phone up and looked at me. She squealed and ran to me for a hug, which I returned.

"I'm so, so excited for you guys," I said.

"Thank you so much, Bentley!"

"You're the perfect piece to our family puzzle." Pop said pulling us both into a hug. We all laughed, and Maria showed me her beautiful ring.

"Can't breathe!" I yelled, and he let go of us both. "I've got to go check something in my office. I'll be back."

"What could you have to check right now?" Pop and Maria both looked unconvinced, but I shrugged and walked away.

I couldn't tell them I'd already been working on their wedding present because if I knew Pop, he'd be snooping on my computer that very night. I made my way to my office and picked up the phone to call Ryan, Maria's son.

"She just called," he said as soon as he answered.

"It was as romantic as a BBQ proposal could be," I laughed. "Your mom cried."

"I figured she would. She cries all the time," he laughed.

"So, are you still moving up here?"

"Yeah, I think it's time for a change. Plus, I know all the girls in this town, so I need to meet some new ones."

"There aren't a whole lot here either. There's always my best friend, but I don't think she's into old guys."

"Like you are?"

"Shut up. He isn't that old."

"He's almost ten years older than me."

"No, he isn't!" I laughed, and Ryan joined in.

"We're going to make great siblings. We already argue like some," he said.

"Your mom is going to freak out when you tell her you're not leaving after the wedding."

"Did you find any houses out there?"

"Just the one, but you can always rent until you find one you're looking for."

"True. I just hate to waste the money."

"There are a couple of extra bedrooms in Pop's house," I suggested.

"Absolutely not."

"Alright, alright. I'll let you know if I find anything else."

"Thank you, I appreciate it," he chuckled.

"It's the least I could do with you moving here. I can't wait to meet you officially!"

"Agreed. I'll talk to you later."

We hung up, and I sat back in my chair smiling. Pop and Maria were going to be so excited when they found out at the wedding. I stood and turned to head back outside and screamed

when I saw Brennan standing in the doorway. My hand flew to my
chest, and I tried to get my breathing under control.

"What are you doing?" I yelled.

"I was coming to ask you a question," he laughed. "I'm so
sorry I scared you."

He walked over and pulled me into a hug. I smiled when he
buried my face into his chest. Since our date two weeks before,
we'd easily settled back into being comfortable with each other.
There was something more this time, though. Since we had no
secrets between us, there weren't any walls up. We were finally
free to talk about anything and everything, and we had. For
fourteen days, we had spent every single night talking on the
phone, even when we'd seen each other hours before.

I started feeling like I was leaving something behind every
time I went home. It was a something I loved because I knew I
couldn't move forward without that feeling.

It may have been too soon, but I trusted him. I cared that
he was involved in such a horrible accident that killed my
sister, but I wasn't angry. I cared because I hated that he had
to be a part of something so tragic at such a young age. I hated
that he had to carry that scar around. I wasn't angry that he
left me to protect his case. I couldn't hold something like that
over his head when he was an officer of the law, and he had been

fighting to make such an impactful change.

What I thought was going to be difficult was the fact that Aaron wasn't coming back but the more time I spent with Brennan, the more I realized he had never really hidden his true self from me. How could I be upset and distant because of a feeling I didn't even have anymore?

"So why did you come see me?" I asked smiling. "Did Sam hurt you?"

"Do you want the truth?"

"She did not!" I said, shocked.

"If I'm honest, getting hit in the head with a rolled up newspaper isn't pleasant."

"She probably had something rolled up in it," I said. He paused and looked at me like I was a genius. She was currently upset with Brennan over a bet they'd made, and he won. She wasn't letting him live it down.

"What a little brat," he said.

"That she is. So what's up?"

"I was wondering if you'd like to go out this weekend? I want to take you to the zoo."

"The zoo? That's like a million miles away from here," I said.

"Close, but it's actually about an hour and a half drive."

"I'd love to go," I said.

"Really?"

"Definitely."

"We can leave Saturday after work if that's okay with you."

"I bet if you asked Pop he'd let us have the day off," I suggested.

He looked at me and the door a few times before he shook his head.

"No, that's okay. We can just leave after work," he said before walking out.

How horrible was it that Brennan's fear of Pop made me laugh?

CHAPTER THIRTY-TWO

Saturday after work I went to the restroom to change into a blue tank top, shorts and tennis shoes. When I walked outside, he got out of his car and opened the passenger door for me. I smiled and thanked him.

Brennan seemed to be extra quiet for the first few minutes of the drive so I asked him if everything was okay.

He sighed. "There's something I've been wanting to talk to you about. I told your dad a few days ago, but I asked that he let me tell you myself."

His tone sent nervous flutters through my stomach. "What is it?"

"The case that I was on, it was what I was involved in when I was a kid. I think that's why they thought I was the best fit for the position."

"Pop told me that your foster brother got out of jail a few years ago," I said. He glanced at me before looking back toward the road.

"That's actually what I wanted to tell you," he sighed again and it made me uneasy. "When we got inside, during the takedown, Will was there."

I sucked in a breath. "What happened?"

"I tried to talk him down, but he came at me with a knife. He was going to try and kill me, and I honestly don't know if I could have pulled the trigger, but one of my partners did."

"Did he survive?" I whispered.

"He didn't. He's dead."

I took a moment to let the news settle into my mind. It was a weird feeling, having a sense of relief and remorse. I felt sad that someone had lost their life, but if Will hadn't changed, maybe it was better that he wasn't alive to cause any destruction.

"I'm so sorry," I finally said. "I'm sorry you had to watch someone you looked up to as a kid die."

"I don't feel like I've lost something special, but I hate that he didn't turn his life around. I hate that he lost his life."

"Thank you for telling me."

"I just wanted you to hear it from me. I didn't want you to ever think I was hiding it from you," he said. "I hope this doesn't ruin your day."

"No, it doesn't ruin it, I just feel sad for you and guilty because I-," I stopped.

"Why do you feel guilty?"

"Honestly, I feel relieved that I don't have to ever worry about running into him. Now, I know he can never hurt another person and it makes me feel like a horrible person for feeling that way."

"You're entitled to feel however you want. He wasn't a good person, even in his best moments, he was bad. He was a part of an operation that probably took countless lives because of addiction. He had no remorse about that."

"I was watching the news the other day, and they said that drugs are almost disappearing in Hillview. They credited the police force that took down the biggest drug ring Ohio had ever seen."

"There were a few small operations around, but I think the Chief has a good handle on them."

"You changed a lot of lives," I said.

"I only followed orders," he smiled.

"You followed orders for almost three years, and you made

difficult decisions that weren't always what you wanted to do. I think you deserve some credit."

"I appreciate that," he said and then changed the subject. "Your dad mentioned a while back that you were in school?"

"Yeah, I started this spring. My goal is to be a counselor of some sort. I think it would be pretty awesome to work at a school, but I'm open to anything." I wasn't sure why I hadn't brought this up to him yet. I think it was partly because he had been the one to make me second-guess my career choice and the other part was because, for some reason, I knew my degree was going to be a part of our future. It was a scary thought, knowing someone was going to be in your life for a long, long time. After such a short period, I was convinced he was my forever.

"That's awesome, Bentley. What made you decide to go back to school for something other than business?"

"You did," I answered.

"I did?"

"Yeah, you made me think about what I wanted for myself. I'd never thought twice about working at Cooper's for the rest of my life, but once I asked myself if there was anything I wanted to do, I realized I wanted to do this."

"How did your dad react?" he asked.

"Perfectly fine. He said I would still own the business one day, but I didn't have to be an on sight owner. Once he retires, if I'm not living in Taylorsville, I'll hire a manager to run the place."

"Sounds like you'll have the best of both worlds."

"I hope it all works out. I would hate for Cooper's to suffer because I wasn't there like Pop has been. If it ever did, I'd have to go back. I couldn't let that happen."

"I'm sure it never will. As you said, your dad will always be there, and whoever you hire to be the manager will take good care of it. You're not going to hire an idiot."

"I was thinking of asking Sam to do it if she's still there. Once I get my degree, if I move Pop will need a new assistant manager. I think she would be perfect for it."

"She really would. She has a lot of excellent ideas for the shop, but I can't convince her to tell you guys. She thinks she's too young to have an opinion that matters."

"That's not true. We listen to everyone's ideas. We actually wouldn't even have a shop if Pop hadn't listened to Jerry when he started talking about opening the business."

"I'll have to try to convince her again."

"Well, please don't tell her what I said. I don't want her to feel like she has to stay because I want her to help me run the place one day. She's too young to think this is her only option."

"I won't say anything, but I think you would be surprised how much she loves working there."

"I know she loves it. I'm glad Drake brought her."

"So, do you think you could be that far away from your dad?"

"Honestly, it's hard to think about. I don't know if I could do it or not but I can't let the fear stop me from actually trying."

"I hope it all works out for you. Even if you do move away, it isn't as if you'll never see him again. You guys can visit each other as much as you want and I have a feeling he wouldn't let much time pass without seeing you."

We pulled into a fast food restaurant and ate in the car on the way. By the time we arrived at the zoo, it was packed with people. We parked in the very back of the lot and made our way to get our tickets.

"There are so many people here!" I said looking around. Obviously, I knew there were billions of people in the world but living in a small town didn't prepare you for being in a multitude. I was elbowed three times, all accidental of course, just from the ticket booth to the man that took our tickets right back and let us in.

"What do you want to go see first?" Brennan asked.

"Do they have tigers? I love tigers!" I answered. I was
getting excited. "This is the first zoo I've ever been to."

He looked at me like I was crazy.

"Your dad never took you to the zoo?"

"Nope. We went to car shows," I said, and Brennan laughed.

"That doesn't surprise me. And yes, they do have tigers."
He grabbed my hand and pulled me in the right direction.

"They have slushies?" I yelled.

"They do," he said looking between me and the slushie
stand. "Do you want one?"

"Only with all of my heart and soul," I said releasing his
hand to get in line quickly.

When Brennan stood beside me, I noticed his body shaking. I
shielded my eyes from the sun to look at his face and confirm my
suspicion.

He was laughing at me.

"Why are you laughing?" I asked.

"Your facial expression was priceless."

"What did it look like?" I asked, smiling.

"I'm not doing it."

"Come on! How will I ever know what my excited slushie face

looks like?"

He wrapped his arm around my shoulders and pulled me in for a hug.

"I guess you never will."

"Party pooper."

When we reached the front of the line, I gave the young girl my order and Brennan paid.

"Thank you," I said. "You didn't have to pay."

"I know I didn't have to, but I wanted to. I still owe you quite a bit of money if my memory serves me right."

"You don't owe me anything."

"I owe you a lot more than you think."

"What do you mean?" I asked. He hesitated before speaking again.

"That first day you left food for me, I was struggling. I was at my breaking point. I'd been there almost two years, and I felt like I had barely made progress in the case. It was like I was on a hamster wheel; continuously running and going nowhere. Then you showed up, and everything changed."

"I didn't know that. I honestly have been so consumed with my feelings over everything I never even thought about how hard it had to be for you to be out there so long."

"Sleeping in a real bed was weird."

"It doesn't matter that you're okay now, it still breaks my heart to know you were sleeping in a parking lot."

"A lot of people do it. It's kind of unbelievable how many people have to."

"It makes me realize how stupid my problems are."

"It puts a lot into perspective, doesn't it?" he asked. I didn't answer because I was already deep in thought.

Of course the things I deemed as problems were small and insignificant compared to problems people were facing in just the next town over. Instead of wasting months being sad over Brennan not being there, I could have been making a difference. He had spent the last three years of his life fighting to make a difference in that town and even longer making a difference as a cop.

I'd started to worry that I'd made this connection because I felt needed. I asked myself what I would have done if I would have met him in a casual interaction. The grocery store? Cooper's? The library? It was hard to say because I honestly didn't know.

The only thing I was certain of was I had fallen in love with this man. Whether he was Aaron or Brennan when it happened didn't matter to me because I loved him. Love shouldn't know boundaries.

"You okay?" he asked after a while, and for the first time since I'd seen him again, I felt confident in my answer. I finished the last sip of my blueberry slushie and threw the cup away.

"Absolutely."

"Good. Turn around."

I slowly turned, and my eyes widened on their own accord. Only a few feet in front of me was the most beautiful tiger I'd ever seen. I'd never seen one in person, but even if I had, this one would outshine it.

She was pacing her exhibit, and every few seconds she'd look through the glass at the people staring at her. I couldn't help but feel sad for her. She was magnificent, and she was stuck in this tiny cage. My joy became a little marred by thoughts of what she could have been in the wild. Very quickly, I realized I wasn't a huge fan of the zoo.

"This makes me sad," I said to Brennan as we watched her. "She's just stuck here."

"It is sad to think about the fact she'll only ever know this place as her home, but fortunately, a lot of these animals are saved from fates much worse than this." He walked to the board that talked about the animal and began reading.

The people started thinning out, but I sat down in front of

the glass, not ready to leave. She walked toward where I was sitting and paced the glass for a few minutes before laying her body up against it, so her back was to me. I guess I had been dismissed. I laughed under my breath and stood.

"What's your favorite animal?" I asked Brennan as we walked away. I turned to look over my shoulder finding that she'd turned her head to watch me walk away. I waved and knew I looked like an idiot, but I didn't care.

"I can tell you honestly that I've never thought about it," he laughed.

"There's got to be something you think is cool."

"I guess snakes are kind of cool."

"Oh, you've got to be kidding me!" I tried to suppress my shudder, but it didn't work.

"Don't tell me you're afraid of snakes when you were sitting less than a foot away from a tiger."

"Snakes are different; they're so creepy. I think it's their eyes," I said shuddering again.

"Reptiles it is," he said pulling me along.

"You're evil!" I laughed.

"No, I'm a man with a plan."

When we arrived at the reptile building, I stopped and took a deep breath. This was not what I thought would be on the agenda for the day.

We walked in, and my face immediately went to Brennan's shoulder.

"Much better," he said, wrapping his arms around me. He walked through the room stopping every few feet. It felt like we walked for forever when I finally started questioning what was going on.

"Brennan?" I asked, not daring to move my face from his shoulder.

"Yeah?" I could hear humor in his voice.

"This building didn't look that big from the outside."

"It isn't."

"Then why does it feel like we've been in here walking forever?"

"Because we have."

"I'm confused," I said after a moment.

"Why would I want to leave the building and have you move away from me?" he asked.

I narrowed my eyes even though he couldn't see it. He had been walking in circles for five minutes so that he could hold me.

What a dork, I thought, but I smiled anyway.

"If I promise you can keep your arm around me, can we go

look at more animals?" I asked.

"Definitely."

We walked through the doors, and when I felt the air change, I lifted my head and smiled up at him. The look in his eyes told me exactly what was going to happen and I barely had a chance to tell the butterflies in my stomach to shut up.

Brennan bridged the gap between us, and I melted into the kiss. It surprised me that we'd only shared a few kisses, and it had been something I missed when he was away.

"Come back to my house tonight," he said, and it snapped me out of my daze. I must have looked scared because he continued. "I have a guest bedroom. I just want to show you where I live. I want my parents to meet you."

"Your parents?" I asked smiling through my sudden nerves.

"If you want to. It makes me sound like a little school boy, asking you to come home to meet my mom and dad, but I guess I don't care how old I am. I love them too much to act like a tough guy. I'm a momma's boy." If there was anything I could understand, it was that.

"I'd love to meet your parents." I'd barely gotten the words out when he crashed his lips down on my own again. I laughed through the quick kiss, and when we broke apart, we just stared at each other for a moment before turning to explore more animals and pizza. We had to stop for pizza.

CHAPTER THIRTY-THREE

Since Brennan lived closer to the zoo than I did, it took us less time to arrive at his home. His driveway was long and on one side sat a large, two-story home, while the other was fenced in. Three horses were running alongside the car, and he rolled down my window to yell greetings at them.

Once we reached the house, he opened the garage door to pull in beside his police cruiser and a four-wheeler. There was still space for another vehicle, but it wasn't filled, and I wondered who usually parked there.

"You ready to take the tour?" he asked. I smiled and nodded in response.

We got out and walked up the few stairs that led to his door, and he opened it for me, allowing me to walk in first.

He took me through the entire house; all three floors.

There were bedrooms everywhere.

"Wow, you are planning on having a whole lot of kids aren't you?" I asked.

"I wasn't lying to you."

We made our way back to the living room, and he opened his DVD cabinet, showing hundreds of different movies.

"I've got my supply of your man's movies for you, stocked and ready for a marathon."

I laughed and walked over to him. He took me in his arms and squeezed like he'd never let go.

"Brennan, this home is gorgeous," I said.

"I'm glad you like it."

"How much of this do you own? The land, I mean."

"A few years ago, I bought out the neighboring field so now I have three hundred acres."

"Oh, just three hundred?" I laughed. "You're so casual about that."

"I rent almost all of it out to a local farmer. Other than the few acres the house sits on there's about fifty surrounding us that's all trees. I use that."

"Maybe this is inappropriate, but how in the world do you afford this?"

"I found out that this would be mine one day when I was

sixteen, so, any money I made from odd jobs I came across went toward my house fund. Then, when I turned eighteen, I started college, but kept saving. By the time I was ready to build, I had a big chunk of the money I needed."

"I need to find some of these odd jobs," I laughed.

"My dad helped a lot. You have to remember, I've been working for fifteen years."

"That makes you sound incredibly old. Not as old as my future husband, but old." When he gave me a weird look, I smiled. "My favorite actor; I'm still holding onto hope he notices me."

"I think I'm exactly the same age as your future husband," he said. He leaned forward to kiss me and when his meaning sunk in, I blushed.

"So," I cleared my throat. "What's the plan for the evening?"

It was getting late and our day walking around in the heat had left me exhausted.

"I figured we could just watch a movie and go to bed. I invited my parents over for lunch tomorrow."

"Oh, my gosh, way to make me want to throw up!"

"Listen, if I can face your dad after everything that's happened over the past eighteen years of my life, then you can meet my parents."

"Oh, whatever! You're scared to death of him."

"With good reason! He could probably choke me out with one hand tied behind his back." I laughed and sat on the sofa while he popped in a movie.

"I'm going to go get some snacks. I'll be right back."

While he was away, I picked up the picture album on the coffee table and started flipping through it. There were more pictures than he had room to show. Some were stuffed behind others on the pages, and there were more in a pocket in the front and back of the book.

Every picture had who I assumed was Brennan's parents. Brennan had told me the story of how they met at college and chose where they'd live. They both wanted a country life, and so after they were married, they put a bunch of towns on pieces of paper and threw them in a hat. They had picked the place they would live when they drew a sheet of paper out of a baseball cap. I loved that.

I thought it was amazing and they sounded like fun people.

Brennan came back, and we started the movie. I must have fallen asleep because I awoke to him picking me up and carrying me to a room on the second floor.

He laid me down and pulled the covers over me before

whispering goodnight and shutting the door behind him.

Only a few seconds passed before I sunk back into a deep sleep.

The next morning Brennan took me out on the four-wheeler. We rode into the woods, and I almost screamed when we scared a few deer out of the trees. I'd seen very few deer in my life, and it was possibly the coolest thing ever.

By the time we got back to the house, there was a car in the driveway and a couple standing, facing our direction. Linda's pale complexion stood out against Phil's dark, brown skin. His arm was around her shoulders while hers was around his lower back, and they were both smiling widely, their joy evident in their shining eyes. Instead of feeling nervous about meeting his parents, all I felt was excitement. I felt like I was about to see two people that were already a part of my family.

"Hey, guys!" Brennan called out, shutting off the four wheeler.

"Hi, Honey." His mom walked over to give him a hug when we climbed off and then she turned to me. I felt like so much was resting on this particular moment in my life and when she smiled at me, it was as if she took all the weight of the world off my shoulders.

"Hello, Sweetheart. I can't tell you how great it is to

meet you finally." She pulled me into a hug, and it felt natural.

"We've heard nothing but great things about the girl that stole our boy's heart." I heard Phil laugh and Linda released me so he could have a turn hugging me.

I didn't feel like I was meeting these people for the first time at all. I may not have known many things about them, but I felt like we were family.

"I'm happy to be meeting you too, finally. I'm not sure if Brennan told you, but I tried making a blueberry pie for him so he could have a piece of you while he was in Taylorsville."

Linda's eyes misted up, and her smile grew. "He didn't tell me, but I suspect he hasn't said a lot of things."

"Let's go inside so you guys can get to know each other better," Brennan said.

We all walked into the kitchen and sat down at the table.

"So what are your plans, Bentley?" Phil asked.

"Well, I'm in school right now to be a counselor. I'd love to work at a school, but I'd like to have my Master's degree first."

"Brennan says you own a car lot?" Linda asked.

"My father owns it, but I'll eventually take over once he retires. That's been the plan since I was a kid." I smiled at the memory of Pop telling me I'd be a business owner one day and me asking him what a business owner was. He'd laughed of course.

"So, you plan to stay in Taylorsville?" she asked.

"I'm not sure. I haven't decided to stay or go yet." I blushed at my thoughts. My decision was going to be based on where my relationship with Brennan went, but that wasn't something I wanted to say out loud.

Phil and Linda gave each other a knowing look and went back to questioning me.

I got to learn a lot more about them, how they met and why they'd chosen their career fields. They told me the story of when they adopted Brennan and even though I already knew most of it, hearing them tell it brought tears to my eyes. Seeing the way they adored their son made me love them so much more than I already had.

After making plans for breakfast the following day, Phil smiled and said, "I think we're going to head home, now, Son. We don't want to monopolize your time together."

"You guys don't have to go yet!" I interrupted. They all smiled at me warmly. I realized I had invited them to stay longer in a home that wasn't even mine. Embarrassing. "Sorry," I laughed. "I just already know that I'm going to miss you guys."

"Awe, Sweetheart, we're going to miss you, too. Please

promise me you'll come back for a visit." Linda walked over and pulled me into a hug.

"I promise," I answered.

We walked out onto the porch, and I hugged Phil and told them goodbye again before they climbed into their car and drove away. Brennan and I were still sitting on the porch swing thirty minutes later when he said, "We should probably head back home."

I looked at my phone and couldn't believe it was already five in the evening. It was going to be a long drive home, but at least I could offer to help with the driving.

"I guess you're right." I sighed.

"I have a question for you." He scooted closer to me on the swing and wrapped me up in his arms.

"What?" I asked, smiling.

"I'd like to know if you'd be willing to date exclusively?"

I smiled so big that my eyes crinkled and I couldn't see.

"Bentley?" he asked. I realized I hadn't responded and laughed.

"You want to be my boyfriend?" Why did that sound like such a high school thing to say?

"I want to be your boyfriend," he said. I could hear happiness in his voice.

"I'd love it if you were my boyfriend."

He pulled away slightly and placed his palm against my cheek. His smile was as big as mine, and when he leaned in to kiss me, we both laughed. Minutes ticked by, alternating between chaste kisses and laughter. There was something different in the way that I saw him now. The openness his eyes held was something I knew he saw in mine as well. Nothing was separating our hearts this time, and I vowed never to let anything come between us. No matter what I faced in my life, I wanted to face it with him by my side.

CHAPTER THIRTY-FOUR

November

The weather wasn't exactly right for a wedding, but no
one's spirits were dampened. It was raining, and on top of that,
the temperature had to be near freezing. Every time someone
opened the courthouse doors a gust of wind blew in, and I
started shaking all over again.

I looked at Sam, in her suit, and for the first time felt
jealous I wasn't a groomsman. When Maria went to her and asked
if she'd be a bridesmaid, we oddly weren't shocked when she said
Pop had already asked her to stand with him. That gave Maria the
bright idea of asking Brennan to stand with me on her side. He
only agreed because he was going to be in a gray suit as well,
any other color and he said he would have run.

Ryan kept eyeing Sam, and I wanted to scream from the rooftops that she was single. She wasn't ready to tell anyone that she and Matt had broken up, though. She was upset about it, as anyone who was in a relationship that long would be. There were just too many differences between them and Matt had ultimately broken her heart.

Sam caught Ryan's glance, and she scowled. She didn't like the attention apparently. I looked at my soon to be step-brother and almost laughed at the smirk on his face. This was going to be fun to watch.

Pop and Maria walked out of the office with all of their papers, and we followed them into another room. The judge greeted us, and the ceremony began.

Brennan stood behind me beside Maria and Sam stood beyond Ryan beside Pop. We probably looked like a strange assortment of people.

Rings and "I do's" were exchanged and after Pop leaned in to seal their marriage with a kiss, he pulled her into a hug and whispered, "I love you," into her ear. Her shoulders started shaking as she cried and laughed at the same time.

"I married you in complete blind faith that you would finally say those words to me today," she said, wiping her tears away.

"I've said it to you in my head a million times," he answered. I won't lie, I had a tear fall down my cheek with that line.

"I guess since you're already crying this is probably the best time to tell you," Ryan walked up to his mom, smiling. "Bentley's been helping me look for a place in Taylorsville, and we finally found one last month. I won't be going anywhere when we get back."

"You're staying?" She started jumping up and down and jumped up to hug his neck. He caught her and laughed while she repeated how excited she was about him finally living near her again. I looked at Pop and felt my heart start to ache. I knew my degree eventually would take me away from Taylorsville if a particular man didn't do it first. He seemed to have the same thought because he looked at me and gave me a sad smile.

Why was walking into your future so hard when you didn't want to leave the people you loved most behind?

"Let's get going. Jerry said everybody's waiting for us," Pop said.

Brennan's mom had sent me multiple texts throughout the last hour asking me questions about the set-up of the room Pop and Maria rented for the ceremony. She'd taken over the task of setting up, and she'd been there since early morning making sure everything was in place.

When we all arrived, the parking lot was already filled with other cars due to another wedding ceremony in one of the other rooms. We parked and ran in as fast as we could to get out of the freezing rain. Pop opened the doors to room R4, and when we walked in, everyone stood. Cheering and clapping overwhelmed us, and I knew if I could see Maria's face, she'd have tears in her eyes. Ryan looked over at his mom, and I must have been correct because he laughed and patted her on the back.

Brennan grabbed my hand, and we walked to the head table on the other side of the dance floor.

The newlyweds shook hands and hugged everyone before making their way to the table and sitting between myself and Ryan. I looked around wondering where Sam was, and I saw Ryan furiously typing on his phone. My phone dinged.

Ryan: What's an acceptable time to ask a girl out after she ended a bad relationship?

Me: Did you google it?

Ryan: Absolutely not. That would be embarrassing.

Me: I don't know the answer to that. It's a complicated situation. You could always ask her to dance, but she might say no.

I sent the message and looked up to see a young woman in a

black dress walking toward our table. The pink hair instantly
gave Sam away, and I couldn't stop my jaw from dropping. She
looked gorgeous! I knew my friend was beautiful all on her own,
but I never guessed she could rock a strapless black dress and
heels.

Ryan: I think I'll ask her out tonight.

Me: She'll turn you down.

Ryan: I guess we'll see, won't we?

I laughed and put my phone away as I watched Sam sit beside
Ryan. He was grinning ear to ear, and Sam didn't let it show if
it affected her.

"I guess we'll be going to their wedding next," Brennan
whispered.

"I hope not before our own," I said. I immediately felt my
face heat up. We hadn't even officially told each other we loved
each other yet. I slowly slid my eyes toward him and saw his
toothy grin. I wrinkled my nose trying to stave off my smile.

"Let's dance," he said standing and taking me with him. We
walked to the dance floor, and I wrapped my arms around
Brennan's neck.

"Why do you look sad all of a sudden?" he asked.

"It's stupid," I answered, but he just stared, waiting for
my reply. "We didn't get our epic 'I love you' moment."

"What do you mean?"

"I don't know. I just hate that I know you love me because you were joking around. I mean, I told you I loved you in a cemetery. It's not exactly romantic."

"Do you need it to be romantic?" he asked. He'd stopped dancing and was looking down at me intently.

"I guess not." I shrugged. "I'm just a sucker for it."

Brennan looked out through the windows that surrounded us and laughed. Grabbing my hand, he pulled us toward the doors and then through the large double doors that took you outside.

He pulled us out into the rain.

"What are you doing?" I yelled. "It's pouring out here!"

"I'm giving you epic, baby."

He grabbed my face in his hands and looked into my eyes.

"Bentley, from the very first moment you barged into my life, I knew you were going to change it. For months, I would lie there and listen to you talk. I'd pray for a reason to respond to you. I'd beg God to give me the courage to sit up and tell you my name, but you were just too beautiful for where my life was. One day you dropped your debit card, and I thought, 'this is it.' I had the reason I'd been waiting for, and within a month you gave me a warm home and showed me more kindness than anyone had in years. I fell so hard for you. Not only because you have an incredible sense of humor and you're beautiful but even your little quirks, like how you say sofa instead of couch."

"Couch sounds like a weird word," I said through chattering teeth. Brennan was shaking from the cold, too and for a moment I thought epic wasn't worth this temperature.

"I love you, Bentley. I love you more and more every single day."

"Getting me sick isn't romantic," I said. The rain was running down my face, mixing with my tears.

"I will take care of you. I'll care for you for the rest of your life if you let me. For forever."

"Forever?"

Brennan got down on his knee, and I gasped. "I had this all planned out, you know? I was going to ask you to play a game of Rummy with me, and I was going to wipe the floor with you," he laughed as well as he could through his shaking. "I was going to tell you your answer would change your life forever, so you had to be honest. Then, I was going to get down on one knee, like this, and ask you to be my wife.

"I don't have the ring with me today, but it's in my apartment. I talked to your father, and he gave us his blessing, so now I need to know, will you marry me?"

Between the chattering and shaking, I don't know how I visibly nodded but Brennan stood quickly and spun me around in his arms.

"Thank God! Kiss me, woman, I'm freezing."

And I did. I kissed him with all of the emotion I'd held for him since the very beginning. All the curiosity that turned into concern. The friendship that turned to love. The love that turned into hurt and then transformed into the feeling that I couldn't live without this man. Something deeper than love.

"Can we go back inside now?" I asked, and Brennan laughed as we ran into the entry hall. We stopped, and he pulled me into his chest, squeezing me tightly.

"I didn't know I could love someone nearly as much as I love you," he whispered.

CHAPTER THIRTY-FIVE

Pete was standing in front of his diner, closing the door
for the last time when he heard someone approaching from behind.
He turned to see who it was.

"Brennan, it's been a long time," he said, taking the other
man's hand in a shake.

"It has. I heard you were closing the place down and I
wanted to come see if there was anything I could do."

"Sylvia's been wanting to move out west, near our boys for
a few years now. I've been putting it off for far too long," he
said looking back at the diner.

"I hate to hear you're leaving. Bentley's going to hate it
too. She's missed Sylvia a lot. She would have been here with
me, but the baby isn't feeling the greatest right now."

"I heard you two had a little one. How old?"

"Jake is three months old now. It feels like yesterday he was born."

"Time will fly by, now that you've started your family. Be sure you cherish all of it, Brennan."

"Yes, sir, I will. You take care of yourself, Pete. Let me know if you ever need anything. I mean that."

"I know you do and I appreciate it."

Pete watched as Brennan climbed into his car and drove away. He'd never forget the day he watched the young man walk into his parking lot and lay down for the first time. Nor would he forget the girl wearing her heart on her sleeve walk out there and do what he'd yet to see anyone else do.

He chuckled to himself as he recalled his wife's comment about them making a cute couple long before Brennan had let Bentley hear his voice.

He was thankful for the changes Brennan had made in Hillview. And even though he was leaving the town behind, he could feel it in his bones; Taylorsville and Hillview had more in store for their futures.

CHAPTER THIRTY-SIX

Bentley - Graduation Day

I was standing in front of my chair in the large room where
the graduation ceremony was being held. I turned to look at the
rows where friends and family sat, proudly cheering for the
graduates. I spotted my cheerleaders quickly.

Pop, Maria, Brennan and my kids were all cheering. Jake and
Ivy had no idea what they were clapping for at three and four
years old, but it made me proud anyway. I knew that one day when
they could understand, they'd know their mom made a tough
decision and went to college. I hoped all my kids would go to
college one day.

I smiled to myself as I thought of the paperwork waiting in
my desk drawer at home. I'd been hiding it for well over a

month, and I couldn't wait to see Brennan's face when he opened
it.

I didn't know what my future held at that moment, but all I
cared about was my family. Present and future.

After the ceremony, I walked toward my loved ones and was
swept up in Pop's hug.

"I am so proud of you," he said in my ear.

I squeezed him and let go to hug Maria, too.

"I'm glad you guys are here," I said.

"We wouldn't miss it for the world," she said, giving me
another quick hug.

I hugged Jake and Ivy before they got distracted by their
grandparents and the snacks we all knew Nanna Maria kept in her
purse for such occasions. I watched them walk to the nearest
bench where Brennan's parents and my brother were seated.

I turned and looked at Brennan. He opened his arms, and I
stepped into them.

"There's my sexy college lady," he said. I let out a squeak
when he picked me up and started spinning. "I'm so happy for
you."

"Thank you," I said when he sat me back down.

"You're going to do awesome." He leaned down to kiss me,
and I felt butterflies erupt in my belly. This man still had an

effect on me that I hoped would never go away.

We joined our family, and Jackson apologized for Olivia, Logan and Callahan not being able to make it. She was at home with two sick kids, which I understood all too well.

My phone went off, and I pulled it out of my purse to see Sam was calling me.

"Hey, Sammy!" I said when I answered.

"Hey, Brat! Congratulations!" she yelled, and I heard Ryan groan before calling her a loud mouth.

"I have got to learn to be quieter," she whispered, and I laughed.

"It'll get better. Ryan will get used to your obnoxiously loud voice, or we'll have to tape your mouth shut."

"He already threatened that," she laughed. "I better go. Ryan's giving me the evil eye because we're about to walk into a movie."

"Okay, well thank you for calling! I love you and miss you!"

"Love and miss you too! Don't forget to call me when you give Brennan his surprise," she said. I looked at my husband and smiled.

"Will do," I said before hanging up.

CHAPTER THIRTY-SEVEN

Brennan - Life After Marriage

Almost two years after the wedding, I was standing in a hospital room holding my wife's hand as she gave birth to our son.

Jacob Isaac Murphy came in at a whopping nine pounds. Bentley swore she couldn't go through that again.

She did, though.

When Jake was four months old, Bentley came running into the bedroom and hurled a pregnancy test at my head.

"Look at what you've done!" she yelled, and I couldn't help but laugh. She narrowed her eyes but started to smile back. I grabbed her hand and pulled her onto my lap.

"So, you're pregnant?" I asked.

"Obviously. You did this on purpose."

"Baby, I didn't do it on purpose, but I'm not sad about it. Are you?"

"No, but I'm scared. Jake about killed me." I couldn't help but laugh again.

"I think you'll be okay. Maybe this one will be little," I said.

"What about school? I still have another year left for my bachelor's, and my goal is a master's. There's no way that's going to be possible."

"It's entirely possible. I promise you; you will get what you want. I'm here to help with the kids. After the baby is born, we can look into birth control so that we won't have any more kids for a while."

"For a while?" she laughed.

"Absolutely, I'm not done having babies yet," I said, pulling her to me so I could kiss her.

Ivy Kendall Murphy came in at six pounds seven ounces. She was her brothers exact opposite in every way. She had light brown hair where his was almost black. She was always getting into anything her hands could reach, and he was content just to observe. They were incredible.

After Bentley graduated with her Master's, we were

celebrating her degree and my fortieth birthday when I got an incredible gift. Bentley came to me with paperwork I'd been dreaming of filling out. Even though I was excited, I was also confused.

"Don't you want to get a job before we have more kids?" I asked.

"Not really, my goal was to get my degree, and I have it. I can apply to a few schools around here, but I'm not in a hurry. I've spent the last six years on school, and now I want to spend a couple on our family."

We started the process to adopt a child, and one day, two years later, we met Parker and Kelly. Parker, four, and Kelly, two, were brother and sister. They were pulled out of an incredibly tough situation and placed into foster care. With a mother that had overdosed on heroin and no idea who the father was, these kids were immediately put in the system.

For a week, we talked about it and tried to decide what was best for our family. We already had a five and six-year old, and we sat down with our kids to see what they had to say. They didn't understand why we hadn't already brought them home, so that's what we did.

It was tough for a while. They didn't understand stability or even eating on a schedule. I may not have ever been in my own biological mothers home, but I'd been placed with enough bad families to understand that. We worked diligently with them and did everything in our power to make sure our kids felt full of love, all four of them.

It took a good year for Parker to come to realize we weren't going anywhere. At first, he wouldn't let us out of his sight. Then, little by little, he allowed Bentley and I to walk into another room where we'd be out of sight, and finally, he was playing in the basement with Jake while I was upstairs and his mom was at work. We celebrated that night because we knew he finally felt like he was home.

Bentley's pregnancy with the twins came as a huge surprise to both of us. Since I didn't know my family and therefore had no idea if twins ran in it, she obviously blamed me. Walking into the bathroom and seeing ten different positive pregnancy tests made me turn tail and run. I didn't get very far when I felt the first test hit my back. I started laughing as she chased me through the house.

"Brennan Murphy! You are so sleeping on the sofa tonight!" she yelled.

I stopped running and turned to grab her before she slammed into my back.

"You've got to stop throwing stuff at me when you get

pregnant," I laughed. "It's sending the wrong message to the kids."

She turned and looked into the hall where all four of our children looked amused.

"Right, sorry. Well," she said smiling at me then turning to the kids. "We're having another baby."

They all went wild and started screaming and jumping up and down. Kelly, who had just turned five, chose to jump on the couch and Ivy was doing a weird little victory dance.

"Santa did it!" Kelly screamed.

"What do you mean 'Santa'?" I asked.

"We asked Santa for a new baby," Parker explained. "He did it, Dad!"

Bentley's eyes were huge. I knew she was going to start checking the letters they sent to Santa in the mail from then on.

Graham and Rosa were born eight weeks early and had to stay in the NICU for nearly a month. The day we brought them home Bentley looked at me and asked if I'd had enough babies yet. At forty-six years old and married to the hottest school counselor in the world, with six kids, I'd say I had my dream life.

I always knew we should have done something a little more permanent than birth control pills, because a year after she had

the twins, she was on a hospital bed again, pushing out another
baby boy.

When Duke was six months old, she made the appointment to
get her tubes tied, and for our anniversary I was gifted with an
appointment of my own.

"We're not taking any chances, Brennan. My uterus loves
holding babies, and you have potent baby makers, so this is it.
You're getting a vasectomy."

Just the thought made my stomach turn, but I did it for
her.

When I built our home in my early twenties, I'd had no idea
who would fill these walls. Now, I couldn't imagine them being
filled any other way.

I've spent more evenings than I can count sitting on my
back porch watching my kids run around and play. It was hard to
remember a time when I didn't have them.

Growing up, this is what I'd always wanted. This was my
most sacred dream, and I never knew I'd end up finding my home
in the same place I found my redemption.

CHAPTER THIRTY-EIGHT

Brennan

May - My name is Aaron

In the years I'd spent away from this place, it hadn't changed a bit. I put my first postcard in the box at the post office and walked through the most vacant town I had ever seen. I was headed to a diner called Bucking Bandits to set up where I would be staying for however long it took.

I needed to be far enough away from the heart of Hillview's residents to remain under the radar but close enough to get involved.

Bucking Bandits looked like almost every other building in sight, well past their years, the only difference was that this one was still in business. I walked into the diner and asked the older man if he'd call the police on me if I slept in his parking lot and I was shocked when the waitress told me to stay as long as I needed. Little did she know I would be there a while.

I walked back outside and laid the scraps of cardboard on the ground. My backpack was filled with newspapers and enough food to give me about two days to find work.

My hair was beginning to fall into my eyes so I scraped my fingers through it, pushing it back. It had been almost a week since I showered and it had already begun to take its toll on my mood.

I sat on the makeshift bed and looked at Charlie. He was already fast asleep, and I got the idea to make us a couple of signs. I pulled two pieces of cardboard out from under us and wrote, "will work for food" and placed it beside my bag and wrote, "I'm friendly" for him. Might as well let people know we weren't going to hurt them.

As I sat, thinking about my next move, I heard a commotion coming from where I knew the town line was. I looked up to see a young girl walking, talking and laughing with a rather large man. She ran up the stairs, leaving only the sound of her laugh behind.

"Bentley!" he yelled. He was smiling, so I figured he

wouldn't hurt her. "Get back down here, you little brat."

The girl, Bentley, came back down and bent over giggling. She finally stood and handed him a wad of towels, and when he turned around, I saw the mess on the front of his shirt.

A few trips and a couple hours later, I assumed she was all moved in. I was lying on the ground when the man walked back to his truck. He stopped and looked over to where I was and stood, staring for what felt like forever. I prayed he didn't come over and start some trouble for me and I breathed a sigh of relief when he finally got into his truck and left.

The next day I made my way back to where I knew I could find some work. I had a few small bags of marijuana with me and started trying to sell it to anyone who would look in my direction.

In no time at all, as I knew would happen, a man approached me, and I had a gun pointed at my head.

"What do you think you're doing?" he asked. I raised my hands up and tried to look like the desperate man I needed to be. Hunger made that easy.

"Just trying to make a few bucks, man. I need some money, that's all."

He contemplated something and pulled the gun away.

"You want work?" he looked down at Charles and narrowed his

eyes.

"Yes, sir," I answered.

"Meet me back here tomorrow night. Seven o'clock. Don't be late."

He walked away, and I made my way back to the diner. There was a good chance I had the right group but only tomorrow would tell. I prepared myself for what I knew was coming my way.

The next day, after getting the crap kicked out of me I was sent back "home" with instructions to come back the next night.

Thankful no one hurt Charlie; I took the beatings for an entire week before I was finally taken to the guy I'd first met.

"I'm Eric," he said.

"Aaron," I supplied my name through a fat lip. I had blood running down my chin, but I stood with all the strength I had. I was weak, tired and sore. I hadn't eaten in three days, and I knew if I didn't get this, I'd be in trouble.

"You keep forty percent," he added.

"Agreed."

In the following months, a little gas station became my best friend, and I bought whatever forty percent of almost nothing could buy for Charlie and myself to eat.

I lost weight pretty rapidly, but soon I was selling more than I was being given. Eric told me it was time to move up and

I took the first step of many in a ladder that seemed to have no end.

One year and ten months later

I was approaching two years on this job.

Laying on the cold cement with a headache that I thought would kill me, I thought about what I was doing. In the entire time I had been there I'd never felt like leaving more.

For months the only human contact I'd had was drug dealers and junkies, and I couldn't take it anymore. Outside of the woman that worked in the diner, not one person had asked me anything other than what I had on me.

I was going to get up and walk away from this. My head was pounding so hard I pulled my too long hair into my face to get rid of as much sunlight as possible. I hadn't eaten in two days because the little money I made that week went to feeding Charles. I couldn't let the dog starve.

I heard footsteps and tried to disappear into the cement.

Just leave me alone, I thought.

I didn't have any such luck.

"Good morning!" The voice said. It was a woman, and it was way too happy for me right now. "Hello?"

I heard her moving around and felt two fingers touch my neck. Despite my headache, I wanted to laugh but forced it down.

"Sir?" she asked. And then she took me by the shoulder and shook me. I felt bile rise in my throat from the movement and I reached my hand out, waving her away.

"Hey! I have some food for you!" I caught a whiff of the food and felt my stomach clench. I was starving but didn't know if I could sit up quite yet.

I heard her moving things around, and before long, she sighed.

"Breakfast is ready, sleepyhead." I tried to move my body what little I could, and I heard her footsteps again. When I sat up enough to look at her, she was walking in the opposite direction.

I looked beside me to see Charles licking an empty to-go box and saw my food. Within minutes I was thanking the angel that brought me breakfast because my headache was diminishing.

I eventually recognized her as the girl who had been moving in on my first day out here and for weeks I tried to think of a way to thank her. Every morning she would drop off two meals and walk away without saying a word, and I had no way to pay her back. I tried to convince myself she would stop eventually but as the days went by, she continued.

One day, months later, she stood to leave, and something landed beside me. I waited until she was out of sight to sit up and see what it was.

She'd dropped her debit card.

I had my in.

I was going to talk to her.

Tonight.

#

CHAPTER THIRTY-NINE

Thank you!

To my husband, thank you for believing in me. You believed in me even at times I didn't believe in myself.

Turkeys, thank you for being the light in my life.

To my grandma, goodness! You have been my biggest cheerleader! Your enthusiasm for my novel was exactly what I needed. Thank you for being on my marketing team before the book was even finished!

Sara, Terri, Barbie, Lanie, Emily, and many others. Thank you, thank you, thank you for being the greatest BETA readers anyone could ask for. Your love for these characters gave me hope! Thank you for giving me hope!

To my incredible Aunt Pam, you deserve the most amazing thank you. You worked your butt off reading, editing, and giving advice. You went above and beyond, and I'll forever be grateful. Thank you!

Mom, thanks for listening to me talk and talk and talk about my ideas. Thank you for raising me to believe that if you want something, all you have to do is reach out and grab it.

To everyone who reads this story that means so much to me, thank you. I look forward to bringing you more characters that I hope you love just as much as you loved the group from Finding Home in Redemption.

<<<<>>>>

67900354R00198

Made in the USA
Lexington, KY
25 September 2017